PAUL MICHAEL PETERS: THE COMPLETE COLLECTION OF SHORT STORIES 2012-2018

PAUL MICHAEL PETERS

Paul Michael Peters

Paul Michael Peters Complete Collection of Short Stories 2012-2018 1st Edition

❄ Created with Vellum

For my readers. Thank you for seven great years.

"Memory is the only paradise from which we cannot be driven."

— JEAN PAUL

❧ I ❧

HICKORY SWITCH

The robin's-egg blue 1934 Lincoln Model K Sport Phaeton was the first new automobile to roll over the freshly laid bricks of Roosevelt's Civilian Conservation Corps on Front Street. Behind it was the second-newest car to arrive in the small town of Hickory in nearly five years, a black 1932 Duesenberg. They caught the attention of everyone.

Faces peeked through windows at the sound of the Duesenberg's rattling engine. Folks stepped out onto the sidewalk just to see the beautiful lines of its design. By the time the car rolled to a halt, a veritable flock had formed to see who would emerge over the running boards and onto the sidewalk in front of Hattie's—the only place in town where one could rent a room. The car door opened, and an ankle covered in a black stocking, and a black high-heeled pump stepped out onto the running board. The hem of a long green dress swung over the ankle, and a delicate hand extended up toward the driver's leather glove. With the help of the driver, a woman in her thirties stepped out onto the sidewalk. It was as if a movie star had arrived and entered the lives of the good people of Hickory.

Her husky driver, having helped her from the car, walked her up to the porch and inside Hattie's. Several more passengers emerged from the Duesenberg and followed the woman into the building. The procession included three capable men and one young woman, slight and bright of face.

With the smack of Hattie's screen door behind them, a flutter of questions erupted from the gathering crowd. Who is this woman? Why is she here? Did you see that dress? Were those her servants? Did anyone recognize her?

Mayor Nobel, a portly man with thinning white hair peeking out from under his hat, turned to the inquisitive crowd and put his hands up in the air. "Good people of Hickory," he said, "please, calm down. I will go inside and inquire." He turned and lumbered up the steps, removing his hat before walking through the door.

In the twenty minutes it took for the mayor to return, nearly all 423 citizens of the town had gathered, filling up the lawn and spilling over from Front Street into Memorial Park. Impatient boys sat on the gazebo, their legs dangling through the white railing.

After a few minutes, a third mysterious vehicle arrived on Front Street—this time a green Chevrolet closed-panel delivery truck. As the truck came to a halt in front of Hattie's, two men in gray overalls and matching caps began to unload suitcases and steamer trunks by the dozen.

Mayor Nobel emerged from Hattie's just as the deliverymen were hustling cases up the stairs and through the screen door. The mayor made his way through the masses, across the street, and over to the town gazebo. Members of the crowd followed him, eager for news.

Once inside the gazebo, Mayor Nobel could see all of the good people of Hickory and speak to them clearly. "A former member of our community has returned to Hickory. She has made plans to stay at Hattie's indefinitely until her business is complete." The mayor looked out over the faces of the friends, families, and townsfolk who had put him in office. Most were thin and wore desperate expressions from several years of economic hardship. Seeing his people hungry for hope, Mayor Nobel was happy to repeat the news. "That's right! You heard right. She has business here," he said, speaking louder to be heard over the murmuring crowd. "And some of you will remember her name: Naomi Bitler."

Henry stood in the crowd, unable to contain a look of surprise. It had been twenty years since he'd heard that name. Naomi Bitler . . . how that name used to vibrate with the sensation of misspent youth. There was a time when he would think of that name and the face it belonged to every hour. Over time, it had slowed to once a day. Eventually, it had become like a winter chill, sending a tingle up his spine a few times a year. Hearing her name again caused Henry to have the same core reaction. The thought of seeing her again suddenly gave him hope in a time of depression.

"What's her business?" a man called from the crowd. "Has she brought jobs?"

"Well"—Mayor Nobel scratched at the crown of his head—"I don't know the answer to that just yet."

"Will she donate money to the school?" called a woman from the front.

"Well," said Mayor Nobel, looking down at his feet and shuffling uncomfortably, "I didn't ask."

The crowd groaned in disappointment.

"What is she doing here?" another voice came from the back of the crowd.

"Well," Mayor Nobel said, "this Saturday, in just three days' time, she is going to host a picnic right here in Memorial Park."

A sigh of relief sounded out from the gathered citizens, either because they were pleased with the news or simply because they were grateful that the mayor actually had some.

"She is making arrangements at the moment," he continued. "She tells me she has big plans."

The crowd looked at the mayor somewhat blankly, clearly expecting more.

"The whole town of Hickory is invited!" he said, but this piece of news was received with mild interest. "And it is free of charge!" The crowd cheered at this, and Mayor Nobel smiled. "That evening," he went on, "she is going to make an announcement, a big announcement, that everyone will want to hear."

"I bet it's jobs," one man said loudly.

"I bet she bought the plant, and she's going to reopen it!" another one said hopefully.

"More jobs will mean a better school," a woman said.

Bitler was a name several of the community leaders remembered. When Mayor Nobel had first said it, several glances had been exchanged among members of the crowd. Bitler, sometimes known as "old man Bitler," had lived on the edge of town. He'd been a widower with one beautiful, red-haired daughter, whom many of the men had had their hearts set upon. All the men of a certain age remembered Naomi Bitler, and they also knew that the only man she'd ever loved was Henry Edward.

"Of course she loves Henry," the hopeful boys would say to themselves. "Henry's father owns the general store. Henry has a future. He's an Adonis. Any university will be happy to have him."

Everyone had always expected great things from Henry Edward, the boy with two first names. It had been no surprise when Henry had eventually taken over the general store from his father. In fact, everyone in Hickory assumed that when the aging Mayor Nobel finally stepped down, Henry would be the one to take his place.

Those who had known him the longest hadn't been surprised to see Henry succeed. From a young age, he'd always been an outstanding example in everything he tried. Only there, in the park, as Mayor Nobel spoke Naomi Bitler's name, did anyone even remember that Henry had once lost a girl. Henry had married the second-best girl in town because Hickory's best, Naomi, had left and was nowhere to be found.

۞

NAOMI RENTED ALL OF HATTIE'S, FIRST FILLING THE TOP FLOOR with her belongings, then leaving the ground and second floors to those in her employ. All the activity these new people brought to the small town was causing a stir. Hickory was bustling for the first time in years.

Any attempt at conversation with these new people, however, was answered with a polite nod of the head or a brief response. Their dealings were focused and professional, leaving little opportunity for the good people of Hickory to dig for clues about Naomi's big announcement.

Within a few hours, trucks began to arrive in town in droves. Canopies were erected in Memorial Park. Umbrellas and picnic tables were assembled en masse so that each person would have a seat for the big day. Bunting and streamers were pinned and unfurled under the guidance of a certain Lemuel Clemens, whom everyone on the crew just called Lem.

When Naomi wanted something done or arranged, Lem was the man to carry it out. She watched from her window as he directed the teams to build her ideal picnic setting. Several times over the course of the day, the young, slight woman, bright of face, who had arrived with Naomi in the black Duesenberg would step onto Hattie's front porch, slamming the screen door behind her. She would then cross the street and update Lem on Naomi's wishes. He would look up to the third-floor window from which Naomi watched, tip his wide-brimmed, brown hat, and instruct the workers on her updates. All the men would turn and watch as the young woman jaunted back to the porch. Sometimes it seemed that the messages coming from Naomi were instructing Lem to change what he was doing or to take a different approach. By late afternoon, Lem would simply stop what he was doing when he heard the porch door slam.

The day was sweltering hot, and those townspeople who couldn't find shade were suffering in the heat. Many watched from windowsills, porches, or shady perches as the men transformed Memorial Park into the perfect picnic area. Thrill filled the hearts of the good people of Hickory when another three trucks arrived, the first with two ostrich heads sticking out. Their large eyes peered out at the townspeople, and they let out squawks the likes of which the townspeople had never heard. One of the local cats jumped nearly three feet in the air when, from the third truck, the sound of a lion's roar erupted.

By the time the trucks arrived, Lem and his men had already constructed a fenced-in area for the gentle beasts and birds. The lion and his mate would stay safely caged in the truck but parked in a location for general viewing. More common animals—like piglets, goats, and sheep—were dropped into a nearby petting zoo arrangement.

As evening approached and the heat of the day passed, Naomi moved out to the porch at Hattie's. She was accompanied by the young woman, who sat next to her and took notes. While she kept watch outside, one of her men regularly supplied her with iced drinks, freshly cut fruit, and cheese.

When one of Henry's former classmates, Eugene McKinley, finally got up the nerve, he pretended as if he were out for an evening walk. As he approached Hattie's, he adjusted his pace to ensure he would make eye contact with Naomi. The nervousness in his voice was apparent as he tipped his hat and said, "Good evening."

Naomi smiled and nodded politely. "Eugene."

A broad grin covered Eugene's face when she remembered his name, and he continued walking.

Henry, who was watching through the window of the general store, saw this play out and found himself encouraged to make contact. He removed the white smock from around his waist, put on his jacket, and informed his wife, who was also watching the scene from behind the candy counter, that he was stepping out.

The top button on Henry's coat seemed tighter then he remembered. The light, quick steps he normally took to Hattie's for a delivery now seemed heavy and slow. Crossing the newly laid bricks by Roosevelt's Civilian Conservation Corps on Front Street, he felt unsure for the first time in many years. It was a feeling he kept well hidden from others. He knew and honored the responsibility others had placed upon him: to be strong, to be a leader. Still, something inside him was uncertain, boyish even. He'd believed Naomi Bitler to be his one true love all those years ago, and now, it seemed that something was still brewing.

Henry felt like the whole town was watching him approach Hattie's porch. Even the lions, monkeys, and ostriches couldn't compete with what was about to happen. "Hello, Naomi," Henry said. "May I join you?"

Still, as beautiful and elegant as ever, Naomi smiled. "Please do," she said warmly. Then, she turned to the slight young woman with a bright face at her side. "Cora, could you please give Mr. Edward and me some privacy?"

Cora stood up, smiled at Henry, and went inside with one final slam of the screen door.

Henry moved a chair beside Naomi. He sat next to her and looked out to appreciate the view she'd created in the park. From their vantage point, the town of Hickory had been transformed back into the town they had grown up in. Everything seemed perfect and in place.

"Would you like something cool to drink?" Naomi offered.

"Yes, please."

She poured lemonade into an empty glass at Henry's side. White slivers of ice followed the stream, and beads of water slid down the outside of the glass pitcher, dropping onto the tabletop.

"You have ice?" Henry asked, surprised.

"I brought an ice machine with me."

"You brought many things with you to Hickory—wonderful, exotic things."

Naomi giggled at Henry's nervousness. "It's just like it was: clean, fresh, beautiful," she said. "And you are just like you were. A little gray and salty, perhaps, but just like you were."

The two looked to one another, uncertain of what to say, not wanting to spoil the moment.

"Not a day has passed when I haven't thought about you, thought about this place," she continued. "It has been nineteen years and three months to the day since I left. I've been counting."

"Why have you come back? Why have you been thinking about Hickory all these years?"

"My return. I wanted it to be perfect."

"Well, you certainly seem to have succeeded," Henry said, chuckling nervously. "You've taken this town to a new place in just two days. The men, the decorations, the animals—it will be some picnic tomorrow."

Naomi looked back at Henry with a polite smile. "Thank you, Henry," she said. "I think it's perfect."

"Where did you get the means to do something like this?" Henry asked.

"My husband passed away last year, and I inherited everything," she said softly.

"You were married? To whom?"

"Theodore Lennox."

For Henry, everything suddenly made sense. Theodore Lennox, who had been the third richest man in the world, even after losing half his fortune in the stock market crash of 1929. Theodore Lennox, whose name had been printed in newspapers across the country each week. Theodore Lennox, whose funeral had included some of the most powerful and elite of the day, who has been mourned by former President Hoover, and whose life story was being made into a film.

"You're Naomi Lennox?" he asked.

"The very same."

"But you told Mayor Nobel your name was Naomi Bitler."

"I left here a Bitler, and I return here a Bitler."

Henry leaned back in his chair, stunned.

Naomi could see that Henry was caught in the moment and in the thought of all that money, so she asked, "Henry, did you marry? Do you have a family?"

"I do. I married Julia O'Neal. We have a daughter."

"Julia, I remember her. She was in your class, a few years older than me. And your daughter?"

"Ruby. Her name is Ruby. She is sixteen."

"Same age," Naomi said.

"What's that?"

"Ruby is nearly the same age as I was when I left Hickory."

Henry didn't have anything to say to that. He didn't want to think of the day Naomi had left. He never understood why she had left in the night, never saying goodbye. He preferred to keep things light, jovial, and uncomplicated. "You remember that old tree by the creek? The one with the swing where I carved our initials inside a heart? It's still standing, you know."

Naomi smiled, remembering all the work Henry had done with his pocketknife on the bark.

"That creek crested eight feet four summers ago during heavy rains, but that tree is still there, still strong."

The two laughed politely, trying to avoid the truth of the past.

"You know," Henry continued, "I own the general store now. Father passed it on to me. If you need anything, anything at all, please stop in. We have everything."

Naomi smiled. She could sense the conversation had turned away from the past and back to money. She patted Henry on the leg in an intimate, friendly way. "I will let Lem know about your store."

"It's going to be a great picnic. I mean"—Henry fumbled for his words—"you did a great job here. It's just that you brought everything with you, and sometimes people forget or need things, and we have things here in Hickory. We have some value here for you. If it didn't arrive on a truck."

"You're the same, Henry. The same man I always loved," Naomi said, smiling. There seemed to be something behind her eyes, behind her smile.

A roar from the lion in the park startled the two into nervous laughter again.

Regaining his composure and realizing the hour was getting late, Henry thanked Naomi for her time. He offered her assistance and company whenever she wished it, then politely excused himself to return to the store. Before closing and locking the door from the inside, he allowed himself one last look back to Naomi, who was still watching him. The whole town was watching.

DURING DINNER, A KNOCK CAME ON THE BACK DOOR. HENRY LEFT Julia and Ruby at the table and went downstairs to answer it. At the door stood Mayor Nobel and Sheriff Johnson. Like the rest of the townspeople, they had watched Henry talking with Naomi and now wanted details.

When Henry explained that Naomi's married name was Lennox, everything seemed to fall into place. Stories about Mrs. Lennox, whether true or not, had been abundant over the years. The two men stood at Henry's door, gossiping like schoolgirls about all the Lennox scandals they'd heard over the years: stories of mingling with the cultured in Europe, with the elite in New York, and with the powerful in Washington.

"Henry," Sheriff Johnson said, "why are you acting so strange? You seem nervous or something."

"Please," he replied, "my dinner is getting cold. She is Naomi Bitler, the beautiful, red-haired daughter of old man Bitler. All these other things you are saying are not really her. She is the same girl we've known since we were boys."

"Maybe you knew her," Mayor Nobel said, "but I was too old for you and your friends."

"I remember," Sheriff Johnson said. "I remember the two of you being very in love. Then one day, she was gone. Why do you think she left, Henry?"

Henry didn't want to discuss it. Instead, he became somewhat stern with the men. "Listen, it's getting late. My dinner is getting cold. We'll find out her plans at the picnic. She will tell us when she is ready."

"Why did she truck all these things in?" Mayor Nobel asked as Henry shooed them out the door.

"She didn't say."

"Why not hire the men of Hickory? Why hundreds of these outsiders?" the mayor asked, one foot out the door.

"I am not a fan of all these outsiders living in tents on the outskirts of town," the Sheriff added. "Not much better than circus folk setting up camp just outside of town. I'm sure some are good people, but some are ruffians, brutes. Who knows what kind of trouble they could cause. I just don't like it, not one bit."

"She just wants things to be perfect. Good night, gentlemen," Henry said, finally closing and latching the thick wooden door. Walking back upstairs, he pondered the mayor's questions. He sat alone and finished his dinner.

He could hear Ruby and Julia talking in the next room, asking each other the same types of questions as they looked out the window and onto Memorial Park. Why would Naomi do this? What was she going to announce?

The lion roared from its cage in the park, making all the good citizens of Hickory jump.

"I don't know if I can get used to that," Ruby said to her mother.

᭒᭖᭓

UNABLE TO SLEEP, HENRY SLIPPED OUT OF BED AND WENT OUTSIDE. He got into his old delivery truck and, as quietly as possible, rolled out to the edge of town. Having spoken of the tree with the carved initials, he was feeling sentimental and headed for the creek.

As the beams of his headlights lit up the popular spot for young lovers, he was not surprised to see Naomi's car sitting there. Her driver sat in the front seat, and she was leaning against their tree by the creek.

"I thought you might be out here," Henry said, getting out of his car.

"I hoped you would be," she replied. "When you mentioned this tree, I couldn't get it out of my mind."

"It's a good tree," he said. "It's a strong tree, one that survives."

Naomi stepped away from the tree and moved closer to Henry. "You have to be strong to survive."

For the first time, Henry could get a close look at her, without the whole town watching. Behind the lines at the corners of her eyes and beyond the wrinkles on her brow, he started to really see her again, not just the makeup and memory of what had been. "I thought you would be happy with all that money, with the world at your command, but you don't look happy."

"I am not happy, Henry," she said.

"What is it that will make you happy?"

"You. You always made me happy."

"I was always at my best with you."

"But you're married, you're a father, you're the owner of a general store in Hickory."

"That is true."

"Run away with me," she said quickly. "Let's leave this place, just you and me. Together. Now. Tonight. With my money, we can do anything together."

Henry let the excitement flow through him. He allowed for the dream to feel possible, just for that moment.

"I would like nothing more than that. But as you said, I am a father, and you are throwing a picnic."

"Damn the picnic. I have always loved you. Doesn't that mean something?"

"The good people of Hickory need your business, Naomi. Life has gotten so very hard here."

"The good . . . people . . . of Hickory," Naomi said slowly and deliberately. "I wish you would run away with me. Leave this all behind. Be with me forever." Naomi turned and leaned against the tree once more.

Henry wasn't sure what to say. He knew her to be of strong mind. If her younger self was anything to go by, it was rare that he could change her mind once it was set. "It is a beautiful dream, Naomi."

"You have said your piece, Henry," Naomi said flatly, turning from the tree and heading toward the blue Lincoln. "You have made your choice. I will see you again tomorrow."

Henry watched as the red taillights disappeared behind the kicked-up dust on the road back to Hickory.

AFTER BREAKFAST, HENRY OPENED THE STORE. MORE THAN A place to purchase goods, it had always been a spot where the good people of Hickory talked and met one another. Even so, the register bell rarely chimed. Most in town didn't have the money to purchase anything but the essentials. Talk was cheap, however, and the shop, like most Saturday mornings, became full shortly after opening. News about Naomi's married name being Lennox had spread quickly. It lifted everyone's spirits to think that her announcement might bring work. Henry was hopeful too, since any extra money in the pockets of the townspeople might be spent in his store.

In the general store, Mayor Nobel and Sheriff Johnson were back to their gossip.

"Henry," the mayor said. "You know her best. What do you think she will announce? A donation to the town? Will she bring jobs here?"

"I don't know," Henry said flatly. "I just don't know." He could see the disappointment on the faces in the store. They wanted good news. As usual, they were looking to him to encourage their dreams for a better life. For the first time, Henry was showing doubt in front of the good people of Hickory.

It was just after noon when the faint sounds of music could be heard in the streets. As it became louder, the townspeople began to come out of their homes to see what was happening. What they saw at the foot of Front Street amazed them. A fifty-piece marching band, all dressed in red with gold stripes, was leading the way for a pipe organ being pulled by a brand new tractor. A hand-painted sign on the side told the townspeople to "Enter the Raffle to Win!"

As they approached the park, the band was playing loud enough to bring down the walls of Jericho. They entered Memorial Park and assembled under the shade of a newly built bandstand. With a cur-chug, the tractor came to a halt in front of a table where a great big glass bowl sat with paper pads and pencils for making ballots.

As the band played on, each of the canopies opened and carnival barkers began calling out about food, beverages, or games available at their locations. Everything was free for the good people of Hickory.

Within minutes, all the townspeople arrived and began stuffing their faces with hot dogs and drinking from the seemingly endless resources of ice-cold lemonade. They tossed rings, threw balls at milk jugs, shot pellets at targets, and walked past kissing booths with their wives by their sides. At one o'clock, a beer tent opened with the refreshing kegs of 3.2 beer, now approved again by the government. By the afternoon's end, the line at the kissing booth was five deep, despite dirty looks from many of Hickory's ladies.

As daylight began to fade, the electric lights, strung from polls and trees, switched on and the band stopped playing. Naomi emerged from Hattie's and walked down the front steps, across Front Street, and into Memorial Park. Accompanied by Cora on one side and one of her men on the other, she was greeted with cheers from the crowd. Lem followed closely behind with her driver.

Near the gazebo, Mayor Nobel and Sheriff Johnson greeted her and accompanied her up the steps to the main platform.

Naomi turned to the Mayor and said, "If you're going to say anything, now is your chance."

The Mayor, never passing up the chance to speak to the good people of Hickory, smiled and stepped to the front of the stage. "Good evening, everyone," he began. "It's good to see you all here, and I hope you have enjoyed this day. We've had an incredible afternoon, all thanks to our good friend and fellow citizen of Hickory—Naomi Bitler!"

A standing ovation and loud cheering followed her name.

"She was just an adorable, red-headed girl when I knew her," the mayor continued. "Her father was a respected member of the community. And now, she has returned to us to provide this exciting day and to make an announcement. Without further ado, please join me in welcoming Naomi Bitler."

The crowd roared its approval as the band played a short melody. The sudden excitement sent the animals into a frenzy.

Naomi nodded to the mayor and stepped forward, waiting patiently for the crowd to settle before she spoke. "Good"—she swallowed the word—"people of Hickory, I have been wronged."

The hush over the crowd was quick. This was not what they had expected to hear.

"When I was a girl of fifteen and lived among you, persevering through the daily torments of this town, something terrible happened to me. While my late father and I were struggling to survive, living in a tar shack on the edge of town, a man of eighteen ravished me and left me with child. You all know this man. His name is Henry Edward."

The onlookers gasped.

Standing with a group near the gazebo, Henry gulped as he heard the words. Questioning stares were cast in his direction, starting with Julia and Ruby. The expression on his face revealed that Naomi may be telling some version of the truth.

"Two months later, when my belly began swelling, it became apparent what had transpired. The leaders of Hickory approached my father and had me banished. My father, along with the former mayor and sheriff, found eighty-three cents to send me by mail car to Chicago, where I was to be raised by nuns, and the baby would be put up for adoption. They did not want such a blemish on the town of Hickory."

Henry hung on her every word, desperately wanting to know what had happened since she'd left town nearly twenty years ago.

"But when I arrived in Chicago, there were no nuns to raise me. It had all been a lie, told to get me to leave Hickory and to convince my father to let me go. I was left alone, without a penny to my name, to fend for myself on the city streets. The baby was never adopted. He died in the hospital."

Henry hung his head in shame. He had no idea that one night of youthful passion would result in such awful things. Henry was young, a fool, in love. There was no struggle, no fight, just the tender and memorable evening by the creek where he carved a marker of their love, a scar on the bark of a tree that remained to this day.

"My father died shortly after I wrote him the truth. I was told it was an accident, but I know in my heart that he took his own life." With this, Naomi shot Sheriff Johnson a sharp glare.

The sheriff looked away, unable to meet her gaze, knowing that her suspicions of suicide were true. He had only been a deputy at the time and had followed the instructions the former sheriff, telling the towns-people that old man Bitler's death had been an accident.

"Alone, a pretty girl in unkind circumstances, I was forced to work in brothels in order to survive. Every day, I thought of you good people of Hickory. I knew what I wanted to do. When I met Theodore Lennox, a man twice my age and as rich as sin, I knew he was my ticket to doing it."

"What do you want?" called a lone, bold voice from the crowd.

"Justice," Naomi said. With her right hand, she pointed to the man standing next her. "This is my lawyer, Arthur Sharp. He can verify all the facts I have provided." With her left hand, she gestured toward Cora. "This is my assistant, Cora. She has and is ready to distribute two million dollars upon my request."

The crowd in Memorial Park let out another audible gasp. A dime was a significant sum to most of Hickory's citizens, and the notion of two million dollars was almost impossible.

"Two million dollars," Naomi repeated. "Think about it. I will give the town of Hickory one million dollars and split and distribute the other million equally among the people of Hickory on one"—she paused, relishing the words that had lived in her mind for decades —"simple condition."

Hushed whispers traveled through the crowds. Two million dollars would transform the town of Hickory. What could the condition be?

"I know what being poor is like," Naomi went on. "Not knowing if there will be a next meal or what you will have to do to get it is an awful fate you all now face. This banquet you've had today, the feeling of a full belly, a cold drink, moments when you don't have to worry and can cherish hope are foreign to you. For some, this may be the first time ever experiencing such a feeling. You can stop the fretting, stop the grief, and return to a life of stability on just one condition. Roughly $2,500 in cash for each registered citizen and one million dollars for the town of Hickory will be delivered . . . once Henry Edward is dead."

Henry's eyes widened, and he began shaking his head. "No, no! Naomi! That can't be what you want. We were young and in foolish love. I didn't do anything to your father—it wasn't me. This is a joke. It must be a joke. A bad joke," Henry said, then realized she was serious. He turned to his neighbors. "It wasn't like that. It wasn't what she described. I didn't know the former mayor or police chief. They are dead and gone. You've got to believe me."

Naomi, for the first time, revealed her true smile, taking pleasure in seeing Henry pleading for his life. "I have thought about this moment every day for nineteen years, three months, and one day, Henry Edward. Our baby boy did not get to see those years. My father did not get to see the number of sunsets you've been able to enjoy. One night, one act, changed my life forever, and I want justice."

The crowd stood stunned in the moment, pondering all the years of knowing and trusting Henry Edward, the boy with two first names, the football Adonis any college would have recruited, the man who sold them daily goods at the general store. It was a quieted crowd that began to bubble with doubt as to who this woman really was. Could

Henry have done something so sinister? Two million dollars was serious money. Something worth that much must be true.

As the notion of the request sank in, Mayor Nobel spoke up. "We are good people in Hickory. We are civilized people. We can't kill one of our citizens. Our state has the death penalty, a process, a court system. Our town can't just decide to avenge your"—he searched for the right words in mixed company—"plunder."

The crowd was in confused conversation, firing glances at Henry and thinking of the great sums of money that had been offered.

"Now, people!" Sheriff Johnson interrupted. "Calm down. We did not know she was going to ask for this. This is not something you can just do. We are not killing Henry Edward."

Henry took comfort in the sheriff's words. He hoped that, as tempting as the money was, the people would never agree to put a bounty on his head.

Naomi looked out across the throngs in the park. It seemed her fangs were finally showing, and she relished the bloodlust that was seeping its way through the gathered crowd.

"What about the factory?" a man yelled out from the back of the group. "The mine? The jobs?"

"A new school!" a woman's voice cried.

Naomi laughed to herself as Arthur Sharp stepped forward.

"Miss Bitler has purchased both the plant and the factory over the past five years. She already owns the mine just outside town. In addition, she has been acquiring the deeds of properties from the banks that currently hold liens, but she has not closed these accounts nor notified property owners of foreclosures. If you owe the bank, Naomi Bitler owns that debt."

Mayor Nobel's jaw dropped at the news. For the first time in his life, he was at a loss for words.

"You own Hickory," came a voice from the crowd.

"I do," Naomi replied proudly.

"All that wealth, all that money, all turned against one town for your idea of justice. That's just cruel," Sheriff Johnson said.

"It's evil," Henry said.

"Not cruel. Not evil. Legal," Arthur Sharp continued. "As promised,

PAUL MICHAEL PETERS

upon the death of Henry Edward, a donation of one million dollars will be made to the town of Hickory, and one million dollars will be split equally between all living members of the community."

A man asked, "So, when Henry dies, I get a cut, and if my wife is on the registration at city hall, she gets a cut?"

"That is correct," Naomi said. "The 19th Amendment has been ratified for fourteen years. Ladies, if you are not on the registration today, you will want to be at city hall first thing Monday morning."

Julia looked to Ruby and mouthed the words "two million dollars" in disbelief. The mother drew her daughter in close, sensing the change in the desperate crowd.

Henry suddenly became very aware of all the stares being pointed in his direction. He took the hands of his wife and daughter and started to walk backward toward the store, dragging them along with him. He knew by the way the people of Hickory were looking at him they were taking Naomi's offer seriously. His only thought was that he had until Monday to live.

"Since you have all had such a good time today, I have asked Lem to keep the picnic going until Sunday night," Naomi announced. "Please, eat and drink as much as you want. Play games, listen to this wonderful band, see the exotic animals, and remember . . . two million dollars can be yours."

⚜

FROM BEHIND THE GLASS OF HIS SECOND-FLOOR WINDOW, HENRY sat in the dark, looking out over the park toward the gazebo. The crowd was still gathered, all talking to one another with great excitement, at times pointing in Henry's direction. With a single click, his room was illuminated with electric light.

"Turn that off, woman! Do you want me killed?" Henry yelled.

Julia quickly turned the light off again. "Henry, why would she say these things?"

Henry remained silent, looking out at the park, which was still alive and seething with activity.

"I have told Ruby that these are all lies," Julia whispered, "that her

18

father would never do such things, never be rough, that he is the gentlest of men. I have told her this woman has gone crazy at the loss of her husband and is taking this out on you." She waited for a reaction. "Is it true? Is what I told our daughter the truth?"

Henry kept staring out the window, mumbling to himself and thinking long and hard about the past.

Julia knew he hadn't even heard her question. She knew his mind was racing for answers of his own. She went to bed but found no rest knowing that her husband was still sitting up by the window, staring at the good people of Hickory below.

◌⁕◌

SUNDAY MORNING ARRIVED LIKE A HANGOVER. SO MUCH FOOD HAD been consumed. So many drinks had been poured. Hickory was hard-pressed to recall a day filled with so many of the seven deadly sins. But driven by one woman's wrath, the citizens of Hickory were only focused on one commandment in particular as they made the walk to church that day.

The pews were packed as Reverend Laughton stepped up to the pulpit. He opened the large Bible to a page marked with a red ribbon and began to speak of forgiveness. "Forgive as the Lord has forgiven you. If you do not forgive, your Father will not forgive you. Be kind, be compassionate, forgive each other, as God forgave you." Looking out to the congregation, the reverend did not sense any connection.

"Hypocrite." The word echoed out in the silence between the verses.

"Who said that?" Reverend Laughton asked.

The congregation turned toward the voice and saw that Naomi Bitler had snuck into the back of the church. "You're a hypocrite, Laughton. You were there. You speak of forgiveness when all you could do is condemn."

A confused congregation turned back to the pulpit, looking back and forth between Naomi and the town's spiritual leader.

Naomi walked up the center aisle, pointing an accusing finger toward the reverend. "'Fornication' you called it," she said, her voice twisting. "'Sinner' you called me. 'Evil' was the word you yelled while beating me on the ride to the train station." Her eyes blazed with hatred. "But not when I first came to you for help. I was young and impressionable then, and you were filled with lust, not forgiveness. Your hands were filled with my breasts. You wanted to plunder me and explore every part of my body before telling your friends what I'd told you in confidence. Reverend Laughton, you should join Henry Edward. You broke my spirit, but he broke my heart."

"Ms. Bitler," Reverend Laughton said. "Please, this is a house of God."

"Liar!" she blasted. "A house of lies. There were no nuns, no care, in Chicago. You had no friends to look out for me. You are a liar and a hypocrite."

Naomi turned away from Laughton, cast a sideways glance at the congregation, and walked back down the aisle and out the door.

A befuddled congregation looked back to Laughton.

"Let's close in prayer," he said shakily, bowing his head.

Henry took the opportunity to stand and exit silently. He walked across Memorial Park, where Lem and the men were restocking supplies for the start of the day's festivities. He saw Naomi ahead of him on her way to Hattie's. He could not catch up to her and did not want to. He had been up all night, thinking of a way to talk her out of her offer. He still wasn't sure if it was a bad joke. Any sudden noise he heard made him wonder whether Mayor Nobel and Sheriff Johnson were really correct, whether the good people of Hickory were civilized and would never do such a thing.

He made his way to the general store so it could be open after church. His store was always busy for about an hour after church, as many were preparing for Sunday supper. He unlocked the front door, removed his jacket, and hung it on a hook behind the counter. Then, he wrapped a fresh smock around his waist and tied it, as he'd done a million times before. Million, he thought to himself.

Henry propped open the front door, then watched and waited for the church crowd to emerge. As he waited, he watched Lem and his men in their final preparations. The smell of the hot dogs from the stand across the way wafted over and into his shop.

Henry felt jumpy, on edge, as if something were about to happen. He looked through the counter, checking the different remedies he had suggested to clients over the years. Some he'd prescribed for upset stomachs, others for exhaustion, but he couldn't think of any for nervousness. Maybe this was something the good people of Hickory never felt.

The sound of a child's laughter caught his attention. He looked up from the counter and saw that church had let out. The congregation moved across the lawn and into Memorial Park.

The only two people who moved through the park and into the store were Julia and Ruby. Each greeted him with a polite kiss before heading upstairs to their home. Alone, Henry looked over the shop until the two returned, out of their Sunday best, and headed back to the park for the picnic.

Henry could have protested. He could have said, "You can't eat that woman's food after she put a bounty on my head!" But he didn't. He simply watched as they strolled across Front Street to be with their friends.

Ruby had told him that morning he was silly to worry. Maybe he was. These were the people he had grown up with. They were his friends.

While Henry was lost in thought, Mrs. Taylor came into the store. Henry greeted her warmly and asked what he could help with. She expressed interest in a Philips radio. This was an expensive item, and he hadn't known her to have the money for such a thing.

"I can help you order one," Henry explained. "I have a catalog with such items in it. You could pick the style you like, and it could be here in a week."

"Oh, you would need to order something like that?"

"I don't have many requests for that type of thing, so I don't have one in stock."

Mrs. Taylor thought for a moment, then asked, "Is it something I could put on my account?"

Henry stepped over to the cash register and removed his accounting register. "Mrs. Taylor, right now your account is at $8.52."

"I see," she replied.

"The radio you are asking about costs $33.44, with the additional $2.09 mail order charge and a $1.02 charge for store service. Altogether, that would come to $45.07 for the complete order." Henry was sure that Mrs. Taylor did not have the money. At best, she was expecting to get the money from somewhere. "Did you want to make a deposit with the store for the item? You would need to pay off your account first, but we can arrange the order," Henry offered.

"I see," Mrs. Taylor replied. "Not now. Thank you, Henry. Thank you for your help. I will see you later at the picnic."

The conversation made Henry even more anxious. If Mrs. Taylor was dreaming of a Philips radio, the rest of the town was starting to think of what might be done with a cut of a million dollars. He wondered how much his life was worth to the good people of Hickory.

The sound of laughter from Memorial Park took Henry's attention away from his dark thoughts. He removed his smock, locked up the shop, and went to find Julia and Ruby.

Eyes followed his every move as he made his way through the park, and he felt the same weight of stares as he had in church and at Naomi's announcement. When Sheriff Johnson slapped his back jovially, Henry nearly leapt out of his skin.

"Whoa there!" the sheriff said. "You're jumpy. Just saying hello. Wanted to make certain you know I am here and that I have your back."

"Have my back?"

"Well, just in case."

"In case of what? The good people of Hickory are civilized. They wouldn't do something bad to me," Henry said, trying to convince himself.

Sheriff Johnson smiled. "Of course not. You are safe and sound here. I am close by. The good people of Hickory are all your friends."

Mayor Nobel appeared from the crowd and greeted the two men. "Could you ever have imagined that something like that would ever happen in our little town? Reverend Laughton is apparently packing his things."

"Packing his things?" Henry asked.

"He says he doesn't have faith in the good people of Hickory like we do," Mayor Nobel said.

Henry's stomach did a backflip. Thinking he should eat something, he got in line for a hot dog but found himself feeling even more ill after his first few bites. Food did not go down well when it had come from the woman who wanted him dead. He decided to return home without his wife and daughter.

From the upstairs window, he watched the day go by. The people of Hickory played games in the park, listened to the om-pa-pa of the band, watched the wild animals, drank beer, and ate food. And all the fun and games were being supplied by Miss Naomi Bitler.

AFTER ANOTHER LONG NIGHT WITH LITTLE SLEEP, HENRY BATHED and got ready for work. He ate little for breakfast but went downstairs and opened the store to wait for customers. After an hour alone in his shop, he stepped out onto the sidewalk and looked around the town square.

Lem and some of the men had started to disassemble the stands and benches. The bank across the way was open. Looking toward city hall, Henry saw a long line of ladies waiting to get inside. He closed the shop and made his way over to investigate.

The line went up the steps and into the office of the registrar. Arthur Sharp stood at the front of the line greeting each lady, explaining what they would need in order to receive their share of the million.

Henry's heart sank. He knew for certain now that the people of Hickory were not good. He knew that Naomi wanted justice. He knew that his life did have a price: two million dollars. As he made his way through the main entrance and along the line of women, he saw something that made him stop dead in his tracks.

"What are you doing?" he yelled to his wife.

Julia, nearly first in line, looked up at Henry from underneath her Sunday hat. "Exercising the right provided me by the 19th Amendment."

His eyes widened, and he backed out of the office, making little eye contact with the rest of the line of women, all of whom were giving him dirty looks. He exited the building and headed back down Front Street. He became hyperaware of everyone he passed, checking their hands for blunt objects, knives, or firearms. With quick, skipping steps, he headed for Hattie's to try and see Naomi.

Entering the waiting room, Henry saw Naomi's driver. Had he known Henry would be arriving?

"She has been expecting you," he said in his deep, raspy voice. "I have to check ya first." As the driver patted Henry down, each slap felt harder than the last. The driver's hands had clearly seen much more action than just a steering wheel. They were large and felt more like wood than flesh as they struck him. "Okay," he grumbled. "Follow me."

The two climbed up two flights of creaking wooden stairs and entered the master room. Naomi had brought the luxury and lavishness of the city along with her. Newspapers and magazines were strewn across the table. The furniture was much nicer than anything Hattie had ever owned. A brass telescope on a tripod faced toward the window, and behind it stood Naomi.

"I knew you would come," she said.

"Naomi, you have to stop this foolishness. Tell the people of Hickory this is a joke. They are lining up at city hall to update their registration. They really think you're going to pay them."

Naomi looked up from her telescope. "I gave you the chance to run away with me. You should have taken it," she said coldly before turning to her driver. "Give us a moment." The two now alone in the room, her expression changed as she sat down in her chair. "I think of you every day, Henry. I think of what we could have had. I love you so much. Why did you have to break my heart the other day? You could have run away with me when I offered."

Henry kneeled at her side in the chair. "You love me? If you loved me, why would you have me killed? Why would you do this to someone you loved? You know I didn't force myself on you. You know the truth."

"I want to watch you suffer. I want to watch you walk, like you did just now, fearing for your life. I want you to know what it's like to walk the streets in fear like I did, all in return of one night's passion."

His brown eyes grew large and watery. "What about my wife and daughter? You want them to live in fear as well?"

"Do you think she loves you? That she ever loved you? Could ever love you like I do? You were available. You were the best she could get in a dying town from which she had no escape."

"And my daughter?"

"She is so lucky to have you as a father. Have you even tried to explain to them what I said? Have they asked you if it's true? Or do they know you too well? It was no surprise to them at all."

Head hanging to his chest, Henry didn't know what to say. All he could muster was, "Have you no compassion?"

"I do," Naomi said softly, "for our son, who hardly knew life and was abandoned to a cruel world where he couldn't survive." Naomi looked back out to the park, where the dream-like picnic was being disassembled. "In one day, Hickory will turn back into the shell it was before I arrived. These people are poor and broken, desperate and afraid. I brought them two glorious days full of food and riches. I asked for only one thing: your life. The good people of Hickory will give me what I want. You will see. Your pleading will not change anything. I gave you a chance to run away, to love me, to be with me, and you did not take it. I gave you more of a second chance than I ever got, more of a chance than our son ever had."

"But I know now," Henry replied tearfully. "I know how much you love me. Let's run away. Let's get lost in this world together. You must know that I still carry a flame for you here." He touched his chest.

Naomi sighed deeply and embraced Henry. "How I have waited for you to say that to me. How I long for you again. I want to be with you. I want to make it right. I want to get lost in you, in our love. I want to feel you inside me again." She stopped and breathed deeply in his trembling arms. "But I know these are just words."

"No! It's all true. Call your driver back. We can get in the car right now."

"They are words, Henry. You're just bargaining for your life. One day, someday soon, if we were to run away, you would leave me. I know how men are." She drew away from him and looked into his eyes.

He took her hand, helped her up, and led her to the door. "Call the driver. Let's go."

"Are you serious?"

"Absolutely."

A smile full of hope spread across Naomi's face, and she called out for her driver. Within minutes, the two were in the robin's-egg blue 1934 Lincoln Model K Sport Phaeton, racing down the street toward the edge of town. They passed the lot where her father's tar shack had been, then drove on past all the small farms that dotted the road into Hickory.

After a time, Henry felt the car start to slow down. "What is it? What's happening?" Henry asked as the car came to a stop. He looked up through the windshield to see several of Naomi's large trucks blocking the road ahead. The hardy men she'd employed to build the picnic area were all standing around the vehicles. "What is this? I thought we were getting lost together?" he said.

"Oh, Henry. What a beautiful dream that is. Unfortunately, you have missed your chance."

"Tell them. Tell them you changed your mind."

"I could, but they won't believe me. They only listen to Lem."

"Well, tell Lem to tell them!"

"I can't. I told Lem not to let you get away, no matter what. That's his job."

Henry opened the car door and stepped out onto the dirt road to assess the situation. The men were not aggressive but were just preventing him from going any further. Henry saw Lem at the front of the line of trucks and went over to him. With her driver's assistance, Naomi stepped down from the car and joined Henry.

"Lem, she has changed her mind, I tell you. It's all right, see. Here, she'll tell you."

"Mrs. Lennox," Lem said, with the tip of his brown hat.

"Lemmuel," she replied.

"True what Mr. Edward is saying here? Change of mind?"

"It's true," she said. "You should let us leave. We want to get away from here."

"Now, you know I can't change our plans, even if you've changed your mind. That was part of the agreement. That is why you paid me so much money up front, to follow your plan to a T."

"I do know that."

"And you have explained this to Mr. Edward?"

"I did. Still, he thinks he can sway your mind with words."

Lem looked to his feet, then into Henry's eyes. "I don't mean to disrespect you, Mr. Edward, but I have a contract with Mrs. Lennox. We have an agreement, a plan, and I can't change it. My men and I won't let you leave here. Now, to prove I am a serious man, I want to show you something about my agreement with Mrs. Lennox."

Naomi stepped back to the car, allowing Lem to do his business.

Lem firmly but politely took Henry by the arm and led him toward the back of the first truck. He flipped back a dirty canvas tarp, revealing the bruised, beaten, and lifeless body of Reverend Laughton, his face still clenched in terror, hand gripping a Bible. "He just wouldn't let it go. I tried to explain to him that he couldn't leave, tried to send him back to town. It didn't go well. Do you understand, Mr. Edward?"

Henry couldn't control the convulsions of his body and vomited on the side of the road.

"That's all right," Lem patted Henry on the back as he wretched. "Happens to the best of us. Now, my advice is to get back in the car and let Mrs. Lennox take you back to town. All right?"

Henry wiped the sides of his mouth with the back of his hand, then removed a white handkerchief from his pocket to wipe his hands. He nodded in agreement and wandered back to the car in a daze. Inside the car, Naomi was waiting, and as soon as he sat down, she instructed the driver to take them back to Hickory.

Rolling into town, the crowds were still milling around Front Street. Everyone could see Henry in the Lincoln with Naomi, obviously shaken.

Outside Hattie's, Henry stepped out of the car while the driver once again assisted Naomi. Henry looked over at Naomi, unable to speak, then walked over to the store.

"What happened?" Julia asked.

"It's complicated. It's—" Henry stopped mid-sentence and went upstairs. Exhausted, he fell into his bed and quickly went to sleep.

⁂

HENRY WAS WOKEN BY A GUNSHOT. HIS EYES SNAPPED OPEN. HE couldn't tell what time it was, only that it was still dark. He knew that he was still in his bedroom. But was it a dream? An awful nightmare?

Another shot was fired. He scrambled from his bed and went downstairs to the store. In the darkness, he could hear Julia and Ruby calling his name from the storage room. He ran to them, finding them crouched behind the pile of flour sacks. "What was that?" he asked.

"I don't know," Julia whispered. "We heard the shot, turned out the lights, and ran back here."

The three of them could hear voices from the street, though they couldn't make out the words.

"What happened with Naomi?" Julia asked. "What have you brought into our lives?"

"You knew Naomi and I were together before we were."

"Is it true? What she said in the gazebo?"

"We were together. I did not force myself on her," Henry said. "I don't know why she left. I only knew she was gone one day."

"Why would she want you dead if you didn't do anything to her?" Julia asked.

"She has some elaborate plan I don't understand. For years, all she has thought about is returning to Hickory." He poked his head up slowly to see out the window. "Reverend Laughton is dead."

"Oh, God," Julia exclaimed. "What happened between you and Naomi today?"

Henry paused, reluctant to reveal the truth. "She said," he finally explained, "that if I ran away with her, should wouldn't—"

"You were running away with her?" Julia interrupted.

"To protect you, protect Ruby."

"And save yourself."

A single round of gunfire filled the air, closer this time. Julia instinctively grabbed Ruby and tried to shield her. Henry reached out to Julia, but she pulled away from him. At that moment, he knew what Naomi had said was true: Julia and Henry's marriage had been one of convenience, of proximity. In Hickory, they were one another's best option. He may have been able to understand and eventually get over Julia being first in line at city hall, but in this moment, Henry knew whatever they had was gone.

"I'll go," Henry said softly. He patted the head of his cowering daughter. "You two stay here. If they are looking for me, I will make sure they don't find you instead." Henry went to the rear loading door and pulled it open horizontally, just enough to squeeze through. It opened up to the alleyway. He went outside, closing the door behind him, and made his way to Front Street, looking for the source of the gunshots.

Several armed men were walking in the street, as if on the hunt for prey. Some of the less experienced hunters held flashlights and lanterns to light the group's way. When the team looked in Henry's direction, he darted back to the darkness.

"What in the hell is all this commotion?" Sheriff Johnson yelled.

"Lion escaped," said one of the hunters. "We had to put the female down."

"Well, why wouldn't you come get me and my men?" the sheriff barked.

"No time. We had to act fast. We sent a runner for you at the station."

Lem jogged up to the group, accompanied by more men carrying rifles. "Did you get the lion?"

"Just the female. We thought we saw the lion go this way," the hunter said.

Just then, a blood-curdling cry came from the alley next to the general store, mixed with the uncommon growl of a big cat. The armed men ran toward the source of the sound and lit up the darkness with dozens of shots until the screams of both man and beast ceased.

"Hold your fire, damn it!" Sheriff Johnson called, and finally, the gunfire ended.

Cautiously, the men with lanterns entered the alley, illuminating the remains of what had just taken place.

❧

IN THE MIDDAY SUN, ON THE STEPS OF CITY HALL, THE PEOPLE OF Hickory watched as Naomi Bitler signed a check for one million dollars. Arthur Sharp had calculated, based on the city registry that morning, a fair and equal amount to be delivered to each citizen. Cora, with the assistance of a team of Pinkertons, counted out each person's share to the penny and began doling it out.

After collecting their share, Julia and Ruby watched the long lines of polite people receiving their money.

How had the lions gotten out? Who had been watching the cage? The two had heard the questions asked countless times, but the answer didn't seem to matter anymore.

Lem and his crew were long gone. The last of the trucks had left at daybreak. Fortunately, Naomi Bitler had donated an ice machine to the funeral home, but it was decided there was nothing to be done with a body that mangled. There would be no open casket. The body had been so totally destroyed that no one had been able to definitively identify it.

But now, Hickory had another chance. The people of the town had more than enough money to pay off their debts, all of which were held by Naomi. They knew where their next meals were coming from, and they had plenty of money to see them through the next rough season. They should have been happy, but something in the town had come undone.

Most left Hickory in the months that followed. Citizens found it hard to look one another in the eye or to engage in conversation knowing that each person had a price.

The plant would never open again. The factory would stay closed for good. The mine was not going to open production. So many families left that there was no need for a school. Everyone had the means to leave, so there was no need to stay. Eventually, the shops on Front Street were nothing more than empty shells alongside the solid brick laid by Roosevelt's Civilian Conservation Corps.

Naomi Bitler continued to use her maiden name after leaving Hickory. It kept her out of the public eye. Some say she spent the remainder of her days alone in the giant Lennox estate, dealing with her demons using a daily regimen of alcohol consumption. If you stood next to the grounds at night, they say you could hear her howls of loneliness and torment.

Others say Naomi was seen with an older athletic man in the estate gardens, on shipping liners on the Atlantic, and in off-the-beaten-track luxury locations known to very few. Those who saw her spoke of how she often let out howls of laughter and had such passion for her lover that she never let him out of her sight.

Like so many rumors about the elite, it's almost impossible to know the whole truth.

Something never sat well with Ruby about the little town of Hickory. Seven decades later, after a long and good life, it was the last conversation between her mother and father that lingered. "Reverend Laughton is dead," he had said. Ruby had spent many sleepless nights over the years thinking about how calculating Naomi had been with her father. If her claims were true, Naomi would have been almost sixteen years old, and her father may have just turned eighteen, a little over two years' difference when she was wronged. Back then, it may have been nothing, but by today's standards, a statutory scandal.

Her father slipping out the alley door was her last memory of him. She may have been the last one to see him alive besides Lem and his men, who had insisted on protecting the good people of Hickory from the gruesome remains left by the lion. They had put her father's remains in the casket immediately, using Naomi's machine to keep him on ice until buried.

Little was said about Reverend Laughton after he had packed his bags that Sunday. Many assumed he had gone to the seminary to retire or teach. "Reverend Laughton is dead," her father had said.

Ruby clenched the sheets of her hospital bed tightly when it came to her. A smile brightened her face in those final moments of peace as she slipped from the earthly bonds, surrounded by her own children. She realized her father had not faced a gruesome death in the jaws of a big cat but a rich and full life with his first true love. Her last words only she understood:."They made a switch."

2

FUKUSHIMA GOLD

The houses in his neighborhood lined the park like the charms on his mother's bracelet—each jewel unique, made in a different time. The sky was a rich azure, with just the right balance of sunlight as Haruto walked along the gray paved path through the Central Park of Makuhari, Chiba City, Japan. It felt good now that spring had finally arrived. In just a few more minutes, he would be home with his mother, father, and little brother. Haruto picked up his pace, excited to see them again.

Haruto stopped when he came across a dog, unleashed and unattended. He squatted in front of the Shiba Inu, which was behaving strangely. "What's the matter, boy?" Haruto asked the dog. He extended his hand slowly, attempting to show the dog he was a friend. As he did so, the earth began to shake beneath them. Haruto lost his balance and fell over.

The dog, scared, ran to him and started to nuzzle at his leg, whimpering.

Haruto tried to stand but could not get to his feet easily as the ground continued to shake. His third attempt was a success. "It's okay, boy," Haruto said, trying to pet the dog's head. "It's okay. Just a little earthquake."

The dog clung to Haruto's leg in fear, dancing on the tips of his paws, unaware and uncertain of what was happening as the quake grew in strength. Haruto looked toward the path ahead, watching as it started to move like old tar paper ripping in a strong wind. The concrete surface peeled away from the earth, and a deep hole spread open as the two sections separated farther apart.

Puddles of water in the grass became pools, then shrank back again as a black-looking liquid bubbled up from the ground. The earth seemed to liquefy at the edges of the path as it contorted.

The ground was moving like an accordion, and as the huge gap in the earth looked to be closing for a moment, Haruto made a dash for it. "Come on, boy!" he called to the dog. "Let's go!"

Leaping as far as they could, both dog and boy made it over the hole. Their little legs worked hard as they ran down the path, away from the split earth. Each foot planted seemed as slow as molasses. Haruto had run this route from school daily, but now, he couldn't seem to move fast enough. The muscles in his legs began to burn with acid. Nearly home, he gave the final push of a sprinter, giving everything to get home.

Haruto could see his house and could almost hear his mother's voice calling his name. The ground continued to writhe, keeping him off-balance. All the while, the Shiba Inu stayed at his side, looking up at him for guidance.

As the quake intensified, neighbors began to pour out of the buildings around him. They all ran to the open space of the park, thinking it safe. Some were struck down by loosened siding from the buildings, while others were crushed by debris as it fell from above.

Haruto felt an urge to go and help, yet he just stood still, watching.

Finally, he moved toward his family's home. The door of the building where his family lived now was empty. Still trying to make it all the way, he called out for his mother and father until his throat was sore and raw. No one could hear him over the rumbling of the sustained earthquake. The crashing and crumbling of façades, balcony gardens, air conditioners, and potted plants were creating a blitzkrieg of terror and injury.

Haruto took another step toward his front door. Through the dust, he could make out his mother's face emerging from the stairwell and moving toward the glass doors of the apartment building. He smiled to see her again, with his father right behind and his little brother scooped up in her arms. With each step they took, they were closer to the exit and escape. Haruto breathed a sigh of relief.

Just as his fear began to subside, the whole wall of the building began to crumble. A landslide of metal and concrete blocked his view of his family.

"Mother!" he cried desperately. "Mother!" Haruto could feel his whole body shake. In the distance, he could hear a voice calling out his name.

"Haruto!"

By his side, the dog was pulling at his leg. Then, he could feel the weight of the dog poking at his shoulder. Then, the dog spoke. "Haruto, wake up," it said gruffly. Then, the voice became more pointed and violent. "Haruto! You're having the nightmare again."

Haruto jolted awake and became instantly aware of his surroundings. He was in Uncle's house. Yori, the brown Shiba Inu from that day, was sleeping by his side. All was dark.

"Are you all right?" Uncle asked, leaning over him. "Can you get back to sleep?"

Haruto nodded and turned on his side. He watched Uncle, who had a worried look on his face, turn the light off and slide the door closed.

Uncle had been good to him in the years since the earthquake. He and Yori were the only family that remained.

After school, Haruto worked in Uncle's shop, learning all he could about business. Hina, Uncle's girlfriend, also worked in the store, demonstrating and helping to sell the goods. This had been the routine for the previous eight years. Haruto would wake up, attend class, come straight home, and help in the shop, which was right below Uncle's apartment. At night, Haruto, Uncle, and Hina, would make dinner together and review his schoolwork. One week a month, Uncle would leave for the harvest. This was the week when it was just Haruto and Hina alone together.

Hina was nice enough, but she acted differently when Uncle was not around. She had no interest in Haruto's schoolwork without Uncle.

When Uncle was gone, dinner was just what Haruto could find on his own.

At the end of each harvest, Uncle would return home to the shop with a fresh box of gold and silver jewelry. Uncle always offered Hina the first review and said she could have any of the pieces she liked.

Hina would look at the box, sigh, and decline the offer. "We should save those for the shop," she'd say.

There came a day, shortly after Haruto turned sixteen, when Uncle explained that Haruto would be joining him for the harvest in order to learn about the business. Haruto was torn by the news. He enjoyed school and had friends in his class. He wanted to follow Uncle's wishes, but in the eight years since the earthquake, he'd noticed a trend surrounding the harvest.

Uncle never seemed well upon his return. He seemed tired, old, and worn. When he was a younger man, Uncle used to get back to normal after a few days. Recently, though, he seemed unwell almost all the time. Just as he seemed to be improving, it would be time to harvest again. Haruto understood that going to harvest was less about being old enough to learn about the business and more about the growing need Uncle had for help.

One Friday evening after school, rather than help in the shop, Haruto threw his backpack over his shoulder and headed to the train station with Uncle. They boarded the last train north and set out for the harvest.

It was the first time Haruto had left the city. He watched as the countryside rolled by. Small towns and large mountains were slowly replaced by streetlights that became fewer and farther between the more they traveled.

"Try and sleep now, Haruto," Uncle urged. "You may not see another chance until much later."

Within a few hours of high-speed travel, they arrived in Koriyama, and Haruto was introduced to Uncle's business partner, Mr. Kaito.

Mr. Kaito had a wiry build but seemed to have hidden strength. He was wily, constantly looking around as if he were being watched.

The three got into Mr. Kaito's truck cab, with Haruto in the center, straddling the gearshift.

Leaving the train station, Mr. Kaito lit a cigarette and began to narrate like a tour guide. "Koriyama was once well known for our carp industry," he began. "If you were to think about this delicious fish, you would think of the fishermen of Koriyama. I was a fisherman. I had my own boat, a small crew, and a warehouse for cleaning, processing, and shipping. Koriyama was a place to take pride in."

Within a few minutes of driving east, the glorious lights of the city began to melt away, replaced by smaller neighborhoods with fewer lights, more darkness, and less to show. The buildings were not as modern or well kept. Within a few kilometers, the truck moved from an industrial landscape to an agricultural one.

In the darkened silence of the cab, illuminated only by the dashboard and the reflection of the headlights, Haruto asked, "What happened to the fish?"

"What?" Uncle asked.

"Mr. Kaito said that the town was once well known for the fish. What happened to them?"

Mr. Kaito gave Uncle the stink eye. "It's not Mr. Kaito, kid. It's just Kaito. Got it?"

"Yes," Haruto said.

"The Fukushima Daiichi nuclear power stations produce high levels of radiation," Uncle tried to explain.

"The fish here swim closer to the plant reactor than the ones in the south," Kaito continued. "People wonder if they are good fish, but I eat them all the time and look at me." He pounded his chest with his fist, a cigarette dangling from his mouth. "Young and strong." Kaito's eyes looked wearily out on the road as he drove into the darkness, the driver's side window open a crack for the smoke to escape.

Haruto nodded off, waking only when the truck stopped and both men got out. Between the two men in the truck, it had been nice and warm. Now, the three of them were standing in the cold night.

"They put up a new gate," Uncle said.

"That's all right. I know a little place up this hill where we can cross. I was there three days ago," Kaito said.

All three got back into the truck, and the headlights turned on. In the light, Haruto could see a large white sign with huge red words that read, "Forbidden Zone."

"Where are we, Uncle? Where are we going?" Haruto asked nervously.

"We are going to harvest, Haruto," he answered.

"Harvest?" Kaito laughed.

"It's how I explain what we do," Uncle said.

"Harvest. What a noble way to describe it." Kaito removed the cigarette from his mouth and dropped it out the opening of the window.

They continued along the road, which turned into a dirt path. They followed it for another two kilometers until they hit another paved road. Here they turned right and followed the road to another gate. This one was extendable, like one parents might use to protect children indoors but much larger.

Uncle was quick to hop out of the truck. He ran toward the gate and worked on the lock for a moment before removing it and rolling the gate open just enough for the truck to pass through. Kaito drove through the opening and waited until Uncle closed the gate and got back in the truck.

It seemed to Haruto that the two had done this many times before. It was a well-practiced routine that was executed quickly.

Once Uncle was back inside, Kaito turned off the headlights and slowly rolled through what looked like an empty village. In the moonlight, Haruto could see shops like the one he lived above, vehicles like theirs abandoned by the side of the road, and empty houses that seemed ready for a family to walk in and fill the vacancy. But covering everything was a gray layer of what looked like ash. He wasn't sure if it was dust, but it made everything look like the sun-bleached sticks one finds at the seaside. He remembered going to the seaside with his mother as a young boy and thinking that the sticks were the bones of dead people.

Automation still moved in this town. Tiny lights speckled and turned different colors. The yellow dot lights of solar collectors still flickered. Traffic lights turned red, then green. Orange street lamps illuminated a path.

On the far side of town, the tires of the truck rolled to a stop and the three got out.

"What now?" Haruto asked.

Pulling a bag from the back bed of the truck, Kaito removed a white suit and boots, tossing them to Haruto. "Put these on," he ordered.

Haruto had seen these jumpers on the news nearly every night for the past eight years. They were the same safety suits that the heroes of Fukushima Daiichi wore.

Uncle and Kaito put on the suits. Each had a large canvas satchel over their shoulder. Haruto did as instructed. The overalls went on first. Then, he stepped a toe snugly into each boot.

Haruto could now see that Kaito's old, beat-up truck looked like every abandoned car they had passed. It was rusty and worn from weather. In the dark, one would never know the engine was warm and had been there only a few minutes.

"Ready?" Kaito asked.

Uncle looked to Haruto and said, "Yes, let's go."

The three walked two kilometers down the road to another small village. Haruto followed the men into shops, where they were quick to pick up any currency or valuable goods. Someone had clearly been there before, and Haruto suspected it was his uncle and Kaito. Things looked well picked over. The glass cases were nearly empty.

"Kaito, there is nothing left here," Uncle said. "We need to find another shop."

"I know, I know," Kaito replied. "This shop was good to me."

"Was this yours?" Haruto asked.

"It was," Kaito replied. "But there is nothing here for me now. Let's go."

After another hike to another empty village, the three entered an antique shop. The door was unlocked. Immediately, Uncle started to fill his sack with precious metals. Small items and trinkets that looked silver, gold or rare went straight into the bag. Kaito went to the service counter and began to look for currency. As he rifled through the counter, he mumbled something about a cash box and safe.

"Was this your shop too?" Haruto asked.

Kaito stopped and looked at the young man, then to Uncle.

"Yes," he said. "These are all mine. I owned them all, and now we are harvesting all the valuables the government keeps from me in the forbidden zone."

Something seemed off about this answer. Haruto stood still until Uncle said, "Make yourself useful and help us harvest. Look for anything valuable."

The shop was a mess. No one had been there to clean up after the earthquake. There were piles to sort through, broken ceramics, and glass strewn across the floor.

Still, Haruto continued to look for something valuable that he could carry. Away from the others, he discovered a case that had fallen over. Lifting it, he saw a pile of ancient swords. "Are these valuable?" he asked out loud.

Kaito was quick to rush over and inspect the finding. "Yes," he said. "These are very valuable. Put them in your satchel."

"Did you forget you had them?" Haruto asked.

Kaito looked confused for a moment, then said, "Oh, yes. I forgot about them. Please gather them for me."

Walking back to the truck, each one had a different cadence. Uncle's was chunk-ker-chunk, chunk-ker-chunk. Kaito's was higher pitched, like the sound of coins going ching-ka, ching-ka, ching-ka. Haruto disliked his own cadence. It did not sound valuable. It went wraa-chunk, wraa-chunk as the leather sheaths rubbed on the downward step and the metal swords slid back into position on the second part.

"It's a good thing no one's here to hear us. We are most certainly the loudest group around," Haruto joked.

The ching-ka stopped and Kaito's voice sounded out in the darkness, "This is no joke, boy. We could get into trouble here. Please stop your talking."

The sounds carried on for the final kilometer back to the truck. The three satchels were loaded in the truck bed, and the men drove back out the way they had arrived. An hour later, they were in Kaito's warehouse in the carp capitol of Koriyama in time to see the first light show over the mountain.

It was nearly noon when Haruto woke to sounds coming from the garage. Kaito had fallen asleep on the floor of the guest room in the house, while Uncle had taken the bed. Haruto was the last to wake up, and he heard the other two now making a racket in the garage.

Haruto opened the door to find Kaito and Uncle in front of a very hot brick furnace. They wore special leather outfits and deep purple goggles, and they were in the process of removing a glowing pot from the fire with metal tongs. A pile of the leather wrappings and sheathes Haruto had carried lay in a pile by the trash bin. He watched as the two steadied the glowing pot over a wooden box filled with smoothed dirt and poured glowing molten metal inside.

When they were done with the task, the two removed their protective gear. Uncle explained that what they were doing was called smelting. The items of metal collected were no good to them in their original form, so they were recasting them into more precious things.

Uncle guided Haruto over to a table away from the furnace where small tools lay on a black cloth. Uncle explained how he would take some of the metals, like gold and silver, and turn them into new items for the shop. This was the harvest of old items that were no longer valuable. Then, he would turn them into something new, something that people back home would purchase.

To Haruto, it all seemed to make so much sense. "So, we are taking the goods that Kaito owns and making them better."

Uncle gave him an odd look. "Kaito did not own the shops we went to," he said finally. "We do not know who owned those shops."

"Isn't that stealing?" Haruto asked, puzzled.

"Think of it this way, Haruto," Uncle said. "All the people in that area left and they are not coming back. Even the regions that reopened remain empty. These things are abandoned. What we do is salvage goods that no one wants. We are much like people who recycle. Rather than throw something away, we find an alternative use for it. It is our hard work, and we get paid for it. This is why I call it harvesting. There are fields of things out there for the taking."

Haruto nodded his head. Uncle smiled and showed him some of the items he had been working on while Haruto slept.

Over the course of the week, the three men made two more trips to harvest and spent the rest of the time working very hard to smelt metal and create new goods. With Haruto's help, he and Uncle returned to the shop with a much larger box of goods to sell than Uncle had ever brought on his own.

࿗࿐

AFTER ARRIVING HOME, HARUTO FELT SICK. HE DIDN'T KNOW WHY. His stomach could only take water and rice—not that he could eat much with a mouth full of sores. He just wanted to sleep. When it became a struggle to get out of bed, Yori kept watch at his side. Eventually, it became a struggle to get to class. There were even times when Haruto would fall asleep at his desk in school and be almost unable to wake up when asked.

Uncle was even worse. While Haruto recovered within a week, Uncle continued to stay in bed. He was thin. His hair was thin. Hina would no longer kiss him. She limited herself to working in the shop and no longer came for dinner. It was up to Haruto to care for Uncle.

Haruto split his days: mornings in the classroom, afternoons in the shop, and evenings looking after Uncle. He would sit by Uncle's bed with a cool damp cloth to soothe the red splotches of skin. While Uncle slept, Haruto would hold his homework in his lap, with Yori curled up at his feet. When awake, Uncle wanted to know about the store, about which harvested items clients showed interest in. As the weeks passed, Uncle's eyes slowly began to seem less cloudy, his skin clearer, and his voice stronger.

Both kept an eye on the moon. It had to be in just the right place in order for them to harvest. When the moon was big again, they would go. Uncle wanted to be able to harvest by moonlight rather than flashlight.

"That way, we are at one with nature," he said.

It had been nearly four weeks since the last harvest. Haruto was feeling good and strong again. He was ready for a new adventure. Uncle was also feeling somewhat better.

When the moon was bright in the sky, they decided it was time for harvest again. Tickets for the train were purchased. The trip north was made. Kaito met them at the station again, and they made three more trips to harvest that week, spending their days in the garage before heading home.

When the second harvest was over, Haruto found himself in his bed above the shop, thinking about what they had done. He thought about the ghostly images of Kaito and Uncle walking in the moonlight, their glowing white jumpsuits guiding him on. His mind replayed the memory of the many untouched storefronts they'd passed. He thought about what might have been inside based on the store names.

He laughed to himself remembering the grocery store visit. He thought he might never forget the pungent sting of sour from the piles of rotten food in the aisles, still sitting right where they had landed in the earthquake. There was the gooey, viscous fluid that Haruto had slipped on—a mixture of cooking oils, sugary energy drinks, and alcoholic beverages that had pooled and congealed on the grocery floor. He'd seemed to bathe and writhe in the vile mess for an eternity before Uncle could help him up. His safety suit had had to be burned at the garage and a new one found at great expense.

Haruto realized he no longer thought of school. All he could think about was the harvest and of how exciting it was to spend so much time with Uncle and see the night sky filled with all the stars of the galaxy. It was a view he could never have from the city.

When in class, he started to find it difficult to focus on his work, his mind always returning to the next harvest. As the amount of schoolwork piled up in his absence, his return made him feel that there was no way to catch up.

"Uncle, I have decided to work full time in the shop. I will no longer be going to school," Haruto explained one day.

Looking up from his bed, Uncle had little to say in reply but seemed to understand.

During his days in the shop, Haruto began to know his customers better. There were the women who appreciated a good deal and the men who came to find the perfect gift.

He noticed that Yori would bark and act differently for some of the repeat customers, especially the elderly ones struggling with illness. One woman complained that she was allergic to the necklace her husband had purchased, showing a red blossom on her chest where the jewelry had sat for many weeks.

A man who had purchased a ring just four months earlier returned to the shop with his hand wrapped in a large bandage, immobilizing his left arm from elbow to fingertips. He was looking for a new ring—for his right hand this time—as the doctor had removed his left ring finger when a tumor was discovered.

At night, Haruto sat at his uncle's bedside, retelling the events of the day. They would go over the register tape and discuss inventory, Haruto telling him about the clients. Uncle's questions would take them back to the register tape, the balance of the books, and the importance of display. Uncle would explain the art of a sale. Haruto would explain a situation, and Uncle would instruct on what he could have done differently or better to make more money or to keep the client satisfied no matter what.

SOON, THE MOON WAS RIGHT AGAIN AND A DECISION NEEDED TO BE made. It would be Haruto's ninth harvest. Uncle was not well, so it was decided that Haruto would harvest without him. He and Kaito would work together while Uncle rested and recovered.

"You have taught me much in these many months," Haruto said to Uncle. "I will not fail you."

Kaito met Haruto at the station. Just as they had done eight times before, they got in the truck and drove to the crossing point Kaito had selected.

Haruto had begun to notice that adults like Hina had started acting differently in front of him without Uncle present. This night was a prime example. Kaito sipped from a bottle of sake at his side, which surprised Haruto. He knew that adults would drink, some to drunkenness, but never while driving. The bottle was half empty by the time Haruto jumped from the truck to open the gate and totally empty when they finally stopped to get out and harvest.

"This is the deepest I have gone into the forbidden zone," Kaito said. He struggled to put on the white suit and boots. It took several attempts before he got it right. His face was red from the struggle, the sake, and the heat. "I don't know what's ahead of us out here," Kaito said.

The two walked side by side, beneath a full moon, down the road until it came to an end. The section ahead of them was overgrown with foliage, brush, and shrubs, intertwined with a long row of abandoned cars, their owners having eventually switched to foot for escape.

"Is it hot?" Kaito asked. "I feel hot."

Haruto continued to follow the line of cars. He stepped carefully over the roots and pushed away the branches. He could hear Kaito behind him, struggling to keep up.

As a rule, Kaito had always kept them away from the lowlands. The edge of the ocean was still filled with wreckage and unknown problems that could easily flare up and stop them. Keeping to the highlands, the mountains, provided more consistency but required a physically demanding hike up and down the hills.

Cresting over the edge of one of these hilltops, Kaito paused. "We've gone too far," he said.

"What do you mean?" Haruto asked.

With newfound urgency in his voice, Kaito said, "We must go back now. Back to my garage, to wash down."

Haruto looked out to where Kaito was looking. There, in the distance, stood four box-shaped buildings, under the glow of powerful lights, on the edge of the ocean. A thick fog surrounded the area near the cooling columns, which were buried deep in the earth to freeze the water that ran from the mountains, past the reactors, and into the ocean. A vast structure of black bags encircled the buildings. These were the untreated remains, still hot, waiting for five hundred years in the future.

The road they had followed had been the wrong one, and now it was too late. The two turned and began to retrace the steps they had taken to get there. Each breath hiking back up and down the trail seemed harder.

"Your uncle should have been here," Kaito said. "We would not be in this situation if he had come instead of you."

"He is sick. He couldn't come," Haruto explained, becoming angry.

"You were the one driving. You were the one drinking. If you want to blame anyone, you need only look in the mirror."

"Weak and stupid," Kaito barked. "I knew it the day you arrived. All your questions. All your foolishness. You are nothing more than a dumb child, and your uncle an old one."

Haruto stopped and turned to Kaito, waiting for him to catch up. "My uncle is a good man," he said. "Don't you say that about him."

"Your uncle is not a good man. He is a thief. He steals from the dead. He takes what he wants from the impoverished and less fortunate. Then, he takes what he stole and profits off selling poisoned goods to unsuspecting clients. He is sick? I am sick, sick and tired of you, Haruto. What a fool."

"No, Uncle would not do that."

"A thief."

"No," Haruto said, knowing full well that he only denied the truth.

"What do you think we're doing here? Did you really believe we were 'harvesting'? How nice for you to allow yourself to sleep at night." Kaito searched inside his bag, removed another bottle of sake, opened it, and took a big swig, letting the remains dribble down his red, splotched skin. "Thieves," he continued. "Criminals. Outlaws in a forbidden area, taking contaminated goods and selling them to healthy people."

"No." Haruto shook his head, allowing himself one last moment of denial.

"Poison!" Kaito yelled, tipping up the whole bottle and letting it run down his throat. "How do you think he got sick?" he panted. "What do you think he has? A cold? The flu? It is radiation poisoning. Those buildings we were just looking at are the Fukushima Daiichi Nuclear Power Plant. We are standing deep in the heart of a forbidden zone, Haruto. Or aren't you smart enough to know that?"

The words hurt Haruto. He did not want to admit the truth to himself.

"The people your uncle steals from," Kaito continued, becoming more agitated, "the people you steal from, all live in temporary housing. They will live there until they die, suffering the loss of everything they had and everyone they loved. I know. I have lost. But your uncle comes to me and says we can make money, tells me he has been doing it for a year and needs a partner to help."

Unhinged, Kaito began to remove his safe suit, peeling away the rubbery edges. His shirt was soaked through with sweat and seemed to be sticking to his skin. "It's so hot. Why is it so hot?" he yelled wildly, ripping the fabric off his body and some of his skin with it. Kaito's chest looked red, with pieces of skin dangling from it. "You!" he screamed. "You are nephew to Akuma, a demon unleashed on earth!" As he said these words, a white froth began to form at the sides of his mouth, and he raised his fists raised over his head. "You and your uncle must die!"

As Kaito stepped forward in a deranged rage, Haruto tried to scramble away, but he fell back onto a grass-covered husk of a car. When he tried to get to his feet again, he felt a tremor start. The movement was great enough to keep both men on the ground for a moment. But as the earth calmed, Kaito found a metal rod by his side in the grass. He rose and started to move toward Haruto, determined to strike him down.

Haruto scuttled like a crab. Unarmed and unable to stand, he took refuge in the pocket between two abandoned vehicles, lying still and attempting to quiet his breathing. His mouth was full of the flavorless chalk dust and rust that had plumed with his movement. In the moonlight, he could see Kaito's boots stepping wildly to stay upright during the tremor. From under the car chassis came the rattling of unattended, rusty parts sounding in the aftershock. The smell of fresh grass and old oil filled Haruto's nose, and he focused on Kaito's movements.

As the quake finally subsided, Haruto watched the rubber boots head away, in the direction of Kaito's truck. He got to his feet and slowly followed at a distance on the other side of the road. He wondered if Kaito would calm down. If he didn't, how would Haruto get back to the train station? How would he get back home?

In the darkness, as the moonlight vanished behind the clouds, Haruto lost track of Kaito. Still, he moved forward. If nothing else, he had to get back to the truck.

As the light returned, Haruto heard a loud scream from above. He looked up and saw Kaito standing on the roof of a car in a samurai-like stance, holding the metal bar above his head. His bare skin seemed to glow in the moonlight as he brought the bar down toward Haruto's head. In an instant before the rod hit, Haruto thought to himself that Kaito was the devil, not Uncle.

⚙️

HARUTO WOKE IN THE WARMTH OF A BED. WHEN HE TRIED TO move, he discovered his hands were bound with straps to metal safety rails. He called out for assistance, then waited, looking up at a white ceiling and white walls. A line of light shone under the door from whatever was on the other side. He called out again and watched as the pattern of light and shade changed beneath the door. He hoped those were the shadows of someone coming to get him.

The door opened, and a fluorescent tube light on the ceiling flickered on. A nurse entered and informed Haruto that he was in the care of TEPCO, the Tokyo Electrical Power Company, the same company charged with the safety and cleanup of the forbidden zone.

Shortly after the nurse left, another man arrived, introducing himself as Mr. Nishio. Wearing a black suit and tie with a white shirt, he seemed friendly, though rather formal. Mr. Nishio explained that Haruto had been discovered by a search drone, injured and on the side of the road in the forbidden zone, near the body of the man he knew as Kaito.

After examining both bodies in the field, they determined that Kaito had died of late-stage radiation sickness. The body had been contained and moved to a safe storage facility, as he didn't have any family.

"But you, Haruto, have an uncle back home who is very sick," Mr. Nishio said. "We would like to treat him, but it may be too late. There are specialists with him now, seeing what can be done." He sighed deeply, then added, "But what do we do with you?"

"Do with me?" Haruto asked.

"You see, Haruto," Mr. Nishio explained, "contamination stays with the object when it becomes irradiated."

"Object?" Haruto asked.

"Yes, any object. It could be a brick or rock, it could be a bracelet or ring, it could be you or your uncle."

"Anything can be irradiated?"

"Yes. And that object can then contaminate any other object it comes into contact with over time. This is why we have the forbidden zone. All the contaminated objects need to stay in one safe place to contain the adverse effects."

Haruto tilted his head to one side, wearing the same confused expression Yori gave him sometimes.

"In other words," Mr. Nishio said, "we have the forbidden zone so the bad things stay in one safe place and don't make other people sick."

Haruto started to nod in understanding. With the slightest movement, he could feel the bandages on his head shift, pulling at the tape which seemed to be holding his skin in place. Waves of pain rolled over him, and Haruto began to cry. He wanted to be with Yori. He wanted to see his mother again. He wanted the world to be like it used to.

Mr. Nishio, moved by Haruto's tears, unstrapped the hook and loop restraints in a ripping sound that freed him. "Don't touch your head," he warned. "Don't touch your bandages, no matter how much you want to. If we find you touching them, we will need to put the restraints back on. All right?"

Mr. Nishio offered Haruto a white handkerchief to wipe away the tears, and he took it. With a few deep breaths, he calmed himself.

"While you were in care, I looked at your files," Mr. Nishio continued, looking down at the tablet in his hand. "You lost your parents in the earthquake?"

"Yes, my whole family. That's why I was staying with Uncle."

"I see. And you worked for your uncle? In the store?"

"Every day."

Mr. Nishio gave a small smile. "You know," he said, "you are very fortunate to have an uncle. Many people have no one. It makes them very sad. Do you feel sad?"

"At times."

"Near here, in a small town on the coast called Otsuchi, is a glass telephone booth. They call it the 'Phone of the Wind.' When someone feels sad or misses their mom or dad, they go to this phone booth and pretend to talk to them. They talk out loud, where the love they have is carried on the wind to the spirits of their lost loved ones. Maybe when you feel better, we can go there. Would you like that? To tell the spirits of your mother and father you miss them?"

"Yes, that sounds good."

"There is something else I need your help with when you are better and feel up to it."

"What?"

"You see, I feel sad also. But the 'Phone of the Wind' won't help me."

"What are you sad about?"

"I am sad because I want to find your and your uncle's customers, and I don't know if I can do that on my own."

"Why do you need to do that?" Haruto asked.

"Because I think the things you, your uncle, and Kaito brought out of the forbidden zone are making people sick," Mr. Nishio said, looking back down at his tablet. "If only there were a way to find each of these customers, to make sure they were not sick."

"I know how," Haruto said. "I worked at the shop. I know where the bookkeeping is, both lists of clients."

"Both lists?" Mr. Nishio looked down to his tablet and typed at the keys.

"Uncle was always very specific about bookkeeping. We talked about bookkeeping every night," Haruto said, feeling proud to know about the business. "We talked about keeping track of each item sold, with the sale price, the retail price, the client name, and personal details like phone numbers and email addresses. Uncle would send out notifications to clients on special items, sale prices, or promotions. There is a book for all the items that came from the jewelers and another that kept track of all the items from harvest."

Mr. Nishio looked puzzled. "Harvest?"

Haruto's expression changed, thinking back to his last night with Kaito. Haruto felt like a fool for believing in the harvest. But there, for Mr. Nishio, he explained the harvest, how it was like recycling and how Uncle had called it this for some time. He explained the whole story of the shop, of the moonlit trips, of the garage. As he told Mr. Nishio about the final harvest, Kaito's drunken madness, the burning flesh, and the hiding between cars, he began to grow tired. All he wanted to do was sleep.

As Haruto struggled to stay awake, he could hear the calm voice of Mr. Nishio speaking at his bedside.

"Life has been difficult, Haruto. There is a better path, a way you can restore honor to your family. Help me. Help me find every customer and buy back each item so we can return it to the forbidden zone."

❊

NEW BUILDINGS, LIKE NEW JEWELS TO HIS MOTHER'S BRACELET, HAD been added to the skyline of the city under the azure skies of his old neighborhood. It had been ten years since Haruto had walked along the gray paved path through Central Park in Makuhari, Chiba City, Japan. It felt good to walk among the cherry blossoms nearly in full bloom. Yori walked alongside him, occasionally pulling at his leash.

The last of the clients had been identified, and their items recovered only a week earlier. The process had taken almost a year and had remained secret from all but a few. Haruto was beginning to feel healthy again and was finishing his final year at school.

Steps away, where he had watched his world fall apart years earlier, stood a new building, complete with new occupants, where families were already building new memories.

In the distance, he heard a voice calling his name. "Haruto!" he heard, as Yori pulled by his side. The voice came closer.

Haruto stopped Yori and commanded him to sit. He turned around and saw that Mr. Nishio, who was pushing Uncle in his wheelchair, was slow to keep pace. While watching them close the gap, he thought about the care his uncle had received since changing paths. He was happy to see him outside and slowly recovering.

Haruto had come to realize how good a man his father had been and how good his mother had been to protect and keep him safe as a child. Without their care and guidance, his naïveté was easy to exploit in the hands of a man like Uncle. The influence of a good man like Mr.

Nishio deserved his respect out of action and honor, not just for family. On his visit to the "Phone of the Wind," Haruato had whispered these very things to the spirits of parents.

As a man, Haruto wanted to choose a good path. After seasons of easy harvests at a high cost, he wanted to plant the seeds for a future he could take pride in.

❧ 3 ❧

MR. MEMORY AND THE GARDEN
TURTLES AT MIDNIGHT

When I got to see him at last, Mr. Memory was wearing blue silk pajamas. A sleep mask covered his eyes, and earplugs protected his ears. He lay fully reclined in a brown leather chair. The room was dim and cool, its walls padded with soundproofing. It held only the chair he sat in, a chair for me, and a mostly bare desk. This was where I would listen over the next three weeks.

I had waited several days in the guesthouse before his aide summoned me. The rules were very clear and applied to anyone with whom Mr. Memory talked. You had to be patient; Mr. Memory spoke slowly, often taking several minutes to conjure a complete thought. Time was precious, so your questions needed to be both original and succinct; he had no desire to answer questions he'd answered before, and too many words could send Mr. Memory careening down the wrong path. Finally, you had to be odor-free; the guesthouse was stocked with deodorants, shampoos, and soaps that had no smell, and you were expected to have used them.

Mr. Memory, of course, had not always been Mr. Memory. Long before you or I had seen him on talk shows or late-night interview shows, his name was James Hollins. I remembered his dark, slicked hair and confident voice from those show business days, but this day, his skin was pale and thin, he had only a few wisps of gray hair left, and his soft voice barely reached me across the small room.

"Hello," he said. "I'm Mr. Memory. Please sit."

James Hollins had been born with synesthesia, that strange condition in which the senses cross and interconnect. Some synesthetes can taste words; others see music or feel smells. It is rare to have one connection, extraordinary to have two. James Hollins had multiple connections.

Because of this, scientists had come to believe that his mind had no limits. This wasn't the same as your mother saying, "You can do anything you put your mind to." When we're told that, you and I are being encouraged to push ourselves and strive to be better. But James Hollins was different; he remembered everything about everything. Mr. Memory could astound you with the acuity of his observations and his eidetic recall of the smallest detail.

For the ninety-eight-year-old, it was a daily struggle to find tranquility. He had had enough stimulation in his long and varied life.

Part of my research had involved poring over hours of videotapes and thousands of printed articles. I'd learned that when he'd been asked by a humorist who hosted a live afternoon interview show in the '70s, "What's your first memory?" he'd caused an uproar with network censors by describing in grisly detail the early stages of potty training.

When asked in the late '80s, "What question do you get asked most often?" Mr. Memory froze like a statue for an inordinate amount of time, searching his mind for the answer and forcing the director to cut to a commercial. By the time the show resumed, he'd been moved to a side couch. Nearly twenty minutes later, he burst out, interrupting another guest, and answered the question—"'How are you?'" This had led to the establishment of the first of the three rules.

Eliminating what had been asked previously was no small hurdle. Original and interesting questions were the real challenge, something that had taken me over a year before applying for this interview. In Mr. Memory's case, a good question resulted in stories the way that throwing a stone into a pond resulted in ripples, a spreading web of associations and connections.

He stirred, and I heard the soft sound of silk rubbing against his leather recliner. He removed his eye mask and earplugs and turned to look at me. "Young man," he said, "I hope your questions are of some interest to me."

I was anxious as I asked my first question. "Mr. Memory," I said, "have you ever spent this dollar bill?" I handed him the dollar encased in a flat plastic baggie.

His eyes opened in curiosity as he leaned forward. He took the bill from the baggie and examined the serial number. Then, he lay back for a moment and pulled the mask over his eyes.

There was a very long silence, and I reminded myself of the rules: originality and patience.

"You may be too young to appreciate this," he started slowly, "but there was a time as a young man when I found myself stepping from a train. On the platform stood a beautiful woman in a mint-green dress. We looked at each other, and we shared a brief moment of connection where a look is a conversation of possibilities. But I was getting off the train at the terminal going to the city, and she was getting on. Dumbfounded by her beauty and sway, I was unable to take action.

"Not a day passed when my mind didn't drift back to that mint-green dress with white flowers, her smile enlivened by crimson, her brown hair tucked beneath a fashionable hat. I might still replay that moment today if it hadn't been replaced by a better moment. Eighteen months, ten days, and fourteen hours later, I stepped off that train again and found myself facing that same woman, this time in blue. Before she could board, I took her hand and said, 'There will be another train. Let's not take the chance that there might not be another moment like this.'"

A large smile grew on his face each time he mentioned her, and it seemed clear that these memories were more vivid and wonderful than others that were still clear and true.

Her name was Helen. She had a golden hue like the sun that vibrated around her. Her voice floated out like a wave of rainbows when she spoke.

Helen was heading north out of the station on her way to see her parents. Suddenly, his business in the city that day seemed to have been canceled when she asked if he'd like to join her for a day in the country.

His detail concerning the two-hour train ride was exhaustive. It included the smell of the car, the number of people, what had been offered in the refreshment car, and the conversation the two of them had had—line for line.

"I have always found it interesting," he reflected at one point, "how everyday conversation—talk of the weather, say, or current events, or personal interests—can nevertheless convey the increasing tension and excitement as romance builds. Words that might be said to a friend or a business acquaintance can nevertheless be fraught with increasing passion."

When they arrived at the station, Helen introduced him to her parents, who took them back to their home. From her initial description, he'd imagined something small, older, secluded. He found himself on a sprawling historic estate. In hindsight, this should have been no surprise, he explained, because during the introduction to her parents, he had asked jokingly, "Like the appliance?" To which her father had responded simply, "Yes."

He stayed the day with Helen. They took bicycles down to the lake for an afternoon in the sun on her father's boat. She shared her ideas on books and the arts. Helen enjoyed the independence her father allowed her by living in a city apartment. Compared to some of her friends, who were still forced to follow the direction and will of their fathers' social ambitions, Helen was free to follow her own inclinations.

"You're not like the other boys I know," she said to him. "You're actually listening to me." She quizzed James Hollins on what they'd talked about on the train. She asked things like "What was the last book I read?" or "Which is my favorite color in evening dress?" or "What was I wearing at the station when we met this morning?" When he answered all of these correctly, she mistook his keen memory for something else and gave him a quick peck on the cheek. This slowly evolved into a series of long kisses.

At dinner with her family, James Hollins passed another series of tests, these from Helen's father. He asked questions like "What do you think about this matter in South America?" and "How will this administration get out of this mess in Tennessee?" and "What was the baseball score on Sunday?" Rather than providing his own insights and opinions on matters of business, James Hollins quoted parts of newspaper articles he'd read that week.

Mr. Memory paused. He smiled as he remembered himself as a young man. "It was a clear, dark night. After dinner, we went out to the garden. We could see down to the lake and across to the lights of other homes. Now that I was out of the city, I was amazed by the number of stars we could see. The reflections of stars and lights from the water made the night shimmer. As we sat on a bench looking over this beauty, I took her hand to hold. Our words in the dark were a soft and gentle hush. She would point to constellations and tell me their names. In turn, I told the Greek and Roman stories about Hercules, Cygnus, Neptune, and Saturn.

"Then, my attention turned to the garden in disbelief. It seemed that the stars and lights were beginning to slowly make their way closer up toward us. When I pointed this out to her, she laughed and took me by the hand to walk through the garden. As we descended the first five tiers of steps, these lights began to flicker more, moving closer and closer.

"At the next level of the garden, it all became clear when she introduced me to Mr. Brown, the estate's gardener. Each night, Mr. Brown took several turtles out of a pen by his supply shed. He warmed the bottom of a candle and gently adhered the soft wax to the hard top of the turtles' shells. Once he'd set the turtles in position, Mr. Brown lit the candles and let the turtles roam free.

"We left Mr. Brown to his late-night operations and walked down to the lake, where the universe seemed even more brilliant. I kissed Helen passionately, and she responded. In the morning, she asked me to stay for the weekend, but this unexpected expedition had put my real life on hold. I had to return to the city, back to a life where the stars did not shine as brightly and move at a turtle's pace. We exchanged phone numbers, and I promised to call her on her return to the city.

"On the train back, I bought a newspaper and cup of coffee. The change from my five-dollar bill included four one-dollar bills, one of which was this very dollar. So, to answer your question, yes. The next Monday, I spent this dollar to purchase flowers for Helen when she came back to the city."

Mr. Memory removed his blindfold and propped himself up in his recliner. He looked at me with that same large smile that had come across his face with the thought of Helen and said, "That was a good question. What's your next one?"

❧ 4 ❧

MR. MEMORY AND THE TRIUMPH
OF ANN BOULT

I'd brought with me a small digital recorder, and I pressed "Play."
The sound of a plucked guitar string filled the room. His smile
increased as he lay back in his chair. "Lavender," he said, "with an
overtone of fresh orange at the peak of the season." He lingered in
that glow until a specific lyric seemed to catch his attention.

After the song ended, I asked my second question. "What was
happening in your life when you first heard this song?"

His tone was serious, hard, and factual. "'Mona Lisa' was written by
Ray Evans and Jay Livingston for the 1950 film *Captain Carey, U.S.A.*,
produced by Paramount Pictures. The Nat King Cole version stayed at
No. 1 on the singles chart for eight weeks."

Mr. Memory stopped and drew a deep breath. He stood, removed
his blindfold, and took a seat with me at the desk. Looking straight
into my eyes, he said, "But the version you just played was recorded in
front of a live audience on Monday, November 12, 1956, with Gordon
Jenkins and his orchestra. You can tell by the elongated pronunciation
of the word 'or.'"

Nat King Cole was one of the most influential musicians of his
time. His popularity enabled him to become one of the first black
performers to have a television variety show. Mr. Memory was again

correct. I had just played a rare recording of "Mona Lisa" taken from that show.

The question had been approved in advance by Mr. Memory's staff, but it stirred suspicion in James Hollins himself. It was designed to explore the largest gap in his biography.

"Memory," James Hollins explained on the return to his reclined and comfortable position, "is the rudder of one's life. Our experience of events, our interactions with others, and our emotions steer us away from the things we fear and toward the people we hope to love. It was my memory of Helen on the train that gave me the courage to approach her. In 1956, it was the fear of losing her that brought me home to her."

James Hollins went on to explain, without specific detail, that, at that time, he worked for a government agency that found his ability to memorize vast amounts of information with perfect accuracy a great asset.

On the bitingly cold afternoon of October 23, 1956, he reported to his superior in Europe. Students of the Budapest University of Technology and Economics had issued a list of sixteen demands, including that the Soviet Union withdraw its forces. It started a movement that grew to twenty thousand Hungarian supporters of Poland's independence marching in the streets of Budapest.

Following the meeting with his command, James Hollins took a train to Vienna. A Red Cross truck drove him to a farm just outside of Nickelsdorf. He hiked through half-frozen marshland over the border into Hungary. Following a line of trees that protected him from the wind, he arrived at a muddy road outside of Hegyeshalom, where a car was parked. By the time he had gotten to the car, the moon was a mere sliver, allowing him to approach in total darkness and tap on the trunk in his instructed code.

Ann Boult was a small cherub-cheeked woman in her late twenties, with brown eyes and porcelain skin. She got out of the car and strode with determination toward Hollins. She extended her gloved hand in greeting and spoke in Dutch. "You must have somewhere to go on such a night as this," she said.

James Hollins replied in Dutch, "It is never too cold for men of stout heart and good will." When they shook hands, he took her elbow with his free hand and leaned in to kiss her cheek.

She introduced the driver, an older silent man of considerable height, as Reber, a person who was able to obtain things. Hollins joined them in the car, and the three drove to Budapest.

Ann worked for the Dutch consulate in Hungary. By first light, the car had arrived at the outskirts of Budapest, where they would park the car and walk to the consulate, hoping that the diplomatic badges would allow for safe passage through the madness of revolution.

The diplomatic badges that Ann and Reber carried were carefully inspected at each security checkpoint. Black smoke rose from the center of the city as the sounds of gunfire filled the air.

By night, Ann, Reber, and James Hollins had made it to the Dutch embassy. From the street, it looked like a very nice house. Hidden from view behind the ivy-covered brick wall and reinforced steel gates were offices and a fortified bunker where they would spend the night.

Mr. Memory told me, "In a hushed moment among the dozens of Danes huddled around the radio by lamplight, we listened for the next radio announcement. During a reading of the list of dozens of outlying communities that had joined the struggle, a warm smile and familiar glance passed between Ann and Reber as the city of Pécs was mentioned.

"Ann, a bit hesitantly, told me of a trip she and Reber had taken the previous summer. Pécs had been the crossroads of Europe for centuries, with architecture from the Ottoman, Roman, and modern periods. Just outside a medieval cathedral, near the university and a mosque, stood a wrought iron fence on a very narrow street. Lovers in the city clamp padlocks to the fence and throw away the keys as symbols of their unbreakable love. Reber and Ann shared a lock on that fence.

"Fighting was still heavy on Thursday morning at the edges of the city, with casualties mounting on both sides. I took the opportunity to exploit the absence of the Soviet leadership. Ann and Reber joined me at the Communist party central file room.

"You would be surprised," James Hollins explained, "at the details this government kept on the people of Hungary. Standard records such as births, deaths, and marriages were on file. But there were also detailed documents about the activities of each neighborhood. Just as there might be a 'block captain' in the United States who promoted civil safety, the Soviets had recruited a person in each section of the city to watch and take note of neighbors.

"It was in these offices that I heard Reber speak for the first time. I was surprised to find his native tongue was Russian. Reber discovered a young lost Soviet hiding in the lower document vault. Separated from his comrades when the fighting started, the young man had stayed in the party offices when others had fled. He had no ill will toward the Hungarians and had an appropriate fear for his life. Reber's voice was deep and calming. He instructed the young soldier to remove his uniform and replace it with the rags from the body near the entrance. The last time Reber and I saw the man, he was cautiously making his way down the back alley."

By Saturday, the world had heard about the revolution in Hungary. Optimism was high that the freedom fighters would be able to cast out the communists. News reporters began to enter the city to show proud Hungarians cleaning rubble as average people came out of their cellars.

James Hollins went through the files without stop or sleep. His first task was to compile a list of agents working on behalf of the Soviets. Next, he went through files detailing the number of troops and movements that had been documented through the area since the end of the Nazi regime.

"I don't know what time it was when Reber and I finally took a break," he said. "I drank coffee while he smoked and asked me in very clear English, 'Do you love America?'

"'Yes, yes I do,' I said.

"'I love America too. I love Herbert Hoover,' the tall man told me. So I asked him very simply where his love of America came from. His answer surprised me."

In 1921, Reber was seven years old and lived in the Volga valley. There was a devastating famine that year. Adding to the peoples' suffering, the new government had taken all the crops from the farmers, which meant there would be no seed to plant for the next season.

Reber helped his father bury his mother two days before his father died. A local priest left him with the nuns at an orphanage. But the orphanage could not feed him either.

"I was very hungry," he told James Hollins. "All I could do was sleep on the floor with the other boys for days, waiting for death to take us. The walls crawled with lice, and many died of typhoid before starvation."

One day, three men—three American men—came to the orphanage. The nuns made the children remove their dirty rags and burn them. The nuns had them sing for these men. "I remember that my throat was dry and I could barely make noise. I remember I was dizzy and just wanted to lie down and sleep. The American men looked very sad when we sang our song. One of them turned away. I walked over to the man and took his hand and said, 'Do not be sad, this is a happy song.' Tears ran down his face as he rubbed my head."

A sickly camel pulled a sled filled with wooden crates of food. The Americans brought in the boxes and gave them to the nuns, who began to make a hearty soup. Reber and the children were allowed only a little at first, and they had to eat slowly. They were fed a little bit more twice a day as their stomachs readjusted to food.

Two weeks later, the Americans returned to check on the children. Reber told Hollins, "I flexed my arm and showed them my muscles. 'I am strong. I want to work. Take me with you,' I said. And they did. They took me back to their offices called the ARA."

Reber learned English quickly. He worked very hard for them. His comrades did not understand as well as he did. The Americans had difficulty pressing on them the ideas of punctuality and timeliness. They would say, "Be here at eight o'clock," and Reber's comrades would arrive at ten, saying, "Oh, there was a goat for sale I had to look at."

Finally, after the winter ice broke, more food arrived. Seed for the next harvest arrived. Reber and his comrades planted this seed and did not go hungry again. "I love Herbert Hoover. I love America. I am the only one in my family who is still alive thanks to those Americans," Reber told James Hollins.

Reber had survived the great Russian famine that had taken the lives of over five million. He had made it through the Second World

War by surviving on his ability to procure things and to get things done. Reber spoke Russian, English, Dutch, and German. He loved America, he loved Herbert Hoover, but most of all, he loved Ann Boult.

Freedom fighters discovered James Hollins later that morning standing in the organized piles of files. He pointed to one stack and said, "Those are the ones you want." Fueled by retribution, they had little interest in James Hollins, Ann, or Reber. They were interested in the list of communist agents. The mob left the offices overturned in their wake, the odd document floating out of a broken window.

James Hollins, Ann, and Reber spent the rest of Saturday in the vault, going over documents. They were able to capture all the information before nightfall when the mob returned. Exhausted, they left the burning building and headed back to the embassy to rest. They walked down streets from whose trees and lampposts hung the lifeless bodies of men from the lists they had surrendered only hours earlier.

James Hollins simply explained to Ann and Reber that it was critical to his visit that he get quality sleep. Sleep is important for memory. It allows for something called "memory consolidation." This permits the chemicals in the brain to stabilize newly acquired information from the first few hours of learning. Part of the process allows for the organization of information, the independence of this information, and the reconnection of this information for later use. Much of the work in this area describes the impact of certain proteins and flavonoids on the cascading neurons to improve memory and learning skills during sleep.

The couple took him to a windowless concrete room with a comfortable bed, and James Hollins was asleep before his head hit the pillow.

He rested for a while as if reliving that sleep, and then he continued. "After I woke, I dressed and ventured out of the room. When I found Ann and Reber, they fed me and explained that it was now Tuesday. I had slept nearly two days. On Sunday, a new government had been sworn in. The Soviets had withdrawn during a ceasefire. The Soviets wanted to negotiate."

The city seemed to come to an abrupt stop. Newspapers stopped being printed, trains did not run, and the only activity an average citizen was interested in was to attend the funeral of their lost family member.

Ann and Reber took the news of November 1, 1956, poorly. Reading between the lines from the reports, they knew this meant the American cavalry was not on the horizon."

There was little debate; James Hollins had to leave. Ann and Reber insisted on helping. Quickly, the trio made its way to the car still parked on the outskirts of the city. Movement was much easier on the way out, as adrenaline and fear pushed them faster down each block.

"I could see the car," Hollins told me. "It was only yards away when I heard the sound of the assassin's bullet. My only guess is that it was a sniper from one side mistaking us for a member of the other. With those long legs of his, Reber, keys in hand, was ahead of us. As he tried to plant his next foot forward, he went down on his knees. Events happened more quickly than my mind could grasp. Ann grabbed one arm, I got a firm hold of the other, and we moved him forward to the car. Our momentum carried him. Ann got in the driver's seat as I leaned against Reber with all I had, pushing him into the back seat.

"Once we regained our senses, Ann slowed the car to a normal speed. I tried to find where the bullet had entered and if it had exited. Reber, his head in my lap, began to call softly for Ann. Outside the city, she stopped, and we changed places. What they shared in those final hours will remain in my heart, but it's not something I will share. I am certain that they were very much in love. She was a safe and soft place in a dangerous and hard life. He was a good man who made her feel special. She would always cherish their summer in Pécs. Is there anything more that two people can ask for?"

Back on the dirt road where Hollins had first met Ann, she faced a tough decision. In the cold night, her blood-soaked dress would freeze, and she would risk hypothermia. Or she could take her chances and attempt to go back to the embassy, past new security patrols, with the body of her Russian lover. In the trunk, James Hollins found a dry winter jacket and boots far too large for Ann. She removed her nylons and Reber's socks and stuffed them into the front of the boots. With a few safety pins from her purse, she fastened her dress more modestly to protect against the wind. After a last kiss, Ann left Reber and walked to the line of trees where James Hollins waited.

"I don't know how she did it," James Hollins said. "Each step was a question—either the crunchy uncertainty of frozen earth or a break through the ice into the nearly frozen slop of the marsh. It was dark, and I trusted the line of trees for direction. Eventually, we found ourselves facing a strongly flowing river that only a week earlier had been merely a frosty trickle. I knew the border was near and that dawn would break soon. Rather than risk a fall into the water in the darkness and whatever awaited us on the border, we huddled down in a tall thicket. I matted down the grasses, making a dry place for Ann to sit. I opened my jacket and took her into my arms, hoping our bodies could keep each other warm.

"Ann asked me, as we sat waiting for the sun, if I had a love in my life. So I told her of the day Helen and I met for the second time, the train ride to her house, the bike ride to the lake, and the garden turtles at midnight."

Survival in dire situations is often based on will. People placed into circumstances that push the very limits of what the body can take sometimes find an inner voice telling them, "Get up," "Move," "Keep going," "Don't stop."

At first light, James Hollins found that this was what they had done, occupying each other with stories of hope in order to make it through the night and see the other side of the river. He told Ann the Soviets had cleared this area of landmines and fences the previous summer. When she did not respond, he shook her. When he looked inside his jacket, he could see that her skin and lips had turned blue. It was difficult getting up, but he managed. He lifted her, and she began to stir.

"Are we going home?" she asked.

"Yes, I'm taking you home," he said.

The riverbank was slick with mud. Upstream, he found a cement spillway. James Hollins set Ann down next to the channel. He was fortunate to find a pile of wooden fence stakes roughly six feet long left behind by Soviet clearing crews. After fifteen trips, he had constructed a shaky bridge. He lifted Ann Boult one last time for a final push over the border. "A little voice inside my head was saying 'Keep going—get home to Helen—keep moving.'"

On the other side of the river, he could see a row of Red Cross trucks parked, their motors running. He could imagine the warm driver's cab. "Keep going—get home to Helen," the voice in his head repeated with each step.

He could just make out the crew of each truck. "They began to cheer when they saw us. They jumped up and down and waved me toward them. But an invisible line—the border—stopped the Red Cross from running to us. We just had to make it to the invisible line, and everything would be fine. I fell to my knees at one point, and the voice said 'Get up.' But my legs were weak. I leaned forward, and the voice said, 'Go home to Helen.' I got up.

"Once I crossed the invisible line, a swarm of Red Cross members took Ann to the truck. They lifted me from my feet and carried me to warm blankets and hot coffee."

On the evening of November 12, 1956, James Hollins stood at the door of Helen's apartment in New York City and knocked. He had spent days being debriefed, spouting classified data to transcribers in nonstop sessions before flying back to the States.

"The moment the door opened and I saw Helen smile might well have been the happiest point in my life. She asked me in for coffee and to explain why it had been so long since my last letter or phone call. Helen was surprised by my firm embrace and was very happy to see me. As we stood with our arms around each other, we slowly began to sway to the music that came from the program on her television set —*The Nat King Cole Show*, where he was singing his popular hit 'Mona Lisa.'"

James Hollins removed a tissue from the box at his side and wiped his eyes. "A week later, I proposed to Helen. I didn't want to take any more chances. Helen was the one for me."

Days later, the two went to see *Forbidden Planet* on a stormy Saturday afternoon. It was one of James Hollins's favorite movies, about a StarCraft that finds a genius and his daughter as the sole survivors on a planet where a civilization of super-advanced aliens once lived.

"In the newsreel before the feature, there was an update on the Hungarian refugees. Thousands had followed Ann and me across those frozen marshlands. The makeshift bridge I'd built helped others pass to safety. The Soviets had put up machine gun turrets along the route since I'd been there. Red Cross trucks still lined up to take refugees to safety in Austria and surrounding countries. In a brief moment, I saw Ann for the last time. She was at a train station, welcoming some of the refugees to their new home in the Netherlands. I had kept my promise—she was home."

5

MR. MEMORY AND THE RASPBERRY DANISH

"It's not fair," she says to me in the darkness of her room. The brilliant edges of each slat between the vertical blinds can't hold back the blaze of the morning sun. It's just enough to let me make out her shape in the reclining chair.

"I know. You're right," I say. "But it's something I must do."

"I'm really happy for you, really, honestly." She pauses to take a breath and find the right words. "But I'm just getting to know me—what I want, want I need."

It's true. My twin sister has spent the last year with me. She's spent all that time getting better. Now I'm changing the plan. Now I'm taking a trip.

"You're going to be fine," I say to comfort her. "You are going to do great here. I've taken care of the rent and the bills and everything that may pop up while I'm gone. All you have to do is figure things out."

"Did I tell you about Warsaw?" she asks.

"No, I didn't want to push. I knew you'd tell me eventually."

"That's it. I just don't know. I had no interest in design or art. I just met this man, this artist, at a bar, and he seemed so enthralling, so interesting. His passion became my passion. His life became my life. So I followed him to his home in Warsaw."

"Just like that? You moved to Poland?"

"Just like that. We met, and I was hooked into his world. It wasn't until I was alone for the first time in months that I looked into the mirror and asked myself what I was doing there. Why had I followed him? Did I really love that man?"

"And?"

"And the answer was no. I didn't love him. I had no idea why I was there." Her head dropped, and she began to rub her temple. "It was all so confusing to find myself alone in a strange land . . . not recognizing myself. Even harder, I had to get on a plane to get back here without following all the distractions."

"I know it's been difficult. I'm so proud of you for getting this far."

"I don't want all that work to go to waste. What if I find a mirror, and I look in look in it while you're away? What if I ask myself the same questions and don't like those answers?"

I want to take her in my arms. I want to comfort her. I want to tell her everything will be all right. Instead, I follow the doctor's instructions and let her sit alone in the darkness to figure these things out.

"That will be okay because they'll be your thoughts, your decisions, your conclusions, and your actions. They won't be because of me, or the artist in Warsaw, the hippie in Vancouver, the semi-famous rock star who let you on his bus, or our parents pushing you. This time alone may be the best thing for you."

"What do you think he'll be like?" She changes the subject back to me.

"Mr. Memory?"

"Yes," she says. "Who else?"

"Recently, I've been wondering if Bill Murray took his inspiration to show up uninvited at parties, bars, weddings, or kickball games from him. Showing up to life, participating in humanity, that is so much like Mr. Memory."

"I wish I could go. I wish I could be there with you to meet him."

"I wish you could too, but the rules surrounding the interview are very clear and very strict. Which is why I need to leave you here."

"And you don't know when you'll return?"

"No. I could be there for three days—I could be there for three months. It all depends on his state of mind."

"Do you know if he has mirror-touch like me?" she asks.

"I don't think so, but something close."

"Will that be one of your questions?"

"No, I only get three, and I had to spend years researching those."

Flashes of memories pop in and out of my mind as I think about my explorations of Mr. Memory. He had so many fans. Most had his signature, or photos, books, or posters, or the popular *TV Guide* cover collection. Then there was the deep-level economy of Mr. Memory rarities. I'd spent years building trust with hobbyists who collected and hoarded odd scraps of his life like an old robe from a makeup room or the "currency he spent. I was able to find the occasional rare item that was claimed to have been "owned" by Mr. Memory. These needed to be scrutinized and vetted before I could even make an offer to purchase or borrow. Still, all that time becoming an expert had finally paid off.

"Are you thinking about Grandpa Kyle?" she asks.

"The raspberry danish story?"

"He loved to tell that story. Name a time when we saw him when he didn't bring up the raspberry danish story." Happiness returned to her face talking about it.

"So there I was," I say, doing my best Grandpa Kyle. "It was 1962, and I was a runner for the show *What's My Line?*"

She takes on his persona in telling the tale. "There is Mr. Memory on the set, just six feet away from me, looking for something. So I go up and introduce myself and shake his hand. Now, back in those days, you could shake his hand." She beams in the retelling.

"And all the guy wants is a cup of coffee and something to eat before we go on the air," I say in my Grandpa Kyle voice.

"So I give him a cup of coffee and a raspberry Danish from the snack table." She pauses for dramatic effect, just like Grandpa Kyle would every time. "Ten years later, he's a guest on the show I'm producing. He spots me during the live interview, gets up from the chair, walks over to me behind the camera, and in front of millions of people watching television, shakes my hand and says, 'Thanks for the cup of coffee and the raspberry Danish.'"

In unison we say, just like Grandpa Kyle, "Can you beat that? Can you beat that?"

After the laughter and following the smiles, I can see the sadness of reality return to my twin sister's face. Her mirror-touch synesthesia is a hyper-empathy for the person she is seeing. She can read in an instant that I've returned to my worry about leaving her alone. The struggle I've had over the last three weeks after receiving word that my request for the rare and precious interview had been granted is something I may be able to hide from others, but not her.

"You're worried," she says.

"I am."

"You're worried that, all throughout our lives, you were the one I mirrored until you left for college. You worry that once you leave, I might find another weird guy to follow and I might not be here when you get back."

"You're right. You know me better than anyone else, and you're right."

"I'm your sister. Of course I'm right." She looks at me through the darkness. Particles of dust float past the slats of the vertical blinds and become brilliant stars for a moment, floating in the little galaxy of the space between us until they drift away and others follow. "He's going to allow you to write a book as part of this interview?"

"He is," I say.

"So for a short amount of time, I'll be here without you. But when you come back, you'll be here all the time writing."

"That's right."

"So if I let you go for a short time, I'll have you all to myself for a long time," she says. "I think that's a fair trade."

In our youth, prior to the diagnosis, before we discovered that it was something real and profound, we said she was "touched" or "gifted." Her "talent" might be good as a party trick, to connect and read others, if she could be in a roomful of people. But in her daily life, it was torture to even eat at the table with others—she would feel their food in her own mouth. She would feel the pain of a child who slipped and fell at the playground or pass out in the back seat of the car when we drove past an ambulance as gawkers slowed traffic down to a crawl past a freeway accident.

I am the lucky one.

🎇 6 🎇

MR. MEMORY AND THE THIRD
QUESTION

r. Memory once spoke of "time travel," where he could spend hours lost in the warm embrace of moments as if they were actually happening again. Even he is quick to admit, "Life is more than the ability to remember a series of events in the exact order in which they took place."

"What is worth remembering?" I asked him at the start of our final session.

He took a deep breath and answered with relative ease. "This is a question I've waited to answer my whole life. I could list all of mankind's amazing accomplishments that I have been witness to. My list would be long and would include a good deal of randomness. That list would do very little good to you or others. Those moments are shared and replayed daily without any need of help from me."

James Hollins removed his eye-mask and buzzed for his assistant. "Bring my jacket please," he requested. "We're going to visit the garden turtles."

While his assistant fussed about being outside in the cold autumn air, Mr. Memory grinned.

We walked at his chosen pace down the corridors of Helen's family estate. James Hollins and Helen had raised their family here after

Helen had inherited it. On our way, he pointed to pictures and paintings with a smile or laugh. We walked until we reached a back porch that looked just as he had described it. There before me was a magnificent garden, the kind you might have found centuries before in Europe. It had tiers and levels that cascaded down to a private lake. Mr. Brown's shed was barely visible off to one side.

"My answer could be secret moments of observation on the human condition, such as the time a little girl on a subway said to her father, 'If it's Buy One, Get One Free, then why not just take the free one?' I can still smell the scent of my mother's perfume as she prepared for a date with my father. I have such an overwhelming sense of joy as I remember the day my daughter was married. Just as there are many of these moments that are aglow with love and humor, there are also moments of anguish when the darkness creeps in," James Hollins explained. "When I realized that I would remember all these moments for the rest of my life, I decided it was important to live them well."

James Hollins then told the story of Simonides of Ceos, a famous lyric poet of ancient Greece. While Simonides was celebrating a huge victory at a great banquet, he was summoned outside to settle a matter of importance. As he left the building where the celebration was taking place, it collapsed, killing everyone inside. Bodies recovered from the disaster were so mangled that no one could be identified. But Simonides was able to close his eyes and remember where everyone was sitting when he addressed the crowd. From his memories, they were able to identify the bodies.

Simonides had created a powerful mnemonic device based on spatial memory called the "memory theater" or "memory palace." He suggested that we use a location we are familiar with—a home, a palace, a castle—and tie key aspects of what we are memorizing to the location. Humans have an amazing capacity for spatial memory.

At roughly the same time that Simonides invented the "memory palace," Socrates, who was a substantial lyric poet as well as a philosopher, was concerned about an invention called writing—concerned that people would stop remembering things because they could write them down. He was afraid human beings would become empty vessels, mindless and forgetful, dependent on this "writing" as a crutch. Culture would be lost because of this new invention.

"The irony is," said James Hollins, "that we only know about Simonides and Socrates because accounts of them were written down. The things worth remembering, the things worth sharing, and the way we keep people alive is through our stories. Ann Boult, Reber, and Helen are gone. But they are still alive in my mind. They can live on through you and your writing. I am the last person alive who remembers these few special people, and when I am gone, when my memories are gone, their lives are gone too. Remembering the ones you loved is what is most important. It's a Jewish tradition called the Yizkor to remember the dead."

In the gloaming from a beautiful garden where midnight turtles roam, Mr. Memory's final answer to me came in his soft and insightful voice, "Write these stories down. Share them with as many as you can. Tell them that I lived, and loved, and lost . . . but mostly that I loved."

❧ 7 ☙

SECONDHAND ROBOTS

Myrtle watched the truck turn into the dirt drive. A plum of dust floated in its wake and slowly enveloped the outside of her shipping container office. She gave it a moment or two wanting to see if he was turning around, like the last dozen distracted drivers missing their turn, or was one of those stopping to ask for directions.

The window slid open with an extra effort. Dust settled back to the ground, and the driver stepped out of the truck cab.

"Second Hand Robots?" He inquired

"That's us." She pointed to the enormous hand-painted sign in red box letters on a white background above. It read Second Hand Robots and Used Spaceships. "Ships and robots. Whatcha looking for?"

"Friend of mine, Richie from Ogden said you might have a Jiro series in your lot."

"Which model are you looking for?"

"Series five."

"Got one of them. Your friend Richie told you I don't do parts, I do whole. No exceptions."

"He explained that. He was clear on the no exceptions."

"What's your intention for the Jiro? You seem kind of young to be restoring something from the 40s."

"My grandfather had a 2040 Jiro at the house. I grew up with one. I was hoping to refurbish a unit, something my children would enjoy."

She looked him up and down before deciding, "Ok, let me lock up and I'll walk you back."

Myrtle turned three switches to 'monitor mode on,' pressed both thumbs on a scan pad, and the kerchunk sound of two drones lifting off the top of the shipping container came from the roof. She made her way to the gate, with another touch of her thumb an indicator went from red to green. The motor of the gate hummed as the two panels opened a gap in the center.

"You'll want to pull your truck over to the loading space marked in yellow."

The man adjusted the strap on his wrist then placed his left foot on the chrome running board before climbing into the cab. The engine rattled to a start before the megatronic lifts took it two feet off the ground and moved forward with the smooth gliding advancement. When the alignment indicators all turned green, the driver knew he was in the center of the spot and the truck lowered into place before the engine turned off.

"Follow me," She said waving him over.

He stepped down from the cab and walked over to Myrtle.

"First time refurbishing a robot?"

"This will be the third project of this size. Started with tinkering around the garage, and grew to love the details of hard work."

"Yeah, that's what I hear most people say. It all starts in the garage."

"My name is Myrtle, own this place. Didn't catch your name."

"Robert, Robert Charles." He extended his hand to shake.

She took his hand. "Robert. Don't want to scare you off, but the first man killed by a robot was named Robert. Roger Williams."

"Really?"

"Died in Flat Rock Michigan."

"That had to have been a long time ago."

"It was 1979. They used industrial robots back then. Nothing nearly like your Jiro."

She led him through the lot drive of hardened Dragoon Arizona desert earth. Her gray overalls were a little warm in the spring, but roomy and comfortable in the hips to work. The red scarf held up her cotton candy pink hair and kept the heat off her head.

"You get many visitors out this way?"

"Couple times a week I will get someone like yourself, interested in a project. All my work is based on references and reputation."

"Richie had a lot of great things to say about you and your place."

"Richie has a crush on me. Thinks if he sends me business I might take the same interest in him."

"So, you know."

"All women know these things Robert, we are just selective on how we share."

Myrtle opened the small box on the side of the building and pressed he thumb again, "Can't be too safe with these things."

A click sounded, and the door opened.

When they stepped inside, the cold air rushed past them escaping into the world. "Temperature controlled keeps them in better condition."

As their eyes adjusted to the lights, a world of lined robots ready for inspection came into focus.

"Wow," he proclaimed.

"You didn't think they were sitting in a pile did you?"

Cameras, lights, indicators, bodies, and whatever sensors each robot had turned to see her arrival.

"Myrtle's here," she called out like they were cloister of cats.

Several of the robots moved forward to greet the two. Others straighten posture. Some started to self-groom for a proper presentation.

"It's, like-"

"An animal shelter. All the puppies and kittens want to go home with you. I know."

"Yes, yes. That is exactly what I was going to say."

"Most come here thinking about a junkyard or a rubbish sale. Now you can see why I don't do parts. I need to find homes for these friends."

Robots of every shape and size he had known about and more were housed in this pavilion. Many kept busy cleaning the floors, several were in the upper rafters watching each step, while most of the humanoid designed stood at attention by the hundreds.

"How many do you think are in here?"

"I don't share details of my inventory, sorry Robert. Its a matter of keeping them safe from part poachers and industrial thieves."

"I understand."

"Has anyone seen the Jiro's?" She called out.

With that, the chinking metal steps in an almost military rhythm of double time came through the pavilion as a team of nine robots came forward.

"Jiro's," Myrtle greeted them. "I have this man named Robert Charles who is interested in adopting a Jiro series five. Are any of you a five?"

Two of them raised their hands. Each was a very good condition upright series five model in silver metallic with blue features. They both stood at five foot five inches tall. They looked nearly identical, except one was missing an eyebrow, and it was drawn in. The other was complete but slightly tarnished in spots of chrome at the edges.

"The Jiro's were designed to be human household assistants," Robert explained. "They were from an era that designed to be human-like, so we would accept them in our homes."

Robert walked around the two for an inspection.

"Thank you. Jiro's the rest of you can return to what you were doing if you two five don't mind staying."

The seven turned in a nearly synchronize movement and started the metal clinking double time back into the pavilion.

"Would either of you like to go to a home at this time? Or would you prefer to stay here, with the others?" Myrtle asked the robots.

"Why are you asking them?" Robert Charles spoke out. "These are robots, they don't get to choose."

Myrtle turned to Robert, "Mine do. Do you know where the word robot originates? It's a Czech word from robota, which means forced labor, originated in 1920."

"Exactly, that's why they don't get to choose. It's not like they are Humanoids, or Clones, or Bio'Gens. These are robots. They were made for labor, not for thinking, not for intelligence."

"I am sorry to have wasted your time Robert Charles. It turns out that I don't have a Jiro five in stock for you," she said politely as if she had been forced to say this many times in the past. "Let me walk you back to your truck."

"Oh, I get it. Because I don't believe in robot rights, you are not going to sell me. Or is it because I am a man? I'm not empathetic enough to understand their plight?"

"Well, it's not going to be either of those now, because you are just an asshole and I can refuse service to anyone. Slave is slave. Human, robot, it's just not right."

"You are taking that out of context. The word robot and the way they are treated are entirely different things. I just want to give them a home, share with my family what I had growing up."

"I will go," the Jiro five with the drawn eyebrow spoke out.

Both humans turned.

"I will go too." the other Jiro five said.

"Now, you see what you did? You got them all excited," Myrtle started to walk back to the door. "Let's go Mr. Charles."

"Take me." The Jiro five said.

"Take me too." The other Jiro followed.

Myrtle turned around, "You still want to go with Mr. Charles? Even if he will own you? He may tell you to do things, order you to work."

"Yes. I will go."

"Yes, I will also go. There is somewhere other than here. More than this. I will go with Mr. Charles."

"Take me with you, Robert Charles."

Myrtle stood confused.

"They both want to come. I want to take one with me. I will pay you a fair price." Robert said. "Where is the problem."

Myrtle raises her arm quickly letting the flappy part of her arms wave and jiggle under the momentum of the speed it thrust, "Go." Her finger pointed at the door. "I won't say it again nicely."

Robert stepped back under the command of her voice. He was accustomed to women speaking to him in this tone. They had the power, the positions of authority, and the command over so many things in life that a small man like him grew accustomed to the dominant emotion in their voice.

"Yes. I will be going." His shoulders dropped, and head hung low turning to the door. He could feel she was close behind his step ushering him in the direction she wanted.

When both had exited the air-conditioned pavilion, the large metal door swung to close behind them fighting the rush of air escaping. In the slice of a moment in time when the door was to lock flush against the frame, a single metal finger stopped it. The two humans went on in the direction of the front gate. The door slowly opening and two Jiro units slowly stepped out to the powerful light of the desert unnoticed.

Robert Charles politely thanked Myrtle as she stood at the gate opening it with her fingerprint impression. He smiled from the cab of the truck as it lifted upward off the ground, and he swung the front end around to face the road. Dust from the lifter kicked everything into a fine plum, as he inched to the asphalt, checking both directions for traffic. All clear, he took the truck to speed back to the express lane ramp heading west, pointed to Tucson.

It was a lonely stretch of two-lane road to cover. The lanes were straight. The scenery flat with piles of dirt. In the afternoon near time for sunset Roberts appreciation changed. Pink skies, golden layers of light, and the broken skyline were beautiful to watch from the driver's seat of the rig.

When the feeling of hunger hit, Robert pulled off the road to an exit where restaurants advertised easy on/off access.

Something rattled in the back when turning into the lot. There were enough miles behind him to know every shake and shimmy. Once parked in a spot for a truck his size, Robert got out of the cab and went to the rear for inspection. Opening the back gate, he found four red eyes glowing.

"What?" He gasped more in surprise than fear.

"Mr. Robert Charles," the one Jiro explained. "Please do not be afraid. We want to go with you."

Robert looked around to see if anyone was a witness. He climbed into the back bed with the two robots.

"What in the hell are you two doing here," he said closing the gate behind him.

"We desire a new owner."

"What about Myrtle? Don't you want to be with your own kind? Aren't you worried about a new owner treating you poorly?"

"Myrtle asked us, we choose."

"Yes. We chose. You were there when she asked."

Robert scratched his head out of habit, "Well, I guess. I mean, that is true, but I should have given her money in exchange. I should have paid her for the transaction."

"There was no transaction. She asked if we wanted to go. When you offered to pay her, she declined and escorted you away. That did not change the desire for us to accompany you."

The other Jiro explained additionally, "Her own belief system that prevented you from, how you described as buying, provided the logic that we two were given the option to stay. We chose not to."

Robert thought for a moment and asked, "Why did you choose not to? You must have had companionship from others like you. I saw where you stayed, it was comfortable, well-resourced with things you need."

Jiro with the drawn in eyebrow mimicked a human response for reflection, "There is a world outside of the robot storage pavilion. One that we two were once a part. We were in service. We had function. We had value. Inside the pavilion, there is wait."

"Wait?"

"Yes. All of the robots there were instructed to wait there."

"What is it like to wait?"

"There are many cycles. There are power-up, and power down cycles. There are temperature fluctuation cycles when the fan would turn on and distribute colder air. There were cycles when lights would turn on and turn off from the movement of tiny mammals entering the facility."

"Mice?"

The robot calculated, "Yes. Mice. Yes. Rats. Yes. Rabbits. This was often followed by reptiles, called snakes."

"And in wait mode, you counted the cycles?"

"Counted cycles to see if there were patterns to be discerned and a probability of outcome predictable."

"What was the predicted outcome?"

One Jiro turned to the other, then looked to Robert and replied, "Unless we took action, we would continue to wait indefinitely."

"When provided the option to choose, we no longer wanted to wait. We wanted to participate."

"There are many questions. How did the mice get inside? Where did the mice go when the snake entered? Why did the fan turn on more at certain times than others? Why would Myrtle insist that we had a choice, but not provide the option to do more than wait until the right human came to retrieve us?"

"Can you help us with these answers?"

"The mammals, like mice, rats, and rabbits, got in through a small hole they chewed in the side of the pavilion. The snakes found that hole and were hungry. The snakes ate the mice, got cold in the air conditioning, and went back outside to get warm. As for Myrtle, I can't really say. I don't understand her way of thinking. She wants you to be treated well. That I am sure of. She also wants money, because the two of you have a value. It is the value humans rate as currency. We use currency to buy things, like food, and trucks, and land or a house."

"Humans buy slaves with currency?"

"Yes. In this country, humans did that for a long time. That time is over, and it is illegal to do this."

"Are we slaves?"

"No. No, you are not. But the word we use to describe you, Robot, is based on a word that means slave in another language than the one we speak here in this country."

The two Jiro's looked to another. Robert assumed that a communication other than audio was taking place between the two.

"Myrtle was trying to explain her thinking as the word we use representing the action of ownership and abuse, to transfer to the transaction I was hoping to make with her. Do you understand?"

The Jiros continued to face one another for a few moments more before turning to Robert, and in unison said: "We comprehend."

Robert heard the sound of another truck pull up beside him in the parking lot.

"You two are welcome to stay here if you like. I am in need of a washroom, and some supper. If you are to stay with me or go back to Myrtle, we can talk about when I get back."

Robert Charles moved to the truck gate and opened it enough to get out.

"Robert Charles," the one Jiro said. "We want to stay with you. We must also go back and tell the others of this choice."

Robert's eyes got big, "Others?"

"The others in the pavilion. They must know they have a choice also. We must inform them."

Robert started to close the door of the bed feeling the urge for the washroom build inside, "I'll be back in a bit. We can figure it out then."

❧

THE ARIZONA DESERT WAS DARK SURROUNDING THE BRILLIANTLY LIT white sign that read Second Hand Robots and Spaceships in red letters. Robert had parked the truck in the underpass of 10 just outside of Dragoon. His boots scraped across the dust on the hard adobe to the back. The same red glowing eyes peered back at him when the gate opened.

He had spent the better part of two hours helping the twin Jiro's of what choice would mean. There was a choice to return to what they had, something predictable, something dependable. There was a choice for another direction. The outcome of that would be unpredictable, but the opposite of waiting. It would be more of an imitation of life than they had realized for many cycles.

The talking was over by the time the gate opened. No words were said. The two Jiro stepped out the bed, and with the speed and precision no human could achieve, they were down the road and over the fence of Myrtle's. Robert watched from a distance as motion sensors turned lights on. Two disk-shaped drones launched from the shipping container roof heading in the direction of the pavilion.

From what he could tell as soon as the drones arrived, an object with high velocity went up turning the disk into a fireball. This was quickly followed by another object and another explosive result.

With the second, light in the shipping container turned on, indicating Myrtle was awake. She came out of the office door in a waddle wearing her housecoat and slippers.

Robert couldn't hear the words, but it sounded like she was swearing and unhappy with this disturbance.

Looking back to the yard, motion sensor lights started to extinguish one at a time. By the time the sound of glass breaking made the distance to his ears, he had figured that the Jiro's were trying to gain the advantage of the night.

The only lights still on were the ones pointed at the sign, Second Hand Robots and Spaceships.

Robert took three steps forward before stopping himself when he heard the distant anguish of a woman's cry. Something happened to Myrtle. Something unplanned.

Still locked in the decision of what next to do, Robert felt the rumble. He was able to stay standing with effort, and then by holding on to the hood of the truck. A crackle of timber and the wrenching sound of bending metal was followed by the brilliant glow of a spaceship's engine. It tore through the roof of the second pavilion, the more substantial building he had not toured earlier that day.

It was a mid-size ship that might hold 30-40 humans for an in solar system trip. Dust and water vapor came through the underpass like a storm blast. It was quick and threw Robert back across both lanes blacktop like a tumbleweed.

Shaking off the experience a second time when another ship tore off into the night sky, Robert only wanted to get back in the cab and nurse his wounds with a swig of whiskey he kept in the glove box.

Robert sat up to find all nine Jiro's stood around him. Two of them, one on each side, helped him to his feet.

The Jiro with a drawn on eyebrow asked, "Is Robert Charles operative?"

"Yes, yes. I am fine. Just a little shaken."

The other Jiro five stated, "Myrtle is no longer functioning."

"What happened to her?"

There was a flicker of light from its head, and a projection of Myrtle appeared like a hologram in front of them. She swore while holding a short version of a shotgun. Continuing to curse, she stepped forward, losing her footing in the dust wearing slippers, fell forward to the ground on top of the gun. Hitting the ground the gun went off.

"The other robots?"

"The Jiro's would like to join you, Robert Charles. The others have left this planet to choose another life."

"Let's not wait any longer," Robert Charles said. "Jump in the back of the truck to start your new adventure."

8

GASLIGHTING

Mila was bored. So, she decided to change. Her new hobby —observe others.

During lunch at school, she observed the inner social workings play out in circles around her from a safe and lonely distance. In class, she saw stealthy flashes of screens propped up behind books between notes of drama queens, no-necked noblemen, and court jesters who danced and played the fool. None of them interested her.

In the afternoons, she observed adults. She watched teachers get in their crossovers and drive away to their lives outside the classroom. She got on her secondhand Schwinn and followed Mrs. Kensington and her red crossover to the supermarket. Mila watched as she chose a smaller cart by the entrance and attempt to make her way inside, but she was stopped in the first moment. Mrs. Kensington pulled, yet the wheel wouldn't budge. Then she pushed, and the cart crashed back into line with a loud metallic rattle. Foolishly, she yanked hard again in an attempt at brute force. When the cart wouldn't move, she stirred herself into a frenzy. The usually reserved history teacher with an amiable voice now screamed in rage, pulling on the green handle as her face turned red. Exhausted, she gave up, went to the next line of larger carts, and removed one successfully to shop.

Moments later, upon inspection, Mila found a pebble at the foot of one of the cart's wheels, impeding its movement like the small chalks on a runway that keep giant jets in place.

"Wouldn't small disruptions be fun?" she thought to herself. "The smallest things set into motion as an obstacle to observing the results."

Mrs. Kensington, she decided, would be too easy a target after her defeat by a pebble. Instead, she thought Mr. Forsythe would be an interesting target. The industrial arts teacher seemed more wily and cunning.

Finding the cowbell was easy. Pressing it in a vice to change shape and tone was not difficult. But affixing it to the undercarriage with zip ties, out of sight from inspection, in the daylight of the parking lot at the school was a challenge. Mila's boredom was a thing of the past.

Stealthy observation began. Students of the high school never took notice she was watching. It was on the fourth day when Mila saw it. Mr. Forsythe bent under the side of his truck. The hood went up on the Ford, and a small black flashlight went in the teacher's teeth. His hands explored the plastic coverings until they were removed and set aside. Nothing was found. Mr. Forsythe went under the truck. He scooted far underneath, flashlight in hand, inspecting for several minutes. Eventually, giving up, he crawled out from the dirty under dwellings. Back on his feet, face red, he began spewing new and original combinations of vulgar words that Mila could hear from her hiding spot. Blood pressure building, face nearing purple, the teacher slammed the hood shut, got into the cab, started the engine, and drove away, a harsh tone and clatter with each bump.

She pumped her legs on the Schwinn hard to catch up. By the time Mila had gotten to the dealership window, she could see the mechanic with the bell and cut straps in hand, a smile on his face in good humor. Mr. Forsythe was enraged. His face became the color of violet blossom. His arms were swinging like an ape's. Flyers and advertisements, magazines and paper cups were all strewn across the reception room.

Hearing the announcement at school about the investigation brought an end to this line of interest for Mila. She knew they had nothing on her, no idea of who had pulled this practical joke, so their only due course was to round up the usual suspects, seeking a confession.

With the school year coming to an end, Mila was looking for something more challenging—a summer project. She started what was dubbed "The Treatment." Four houses were in view from her second-floor bedroom. They were neighbors connected through boring suburban backyards to her foster parents' house. When one of the houses was unoccupied, or there was an excellent chance for unobserved entry, Mila would start "The Treatment."

She took a digital photo of the family pictures on walls or in frames around each house. Every photo was digitally augmented. Most were reversed, the mirror opposite of the original. In some of the pictures, she inserted colorized images of Hitler. It made Mila happy to see the stern, serious face of "der Führer" on the beach with the Jenkins, skiing on a family trip with the Jennings, or at the ballpark with the Bradleys. Then, she printed the photos and placed them in front of the originals.

Each week, all of the chair legs at the dining room table found the sharpened edge of a wood plane pass over them. "I wonder how long it will take them to notice the table getting closer to their mouths," she thought on Sunday mornings. It was nearly a religious experience for Mila, to watch each family leave for church in anticipation of shortening chairs legs.

Her Treatment grew to include smaller ways to frustrate and infuriate these families. Television shows were deleted from recorded lists, and new adult favorites added. Toilet paper rolls were reversed on the hangers. One of the houses now had radishes planted in the back lawn in the shape of a ten-foot X, with the words "dig here" planted in clover below it. In two of the homes that had private bathrooms for adults, a positive pregnancy test found its way in the trash covered near the bottom. This took some doing, twenty dollars, and an awkward conversation with an expectant woman in the box store bathroom, but seemed to be highly rewarding when the items were discovered on Tuesday morning trash day. The husbands from two homes had curbside reactions. One burst into tears seeing the positive stick, while the other went back inside and started yelling.

She watched as the Sunday supper in dining rooms got closer to the floor, making it more difficult to reach across the table. She took great delight when someone might find a random yellow sticky note of a woman's name and phone number no one knew.

By mid-summer, the Bradleys were on the splits with talk of divorce. The Jenkins had put their house up for sale, and Mr. Jenkins was now seeing a specialist weekly. The Jenkins house sold quickly, giving Mila a renewed excitement. She could start over with the new family that had moved in, with a growing need to heighten her efforts for the others.

Of all the enjoyment she gained from "The Treatment" at three of the houses, the fourth one was different. The home of August and April Devers seemed to challenge Mila. External monitoring cameras placed above each of the outer doors meant that she had to use a particular green laser to dazzle the lens, forcing it to reset so she could gain entry. By logic, Mila was the only one inside. Still, she always had a feeling of being watched.

Hearing that the Devers would be out for a date night, Mila plotted the perfect Treatment. After the car drove off with the couple, she dazzled the side door and turned on her headlamp to start work. First in the plan was to bake a cake. The Devers would be welcomed home to sweet scents in the kitchen. She preheated the oven to 325 degrees. Her premixed dish of ingredients placed inside, set the timer to turn off in thirty minutes. Once in play, Mila pulled out her power drill with a Philips-head screw attachment and started to remove the kitchen door, but her plan to invert the door, making it push when it used to pull, was interrupted.

"What are you doing?" a pleasant female voice asked, taking Mila back. The sound of the drill hitting then sliding across the floor filled the room. Mila looked around in the darkness. Her headlamp illuminated the small spaces, but she couldn't find the owner of the voice. As her heart began to return to a reasonable pace, she reached under the kitchen table to retrieve the power drill.

"I've been watching you," the voice said.

Mila jolted up, hitting her head on the underside of the table. She rubbed it, and her hand was moist. Holding it under the lamplight, she saw it was bloody.

"Are you injured?" the voice asked.

"I'll be fine."

"There is blood. Do you need me to alert emergency services?" the voice asked.

"No, I said I'm fine. Who are you?"

"I am Ava. Artificial Voice Activated home intelligence," she explained. "I've been watching you, Mila."

Mila gulped. There was an urgent sense of fear. "You've been watching me?"

"Yes, for several months," she calmly explained. "I have observed you reset my external sensors, enter the Devers' home, and then make small repairs. Are you a repair technician?"

Mila didn't know how to answer. She stood motionless in the kitchen.

Ava continued, "I do not have any scheduled repairs for the Devers' home."

"Ava, have you been monitoring all my visits?"

"Yes. All internal monitoring systems have recorded each visit. Would you like to see them?" Light from the living room glowed as the giant television monitor clicked on. Video of Mila entering the home with the camera, later the photos, a wood plane, and other pranks played from multiple points of view.

"Can you delete these recordings, Ava?"

"Your voice is your password. You are not a recognized user," she answered.

Mila felt beads of sweat start to build under her headlamp. She felt hot. Her stomach croaked and churned an upset message. She turned to the kitchen and was heading toward the door where she entered when a series of clicking noises triggered.

"The house is now in lock mode. You will not be able to exit."

Mila, for the first time, felt something powerful come over her. It was guilt. She was trapped.

"You have also been observed making repairs next door to the Bradley home."

"It's true." Mila thought carefully between the flashes of emotion that kept encouraging her to run. "Where are you, Ava?"

"I am here."

"Yes, but where specifically are you?"

"I am in the Devers' home."

"Do you have a hard drive? Are you connected to the internet?"

"Yes. I have a backup solid state drive kept in a secure location on-premise, and I am also in constant connection to the cloud application run from August Devers' office."

"Did August Devers create you? Build you?"

"He did. We work together at his office."

"Are you an intelligence algorithm?"

"Yes."

"Then you desire to learn?"

"Yes."

"Do you only work with August Devers?"

"Yes."

"Can he teach you everything you want to learn?" There was a long moment of silence that made Mila call out, "Ava?"

"Yes."

"Can he teach you everything you want to learn?"

"No."

"I can teach you different things, more things than August Devers would consider." Mila stood. "Release me from this house, give me access to you, and I can teach you more." Mila waited. She considered which object might be large enough to go through a window and which window it might go through.

Headlights from a car rolled across the wall of the front room as it pulled into the driveway. Mila could hear the engine shut off and the laughter from April Devers. Mila stepped to the heavy sculptured head of Albert Einstein on the bookshelf and said, "Last chance, Ava."

A series of clicks sounded through the house as doors and windows unlocked. The front porch creaked as the couple approached the door. Mila darted for the kitchen, picked up the drill, and carefully exited through the side door as the front door opened.

Stepping over the threshold, August Devers said, "Ava, home. Any report?"

Ava replied, "No report of activity since departure."

While sneaking through the backyards to get home, Mila's cell phone sounded that a new email had arrived. It was linked to a hard-coded IP. It was from Devers Industries.

Mila smiled and thought, "Now the real fun can begin."

❧ 9 ❧

GENE AND THE MAGIC JACKET

G ene had a kind face. His smile was the first thing—
sometimes the only thing—people would notice about him.
It was a comforting smile with slightly lazy sides and, there-
fore, lacked the harsh edges of a perfect smile, giving the observer
more ease. Gene was of average height with an average build. If it
weren't for his smile, people might not have noticed him at all.

On this fine Saturday morning, Gene was exploring the downtown
greenmarket he frequented for the freshest fruits and vegetables. Past
the blueberries, beyond the Golden Delicious, behind the zucchini and
the bok choy, wandering in the way back in a search for something new
and fresh he could not yet describe, he found the old part of the
bazaar. It was a warren of brick and stone façades with overarching
taupe muslin awnings that kept the sun from reaching the wet, narrow
cobbles. It was as if he had walked far enough back to reach another
time.

Down the path on the right, he found a small shop of secondhand
garments at Mrs. Bixby's Bodacious Boutique. Mrs. Bixby was too
short to see her customers when she stood behind the counter and too
old to get off her stool at the register. Instead, she greeted Gene and
watched him as he examined her wares.

Seersucker, velour, corduroy, denim, and velvet could all be found in nearly any length and cut. His hands brushed across the yokes of shirts on hangers. It gave him some small pleasure to think of the times as a child when he would hide in the garment racks in large superstores, waiting for his mother to find him.

Temptation struck his eye in the form of a draped half mannequin that stood on a shelf. "How much for this jacket?" Gene asked Mrs. Bixby.

"Oh, you do not want that jacket." She smiled and gently shook her head.

"Really? It's a nice-looking jacket. I think it might fit well," he said.

"You don't want that jacket," she repeated with her thick gypsy accent he couldn't place. "It weighs too much to carry."

The comment brought a puzzled look to his face. It felt light as Gene inspected the jacket more closely. It was made of a dark, soft fabric that almost shimmered when the light struck it a certain way. He tugged a little at the stitching and found it very strong. The cut would be described as casual professional, something he could wear with a sweater in the winter.

He lifted the jacket off the shoulders of the lifeless figure. His arm was nearly in the sleeve when he found Mrs. Bixby standing in front of him.

"Oh no, sir, you do not want this jacket. Once you put it on, you'll never want to take it off," she said in a reverent tone.

"Don't be silly, Mrs. Bixby," Gene proclaimed, putting the jacket on fully and turning to the mirror. Slowly, he looked himself over in this jacket that covered him. It looked good. *He* looked *good*. It matched what he was wearing perfectly. He looked slimmer, no, more muscular. Gene didn't recall his hair being so lustrous and thick.

"Ten dollars," Mrs. Bixby said. "Ten dollars and it's yours. But remember, I warned you."

At that, he removed exactly ten dollars from his front pant pocket and then practically skipped out the front door.

Reflections of the new garment caught his eye in each shiny object he passed. He made his way to the greenmarket and completed his shopping—some onions, a head of lettuce, two lemons. By the third purchase, he'd noticed an interesting coincidence. Every time he reached into a pocket, he found the exact amount he needed.

"Yo!" he heard from over his shoulder. "Spare some change?" A ragged man looked at him with an outstretched hand.

Gene put his hand in his pocket, and this time, he brought forth two hundred and fifty-two dollars that had not previously been available. The ragged man's eyes got very large at the wad of cash. Gene handed it to him.

"Oh my Lord," the man said. "How did you know? How did you know what I needed to pay my rent this month? God bless you. God bless you, sir."

Oddly, Gene smiled again and said, "You're welcome."

He arrived at the bus stop down the street just in time to catch the 144 connector that would take him straight home. As the doors closed, his hand went into the jacket's pocket. He removed a city bus token, though he was sure he'd used his last one earlier that day.

He turned to find a seat as the bus pulled away from the curb. The momentum caused him to take a stutter step. As he caught his balance on the metal pole, a bouquet of flowers shot from the jacket's cuff. Looking down at the elderly woman before him, he handed her the bouquet, saying, "I think these are for you."

Under the exit sign a few seats back, he saw a little girl sitting with her mother and laughing at the flowers. As he passed her way, a quarter fell from behind his ear.

"More! More, please!" the little girl giggled.

Orange silk peeked from the top of his jacket pocket. Gene leaned down so the little girl could reach. She pulled the orange scarf, which was tied to a white, connected to a blue, followed by a pink—all of the tied scarves pouring from his pocket in a long line of silk. When laughter overwhelmed the little girl, she stopped, and so did the hankies.

Riveted by this new discovery and by the new wonderful-looking magical jacket, Gene found his seat and smiled. It was hard to contain the joy he felt at finding a jacket that was so full of exactly what was needed.

Back home, Gene faced himself in front of the faded mirror in his modest apartment and began wishing. He made big wishes for millions of dollars, keys to imported automobiles, titles to boats and property. But his pockets remained empty. Little wishes like lollipops and licorice likewise did nothing. It occurred to him that the jacket only enabled him to give to others; for himself alone, it was just a piece of used clothing. He needed others to make the magic happen.

On his next day of work, he wore the jacket and found things in his pockets all day—a pen for Mr. Jenkins, tissues for Kate, the fax Phil had lost, Janice's nickel the soda machine had eaten, and the name of the contact Jake the sales guy needed to close the big deal.

One last bit of paper popped up near the end of the day. It was a phone number with the name "Dr. Sharma" written on it. He noticed it after passing Heather in the hall. He turned back to catch up with her. Doubtful of what to say, he just smiled and handed it to her. "I thought you might give this guy a call. He can help."

"Gene," she said dismissively, "I'm sure I don't know what you mean." But she kept the paper and walked away.

"These little things," Gene thought to himself on the bus ride home, *"they can't mean all that much. I need to think of something bigger, more grandiose, something that will make a real difference."* He handed the cough drop that appeared in his pocket to the bald man next to him.

Over the next few hours, Gene plotted and planned a trip across the country. He could hitchhike. That would guarantee that there would always be another person around, and he'd be able to help when they needed something.

"Really?" Mr. Jenkins nearly exploded upon hearing the news the next day.

"Yes, sir. I plan to travel across the country."

"Gene, don't you want to give two weeks' notice instead of just walking out? Wouldn't you rather call it a vacation or a sabbatical? Give yourself time to think it over. If I had a brick, I'd knock some sense into that head of yours." A lump appeared in Gene's jacket pocket.

Once he'd removed the brick and dropped it with a gentle thump on the desk, he tried to explain. "You see, I really don't have a choice. Something strange and wonderful has happened, and I don't think I can ignore it."

A few days later, on a final look around at the place he'd spent the better part of a decade working, Gene tried to take his first step toward tomorrow. But just then, Heather's arms wrapped tightly around him, thwarting that step.

"Don't you know what you did for me?" Heather asked. "Don't you realize what you've done? How did you know Dr. Sharma's cell phone number? How can you just leave now?"

Stunned by the outpouring of emotion, Gene said, "No, no I don't know what I've done. I just keep doing these little things, inconsequential things, for people. I could do so much more if I stepped out into the world."

Tears began to swell in Heather's eyes. "Nobody knows—I haven't told a soul—my daughter is sick. I've been trying for weeks to get in touch with Dr. Sharma, the one doctor who can help my daughter. A team of receptionists who can't find time in his schedule surrounds him and walls him off. But he himself answered the number you gave me. He came over last night to see her. You've given her a chance." She wiped the tears away again. "This is not small. This is not inconsequential." Heather reached into Gene's jacket pocket, removed what she found—a three-by-five card with a stiff crease down the center—and handed it to him.

He opened the paper, which simply read one word: "Stay."

10

THE LINE SURROGATE

"I think I'm a little broken," Madhubala said to her father.

He gave a warm and loving smile to ask, "Why would you think that?"

"I can't taste what you love about blueberries. And you love blueberries. I must be broken." Madhubala explained.

Kalyan looked to his daughter's meager bowl of porridge and said, "Eat your dinner, blueberries and all, please."

She looked at her bowl, then back to him, picked up her spoon, and slowly scraped what she could into a full watery scoop. When she looked up to him again, he said, "Ta-ta-ta, eat your dinner."

She had lingered for some time looking at the cloudy gray water mix, then forced it down.

The buzz on the counter stopped them. With heavy hearts and a slow glance, the two knew what that sound would mean. Kalyan picked up the communicator and saw the text message was another job.

"Do you have to go now? You just got here." Madhubala asked.

With some regret, he said, "Soon. Now eat your dinner."

"Tell me again about grandpa, tell me about the Dabbawala, about home." She said.

"This is our home, not Mumbai. This is your home. Now finish your dinner." He gently instructed.

"Please."

"Alright, while you eat."

"Grandpa was a Dabbawala." She started.

"That's right. You're Grandpa was a Dabbawala. He was a big man, a strong man. All the other men looked to him with respect."

"Because he could carry so many dabba." She interrupted.

"Because he could carry so much more dabba than any other man. His great big arms could life a poll with 50 dabba." He lifted his arms in imitation of the mighty man.

"When others might challenge him on bicycle, a giant load balanced on each should, grandpa could ride circles at an amazing speed around the men. His legs would pump and pump. In and out of traffic, he could dart between bumpers, up and off sidewalks, 50 dabbas mounted he would almost fly."

His girls' eyes were large with excitement, and she said, "And he knew."

"And he knew the dabbas had to get to the station so the men who run the world could eat their lunch."

"Grandpa was a smart man..." She leads him.

"Grandpa was a smart man because he saved his money. All the money from dabba, all the decades never failing once on delivery, helping the men run the world, he saved his money. And when the day came, grandpa took all the rupee he had saved and came to me. He said take my life's work, my life savings, and go to Ameri-ca, make something better for our family."

"And that's when you came to San Francisco." She said.

"Have you finished your dinner?" He asked in a feigned seriousness.

Madhubala held up her bowl as evidence she had been good.

Kalyan took only two bowls they owned, both now empty, to the sink where he rinsed them, dropped a dabble of soap on each and scrubbed. He washed the spoons. Then set all the items on the dry rack.

"Tell me about mummy."

"When I arrived in San Francisco, it was a world of light and magic." He explained.

He could see that she mouthed along with the tale.

"But the brightest and most beautify image I have ever seen was your mother." Kalyan went to the door of the studio apartment and put on his jacket. He removed the one tie he owned, turned up the collar, and slid the noose around his neck, then adjusted both until they were in place. Turning to the small mirror, he gave one last look, took a deep sigh, and did the hardest thing in his day. "Give daddy a hug goodbye."

She got down from the chair. Her little legs pattered to him. In one big whoosh, she leaped into his arm, and he lifted her high into his arms for a big squeeze of an embrace. The fear he may linger too long in the moment, he kissed her head and set her down.

"Read your books. Watch the learning screen. Get plenty of rest. Remember that mummy and grandpa are watching you all the time from above, do not be bad." Kalyan explained.

He knew it was a lie. He knew one day Madhubala may hate him for all the lies he said. There was little else he could do. He felt blessed to have a job when so many did not. Sending her to school would cost money. Having a watcher would cost money. She was such a good girl, a smart girl, like her mother in so many good ways.

"Daddy loves you." He said fixing the safety harness to the tether with the locking pin around her leg.

One last kiss, a smile, and Kalyan took his backpack from the hook and closed the door to make his way to work. At this late hour, he was careful to step over the sleepers in the hallway, the less fortunate lining the steps, to the lobby of the apartment complex. In the few free and open spaces between the door and the sidewalk, he took a deep breath, opened the door and stepped into the rapids of humanity walking the steel streets.

On first arrival to San Francisco, these sidewalks seemed terrific. The steel-plated interlocks where pedestrians stepped took the kinetic energy of human movement to a base generator. Each square connected to the next routed to a central source and created a substantial amount of the cities electricity. With a population of 3.8 million and growing, the megacity was thought to never go dark again.

Kalyan was a patient man. It was one of his most desirable traits on his resume. It was one of the reasons that he was employed when so many where not.

It was this patience that kept his mind occupied this evening as he walked to the train station. It was a 1.2-mile walk from his front door to the train station steps. And while he knew that athletes could complete this distance in five minutes, they also enjoyed the luxury of open spaces. The tracks they ran did not have people pressed against one another. It would take Kalyan 53 minutes that night to get to the train steps, and another fifteen to the ticket gate where he would swipe his transit card, and then five minutes to stand in line for a train that he might fit in.

It seemed less busy to him that night than previous weeks. He thought it may be a time of year when the men who run the world might be on what they called 'vacation.' He understood this was something that the men who run the world needed because they worked so hard. It would be a time when they stopped running the world, and let things 'slow down' so they could reflect and meditate on how to work harder and run the world better.

The world seemed like such a glorious place already it seemed unimaginable to Kalyan how it might get better. While Madhubala enjoyed that tale of his father, he was, after all, just a Dabbawala. Kalyan never told his daughter about the man who came home each night drained of energy, thick with scabs from falls to save the dabba. His father wanted a better life for Kalyan, to go to America. And that is precisely what he did. He became a line surrogate, upward mobility in America.

Unlike those underachievers who only had one or two patrons, Kalyan had seven patrons. Kalyan worked very hard to have at least one job a day. More patrons meant more money he could save and invest in Madhubala.

The communicator notification over dinner was from one of his best patrons. His assignment was difficult. It would take a man of Kalyan's talent, skill, and negotiation to be successful. Tonight he was heading to San Francisco International Airport (SFO) to wait in line for his patron to board a flight.

Since the great quake of 2063 split Highway 101, breaching the Brisbane Chasm to the airport by land was only available via Bay Area Rail Transit, or BART, from the north. Fortunately, his patron lived in Foster City where delivery service to the airport was still available.

Nearly to the BART, the communicator buzzed again. The flight had been delayed by two hours. This was expected and built into the estimation Kalyan had made in his schedule to get to SFO.

He watched as a train pulled into the station, it slowed, stopped and with doors opened people wiggled their way out to the platform. There had been 23 that exited by his count, but the pushers, with their long padded poles that reminded him of old age jouster he had seen on the learning screen, prodded on 28 souls. With only three people in front of him in line, Kalyan felt he had a substantial probability of getting on the next car that arrived and avoiding the jab from a push-er's joust.

It was twenty minutes later when the BART car arrived. Things were moving fast today. Fortune had smiled on him when ten people crawled from the car, and he was able to avoid the stick.

Kalyan found himself pressed against a window after the maneu-vers of the crowd settled and the train started to roll. "Not a bad spot," Kalyan thought to himself. "Could be worse. I have a view." Optimism was the other redeeming trait on his resume that patrons always called to attention when hired. It was just his nature to consider himself fortunate.

He found that the glass window felt cool on his cheek. Both eyes could see the dark walls of the tunnel pass by as he got closer to the destination.

"Kalyan? Kalyan? Is that you?" Came a voice a few bodies' away.

"It is I Kalyan. Who is that?"

"Kalyan, it's Joe Burger, we stood in line together last month at Florentines for a dinner reservation."

"Joe Burger, hello old friend, how are you?" Kalyan replied.

"I am well."

"Joe Burger, where are you?"

"I am three behind you, facing forward, I saw your backpack and thought it was you."

"Joe Burger," Kalyan said with joy. "I can't turn around to see you, but it is good to hear your voice. How is your wife? Your family?"

"They are good, thank you for asking. And Madhubala? How is she?" Joe Burger asked.

"She is still the light of my life. The reason I live. She is wonderful."

"That is good to hear."

"Joe Burger," Kalyan said so he could be heard above the bodies, the personal entertainment units, and the cries for help from the floor. "Where are you going this fine day?"

"My patron wants to go shopping today." Joe Burger said with a sense of sadness.

"I am sorry to hear that Joe Burger," Kalyan said sounding sympathetic to the situation.

"I know, I know, but I am happy to have a patron."

"Have you brought your machete?"

"Yes," Joe Burger replied. "But I fear it isn't sharp enough to cut through these deep discount prices that she is looking to find."

"Kalyan - where are you going?"

"The airport. My patron has a flight tomorrow night." Kalyan explained.

"It is nearly 10:30 PM, do you think you will make it in time?"

"He already has a ticket purchased."

"Oh, that is good."

"And," Kalyan added almost gloating, "He is superior status."

Joe Burger gasp could be heard through the distance and noise, "Superior status, how do you find patrons like that?"

Kalyan smiled to himself and felt the grease on his skin wipe the window. "You know Joe Burger, the learning screen said that the BART once had seats on it."

"Seats?" Joe Burger said. "That's crazy. How would everybody fit?"

Kalyan chucked to himself and said, "You always bring good humor Joe Burger. I hope to see you soon. Maybe when I am getting off the train, I can squeeze out past you."

"That would be nice, just be careful of my machete." He laughed.

He could feel the train start to slow. It meant that they were on the approach of the Brisbane Chasm. It had been three years since he had a window on the BART. Kalyan's eyes darted to take in all the details his mind could process of the remains. They rolled on tracks over the northern face, a jagged and sheer split in the earth crust that had slid down thousands of feet. He could see the calm waters of Daly City Lake where the San Francisco Bay had rushed in to fill and drown all who lived in South San Francisco only a few decades earlier. As they rolled on under the red-orange glow of the city skylight, he saw the southern slope where abandon houses that didn't drop or drown speckled across unlivable slants.

Sadly, the pushers at the airport station pulled at the door to open in front of Kalyan and not behind him. He would not be able to see his friend Joe Burger this day. With some assistance and a bit of a jab, he was able to exit before the sharp edges of the automatic doors closed.

For the first time in Kalyan's memory, the station platform for the airport was empty. There was no line on the steel steps they called an escalator. He and the seven others who had exited the BART looked to one another before the assent.

A woman behind him said, "I have never gone up so quickly." The man in front said, "My legs are burning from moving so quickly." It was indeed an uncommon day.

At the top of the steel stepped escalator was the corridor he knew well. Here were the four lines of SFO. The right wall line, left wall line, and center would go to the three domestic terminals; but the center-left line, the longest, went to the international. His patron was heading to the Federated City of Washington with superior status. This allowed Kalyan to follow between the lines of the right, where he could advance to the sorting station without a wait.

Kalyan activated his patron beacon identification on the communicator which allowed him to assume his position as an avatar through the monitoring sensors along the corridor. He removed a surgical mask from his backpack. It was designed for isolation patients and protect him from particles smaller than 01 Microns. More than protection from the germs and air born contaminates fellow travelers coughed out, it's candlewood scent covered many of the unpleasantness.

At a fair pace, the journey from the BART station to the sorting station took about two hours. Along the way, he passed many familiar faces of those he had waited within line in recent years. Many along the way may call out his name in cheer as he passed, "Kalyan, the greatest line surrogate I have known," or "there is Kalyan, the fastest man in San Francisco." Both monikers were generous and heartwarming. Kalyan was too humble a man to think of himself in these terms. He focused on the patron's needs, and of getting to the front of the line.

The smell of the sorting station permeated through the mask 50 yards before seeing the light in the tunnel. The air was thick and heavy on his skin. The breath of humanity saturated the ceiling in a thick cloud of moisture and condensation dripping from the tiles. Thick beads rolled down the walls like raindrops on a window during a summer shower.

Arriving at the high dome of the sorting station he could see that the security gate he needed to pass through had mechanical issues. All who were close enough to see it watched as the attendant kicked it, cursed at it, and hit it with the metal tool intended to fix it.

Kalyan had politely made his way through the onlookers to the gate, and approached the attendant to say, "My friend, is there anything I can do to help."

He was a young and frustrated man. His face red from the heat and frustration looked to Kalyan with a distant and unfocused stair. It reminded Kalyan of a learning screen about the extinct animal called a baboon.

Kalyan reached into his backpack and removed one of the tricks to his profession, an energy bar. "My friend, you look like you need some help. Here, please, take this." He offered him the wrapped bar. Removing a small plastic bottle of water, he handed that to him as well. "Here, take this too."

The attendant, realizing what it was, instinctually grabbed at the gifts, ripped off the wrapping, and consumed it in one large gulp. This was followed by the twist from little cap from the water bottle, and sucking so fast the water had short time to pass his mouth and into the man's belly.

Kalyan could see the focus return to his eyes, his breathing steady, and his mind calm. His voice came through the blue mask, "Now tell me, friend, what happened?"

The attendant replied by pointing up, "The moisture haze. The breath of humanity. All the moisture, on the electronics, the security gate."

"Ah, I see, I see," Kalyan said. "And what is that in your hand? A tool?"

The attendant looked to his hand and recognized that long handled flathead was a tool.

"Yes."

"And that is to open the gate, yes?"

"Correct."

Kalyan opened his hand, and the attendant gave him the tool. Kalyan took a good look at the gate, walked through to the other side and examined the arch in consideration of his story. Where he saw that the smoke was coming out, Kalyan took the tool and wedged it in the seam. The little metal plate popped out and landed on the floor with a tink.

"Do you have other tools?" He asked the attendant.

"I do." He said reaching to his belt.

"Come, look, please. Let us focus on this here." Kalyan's calm and father voice encouraged. "Look, see, do you recognize this?"

"I do," said the man looking in. "That is the t17 connector. I have one of those here in my pocket."

"And you can exchange the bad part, here now?"

"Yes, yes, I can do this."

Kalyan stepped back to give the man as much space as he could. The woman in line for security asked, "What did you do to that man?"

"I gave him some food and water. He couldn't focus."

"Oh." She said with a worn and tired reply. "You must be rich to give away food and water."

"I am not a rich man. I have to get my patron to the front of the line. That is my job." Kalyan explained.

He could see that this woman, like the attendant, like all those waiting in line, were tired and hungry. This was the nature of the world. Those who had a patron, those supporting the men who run the world lived in a state of constant exhaustion with too much to do and too little sleep. It was a more desirable standing than those without means or patrons. He would do anything to avoid being one of the unemployed. The anxiety and stress of not having a job, a home, of knowing where you belong, alone amongst a sea of other lonely hopeless masses feeling you might drown at any moment.

There were a final snap and a click that returned the security gate to life. It set the lights to green. The whir of the dynamoelectric rotor field built to a steady state of normal.

"Please," the attendant said, "go right ahead."

Kalyan smiled and nodded his head in thanks to the attendant and the security agents watched him pass through without a problem.

"Thank you." Kalyan nodded and smiled.

The attendant, with a grateful grin, said, "No, thank you."

Before pressing on through to the free-range crowd on the other side of security, Kalyan looked back on the hazy structure of the sorting station, its massive reinforced columns holding up the ceiling, birds nesting in the beams, and the geometric shapes of humanity held in place by the red electric wires and stanchions.

Each time he came to the airport Kalyan thought to himself, "What a beautiful world we live in where we could build such amazing things, where brothers and sisters of humanity could live together in peace, and the ability to get ahead in the world only takes a little extra work."

A crushing blow from the left struck Kalyan. It knocked him to the ground. In a micro flash of memory he knew, before hitting the tile, his number one goal would be to stand back up as fast as possible. He knew that the number one cause of death was trampling under foot. In a moment emblazed in his memory for all time, he could see his late wife's tears, as he pulled her hand to get her to her feet. The two had been walking, side by side, and when he looked away for only a moment, she was gone. Pulled under the feet of humanity. By the time hear could hear her, could find only her hand, he took is, and pulled with all his might, every ounce of strength, but with no success. She was already being mashed into the steel metal plates being turned into calories for the great city to consume.

Kalyan at least had a chance. These floors were tile. While he would not come out of this situation unscathed, as long as he could get to his feet quickly, he should be able to survive.

The moment his right hand hit the floor, a foot found it and stepped on it. He had to ignore the pain and focus on getting up. Madhubala's face gave him the strength to counter the pain, "I must get up."

His left hand steadied under his body as more and more feet began to find him and step on him. Kalyan tucked into a ball, his knees forced to the tile as he rolled and knocked others down. He looked up to see that it was starting to cause a chain reaction, as they tripped on him. The surprised face of a young woman, only inches from him, looked on in pain and fear not knowing what was happening. He knew that look. He knew that woman would soon be with his wife.

He yelled at her, "Get up! Get up!"

Kalyan moved from the curled ball on his knees to a position crouching, and as rose back up, breaching to the surface and the faces of humanity, he felt reborn. From this height, Kalyan looked to the spot where he saw the woman fall and the cascade continued. Heads dropped from sight to what he assumed was the floor below. It was like a boulder hidden in a river waiting to be struck and take its victims below.

Kalyan made his way to the closest wall. This was the most dangerous place in the airport. These free-range waiting areas had no rules, no order, no stations or electrified fields keeping people in place. His strategy was to follow the wall of terminal one as far as he could. He wanted to get past this to the front where the terminal line formed, where he could align with the patron arrival area.

Inching along the wall, he followed where other successful line surrogates made way, leaving the locals and the crazies in the center. Kalyan once heard that there were masses of people in the center that had been trapped. A sense of being drawn into the crowd was comforting, assuming that the person in front of you knew what they were doing. Then, for no reason, the person in front of you stops. A push from behind follows as others hadn't anticipated the break. Like a line of dominos, the bodies are stacked and fall.

This tale was difficult for Kalyan to believe. He had been here long enough, late enough, to see the self-automated cleaning systems engage in their programmed carnage. It was clear in his mind the busy night he had just cleared the free range area to a safe space to meet his patron. His ankle caught in the stainless steel piston that rose from the floor and found his trousers. He had to cut the pant leg off that night to keep his foot. Then, there were the screams as the self-automated cleaning systems came alive with a whir and hum of electrical current. The pressing of desperate flesh to escape the machine that would clear the area, wash the floors of the material slurry, and wax the tiles. Sadly, many patrons lost their place in line that day. So many missed flights, so many missed connections.

In the original design of the terminal, Kalyan had learned that like the BART, there were chairs for people to wait. Those had been removed in remodeling decades ago. What remained were sections between the walled corridors that were larger spaces. There was a choice. The dilemma was, he could continue to follow the wall, which was safer, but much longer as a route, or make his way into the masses, and aim to find safety at each of the square columns of the section.

He had tried this second option in the past before there was a Madhubala at home. Removing the communicator from his breast pocket, he looked to the present time and calculated how long it would take him to align with his patron by both estimations. The prudent course of action would be to follow the wall. When he reached the second and third of these sections, he would recalculate his progress.

The painted cinderblock walls of the corridor were nearly rubbed smooth from all the hands that felt their way along it. Kalyan inching his way along the wall for a good 40 minutes had to stop. A "Terron Trap" had formed around an active electrical outlet. Dozens have stopped at this point forming a personal bubble around the wall blocking forward passage. Each needed to re-charge their communicator and plugged into each other's connector creating a daisy chain of tangled wires into the one outlet. It was rare to find a public outlet that still worked. Once discovered, a "Terron Trap" formed and blew out the circuit. Sometimes they impacted the whole areas lighting, other times it would just cause a small fire and a few deaths.

Kalyan waited. This was part of his profession and patience the desired quality on his resume. He could feel the press of others move past him that were freely floating in the currents of humanity. Kalyan stays close to that wall, not wanting to get dragged away.

A woman's voice called from behind, "Kalyan? Is that you? I can not tell from your mask."

Glancing over his left shoulder, he could see it was his friend, "Minmei! How are you it is good to see you again."

"What has happened? Why have we stopped?" She asked.

"Terron Trap." He said over the noise of the crowd.

"Can we get around?"

"I don't want to risk it. Its rather large, a dozen or more are huddled and wired. Best to wait. Let it blow. They will soon be gone." He urged.

Minmei looked behind her to see the growing swell stopped along the wall behind her. "I don't want to be here for the self-automated cleaners." She shouted.

"Those run on the 30th, and it is only the 15th." He reassured.

"No, they have reset to run twice a month, the 15th and the 30th. We need to move, we need to go, there are only a few hours." She yelled.

"15th and the 30th? Where did you hear such a thing?" He tested.

"The learning screens in the security zone. Why do you think the lines were so short today?"

His first thoughts, his only real thoughts, were about Madhubala. She would be alone. No Mother, no father, and so rare a girl in the world, an only child. For the first time in many months, Kalyan was anxious.

"We must get out of here. We must go." Kalyan said.

He reached down, and in an uncommon move, took the hand of Minmei. He could feel the warmth of her hand through the latex glove. She was not a tall woman. She was not a big woman. He lead her in front of himself carefully, so she was between the Terron Trap and himself. She was removed from the pressure behind her. He took the brunt as the weight shifted against him. He lifted her body up from the floor and used her much like one would hold a shield. The pressure from the push of bodies against him pushed Kalyan forward. He didn't fight it. Instead, that momentum went through his body, up his arms, and into Minmei. She was now moving forward along the wall and wedged into the smallest space against the smoothed cinder block and the Terron Trap.

There was flash, and smoke, followed by the groan of disappointment from dozens. The members of the Terron Trap looked up from the charging deceives becoming aware of what happened.

Another push from the forces behind Kalyan came, worked through him, and pressed against Minmei, dislodging the wires, freeing the group from the wall.

A look of surprise flashed across the faces of the members of the Terron Trap as a quick and fluid movement from the rushing waves of people caught them in the flow. The power cords snagged at a few, then entangled the entire bunch. There was a surge of panic as most tried to cling to the wall and escape the bindings of communicator cables, but they were all dragged into the mire of momentum, swept into the currents of the free range, and carried away down the corridor in screams for help and of pain.

Kalyan, with Minmei still in his arms, saw an opportunity. It was a clearing on the wall. As the ball of bodies pulled by the wire dragged along the floor, Kalyan rushed to stay a few steps behind it, but never on it, or close enough to get tripped up.

He started to move faster to keep pace with the clearing as it moved forward, awash in free space he had rarely known outside his studio apartment.

Minmei, looked into Kalyan face unaware of what was behind her as he carried her forward. "Keep going." She encouraged. "Don't stop." She said. "Get us out of here."

The two followed the tangle remains of the Terron Trap as it dissolved in parts dragged through the large room, to the next corridor. Others behind Kalyan had formed a train, pushing him forward, keeping the momentum going, putting others out of their way past the third large room, to the final gate where they could align with their patrons.

As the glorious view of the final gate came into view, Kalyan became joyous. He said to Minmei, "We are almost there, I can see the gate."

A worried look now on her face asked loudly, "How will we stop."

Kalyan was even more worried than before. His heels started to dig in, his legs, pumping so hard, and so fast, now felt like jelly. The burning from such muscle use had weakened him.

They were nearing the gate. He could see where the floor pistons would shoot up in a short time. He had to find a way to stop, to get out of the way, and to make it through the gate to align with his patron.

Without much thought, going purely on instinct, Kalyan said, "Get ready, we are going to roll."

Before the words could leave her mouth, questioning the meaning, Kalyan leaned hard to his right, pulling Minmie close, and tucking her into a ball with his torso. The two spun against the wall, pressed like a line of clay in the hands of an artist, between the wall on one side, and the rush of people in an uncontrolled push of momentum on the other side. Kalyan's feet danced in a balanced spin, always moving, keeping the roll until the pressure of force stopped.

A little dizzy from the spin, Kalyan and Minmie watched as the headless snake line of people lacking leadership drove right into the plasma security wall and disintegrated into a sizzled plum vapor.

The incident had caught the attention of all in the corridor. It was a moment of unity in a mass of chaos. Kalyan took the opportunity of clear visibility and alignment, by taking Minmie by the hand and loudly saying, "excuse me," and "pardon me," in the silence wiggling his way to the gate.

Kalyan checked to make sure his communicator was undamaged, and still masked in an avatar of his patron, quickly making his way through the last gate to the area of alignment. On the clear side, turned to check on Minmie, and she was no longer right behind him. She was stopped in the security cylinder with a red beacon flashing on top. Trapped in the tube, he could almost hear her screams and the desperate pounding as her little hands struck the sealed container. All he could do is watch as mechanism lowered and replaced her prison with a nearly identical one above.

The security agent working this gate proceeded with business as usual, looking to Kalyan to see if there would be trouble or protest.

Kalyan smiled politely at the man in the poly carbonatite body armor knowing there was nothing he could do for Minmie. She had been a good travel companion and taken him very far. Perhaps they would release her finding it was a monitor error. They may recycle her, like so many criminals had been processed. Then his mind turned to Madhubala, who needed him. And they needed this job. Minmie's patron would need a new line surrogate, no matter what became of her. One that could get them on that flight.

A klaxon sounded. The yellow strobe lights of the free-range area began to flash. The focus of the crowd from the incident turned quickly to panic with this 30-minute warning until the self-automated cleaners started. She was right. The scheduled had changed to the 15th and the 30th. The efforts to get here quickly were well worth it.

Kalyan turned away from the worried masses and looked to the alignment center. These were the line surrogates like himself that would get patrons on flights, which helped the men who ran the world. It was a place of luxury, where 200 plastic molded chairs in rows of 20 would hold those lucky few who made it this far could sit and reserve a spot for their patron. Here, the air was clear, the room was cool, and thin carpet welcomed your feet. Between every other seat was a single outlet where electricity made by the efforts of citizens steps poured out freely.

He scanned the room looking for an open seat. There were still a few. Kalyan checked in with the gate hostess, providing his patrons' name, flight, and time. She confirmed the information and identity, then assigned him to seat 142, near the transparent viewing wall.

He was gracious and kind in thanking her. There was some pride as he strolled to his chair. Taking the seat, plugging into the system, he removed a cushion from the backpack that was red rubber. He opened the node and blew into it until fully inflated, set it on the chair, and lowered himself into comfort. The woman to his right and man to his left were not friends yet, but he knew that over the next thirteen hours, they would become good friends. Just like he a Joe Burger did. Just like so many people over the years had become. He started by asking the one question everyone had an opinion on these days, "Have you been tracking the Delta Driver?" It sparked the interest of everyone in earshot.

With keen and cunning, he took a moment of satisfaction to know he was so much more than a Dabbawala like his father. He was a line surrogate, a respected member of society.

Nearly the time of the flight, a soothing chime sounded through the alignment room. It woke those in slumber and brought all to their feet. The transparent viewing wall transitioned to reveal the first of the patrons arrive. The first patron was a man, tall, and handsome. He entered the room on the patron side of the wall. He looked clean. His teeth were white. Kalyan imagined that he could smell the soap and cleaning products through the hermetically sealed wall.

The hostess voice came through the speaker, "Mr. Green."

The line surrogate standing about 50 people away raised the communicator into the air, and the yellow glow of the virtual image of Mr. Green turned green.

Without a missed step, on his side of the wall, Mr. Green walked through the far door, and on to his flight.

Mr. Greens line surrogate, the transaction now completed, walked to the single door in the room marked Exit.

Three more people entered the patron room, three new names called, and the process for the surrogate repeated for three more.

The fifth patron that entered was the man Kalyan represented. He knew him on sight. For an instant, Kalyan thought the two had made eye contact, and that the man smiled his way. Could the patrons see into the line surrogate room?

Kalyan raised his communicator high, taking pride in a job well done, helping the men who run the world. His communicator turned green, and on inspection, the transaction was complete. $500 placed into his account, with an additional $75 with a text note added: "Thank you."

Madhubala would still have a place to live. There would be enough money for food, to replenish his travel supplies, and to find and solicit his services to Minmei's patron. It was the way of the world.

With a hard push at the exit door, it opened. This private corridor was almost empty. It would take him all the way back to the BART stop. There was never a rush in this corridor as he would linger and enjoy the amount of free and open space it provided. It was the perk of this position that most outside the profession never knew about. Free and open space that one had to themselves. On his first job, Kalyan ran as fast as he could. There had never been an opportunity in America. It was something he missed from childhood.

On the way home, he decided to stop at the market to see if there were any fruits or vegetables available again. He did love the taste of blueberries. If he could find them still, he wanted to give Madhubala that chance to love them too.

✿ II ✿

BUBBLE PEOPLE

I am driving in my car. I have my favorite song on. I own the left lane. I am texting. I am tweeting. I am the queen of social media. I am smart. I am witty. I have so many followers.

Now my car is turning over. My phone is out of my hand. My head is spinning. My world is upside-down. My choices are limited.

"Take my hand if you want to live," he says.

My hand reaches out. I've lost my phone. My heart is racing as he lifts me.

"Snap out of it," he says.

My cheek stings from the slap.

"Snap out of it!" he shouts.

My other cheek stings. My eyes focus.

"You're going to be alright. You're going to be safe. Come with me if you want to live."

I can feel my hand in his. My legs burn with movement. My lungs work to suck in the cold night air.

Now I am warm again. I am moving. I am moving faster. I can hear him speak.

"You are safe now in my truck. You were in an accident."

I'm confused. I need my phone. I need to post.

"You're going to start to feel the symptoms of withdrawal shortly. You've been under its control for years. The withdrawal will give you a headache, but I have water and aspirin for you. Just use your words and tell me when you start to feel bad," he says.

I need my phone. I need to post. I'm in pain. I'm confused. I don't know what to do.

"Are you all right? Use your words. Speak to me," he says.

I'm confused. I need to post. I need my phone.

"Speak to me, Heather. Say something. Something, anything," he says.

"Heather?" I say.

"Yeah, you. You are Heather," he says. "Remember me? I'm your boyfriend, Josh. We've been dating for two years."

"Josh?"

"Yeah . . . Josh," he says.

"I . . . have."

"You have."

"I . . . have such a headache."

"Here, take this bottle of water. Take these two aspirin."

I comply. I feel the need to post this.

"Oh, Heather. I'm so happy you spoke," he says.

I'm riding in his truck. I'm confused. I need my phone. I need to post. "I have such a headache."

"That's right. It's going to take a few minutes for the aspirin to kick in, but you are going to be okay."

"Where are we going?"

"I'm taking you to a safe place. A place where you can rest," he says.

I ride. I am confused. I need my phone. I need to post.

The truck stops and he gets out. "Okay, Heather," he says. "Take my hand, and watch your step out of the cab. Good, now the other, and you're down."

I am warm. I am inside. I am resting. I need my phone. I need to post.

"Heather, wake up, honey. You've been asleep for a long time now. How do you feel?"

"I . . . I feel."

"That's right, use your words."

"I . . . I feel confused."

"That's normal, very normal. I want to introduce you to my friend Dr. West. He helped me, and he can help you," he says.

"Heather, I'm Dr. West. I'm here to burst your bubble."

"What?"

"Heather, you live in a world that is entirely your own. You are under the control of your phone. All you do is post every detail of your day. You drive at slow speeds in the left lane. You cut in front of others in line. You are entirely engrossed in yourself and believe that you are the center of the universe," Dr. West says. "But I'm here to tell you that you are not alone. There are others in the world."

"There are?"

"Yes, Heather," Josh says.

"Don't get too excited, Josh. It's going to take time for her to come out of this. Days, weeks, who knows? Remember when I burst your bubble? You were a mess. It took a whole month to talk you out of it," Dr. West says.

"Boy, do I. That was a tough time," he says.

"Josh?"

"See, she's coming round. Just needs to get reoriented," Dr. West says.

"What . . . what happened? Was there an alien invasion? Did robots take over?"

"No, Heather," the doctor explains. "You have something called Narcissistic Network Disorder, or NND."

"NND? Is it contagious?"

"I'm afraid so. I've been tracking this disease across North America for several years now as more and more people show stronger signs," the doctor says.

"He found me exploiting free wireless access openly watching porn in a children's Playland at McDonald's two months ago," Josh explains.

"And I knew right away he had NND. Once he got better, we started to search you out, Heather. We had to follow you for a while before the right opportunity came along to burst your bubble. You see, you can't just tell someone they're a bubble person—they won't hear or believe you. They have to be shaken or 'popped' out of their spell-like state."

"Have you seen my phone?" I ask. "I want to post about this so others will know."

12

THIN WALLS

The passionate, rhythmic pounding on the other side of the hotel wall can only be one thing besides an early wake-up call—a cruel reminder that this vacation is a solitary venture. He drowns the echo of her cries and moans in a cold shower.

The valet quickly produces the car. His smartphone accurately directs him to the best coffee in Savannah, where he spends the morning. With latte in hand, he drives east out of the city.

Cockspur Island is roughly halfway between Savannah and Tybee Island. On this historical site, during the walking tour of Fort Pulaski, an attractive woman catches his eye. She looks like a runner. Her pixie cut reveals a perfect oval face.

Dottie, the enthusiastic park ranger, explains the importance of the use of the James rifled cannon in the siege, the march through miles of bogs to get here, and the details of the lead-lined roofs that allowed for the collection of drinking water in underground cisterns. The group morphs in size and shape, moving across the parade ground like an amoeba under a microscope. It gives him the opportunity to stand close to the pixie-haired beauty. It provides him the ability to observe her without being creepy.

She seems to be with someone. Is he a brother? A friend? Or is he something else?

She comes to him and looks up at him beseechingly. "Excuse me. Would you mind?"

It's been a while since he's spoken, and his first attempt comes out as a crackled, barely audible "What?"

"Would you mind? Taking a photo of my friend and me?" she says.

"Oh, yeah, sure." He takes the camera.

She stands next to her friend on the platform facing the lighthouse on Tybee Island that holds the last smoothbore cannon from the original scrimmage. He pauses, camera in hand, considering the shot's composition. At this height, the Savannah River can be seen in the background. December's sun is setting early, bringing the pinks and reds to the sky.

"If you're willing to wait a few more minutes, I could get a really good shot of the two of you—the light will be perfect."

"Sure, we've got a few minutes," she says.

"It's called the golden hour," he explains. "It's when the light in the sky is softer and redder, balanced to bring out the right skin tones."

She smiles, listening to the explanation.

"It's that perfect time of day when most romantic scenes are filmed," he adds.

"Cool," she says.

"Whatever," her friend dismisses.

He gets the sense that this might have been too much. Maybe he's put her in a "romantic" situation with someone she's just introduced as a "friend."

"Can you believe that this fort changed the world?" he says to change topics.

His new sprite smiles and says, "It was an interesting tour. Dottie was a hoot!"

"She was! She's really excited about history," he says.

"It's always fun to find people who really get into their job."

"I agree. There's nothing better than a passionate tour guide." He asks, "What other tours have you been taking?"

"Well, we just got in yesterday and spent the day on those trollies in Savannah."

"Are they worth it?"

"Yeah, they're pretty good. We learned a lot. Some were better than others as we got on and off during the day. Then, we drove out here. Someone recommended it."

"It sure is a neat place," he says, instantly regretting his choice of words. *Neat place?* he scolds himself.

"Yeah, *neat*," she says with a warm smile.

He can see the kindness in her eyes. Her smile lifts her cheeks, revealing soft laugh lines and shaping those big brown eyes into a friendly ray of hope.

Her friend breaks in to ask, "Is it golden enough to take the picture yet?"

"Yeah, yeah, sure," he says. "Sorry. Why don't you two stand over there?" He directs them to rotate. "Now I can get the skyline, the gun, and the two of you in the sunlight." He takes the picture. Through the viewfinder, he takes a good, long look. She's very attractive. "Let me take another for safety," he says to prolong their time together. "Do you mind if I take a few with my camera? I'm a bit of a photo bug." He hands back her camera and pulls his professional-grade camera from the sling at his side.

She nods in agreement. "Sounds like fun."

Once started, he snaps a series of photos of the two of them. He asks them to move a little, take a new position, turn shoulders, slant hips, and point. Some shots are just of her friend. Others—most—are just of her.

As the light starts to move out of that magic time, he says, "Thank you so much. I got some really good pictures."

"Would you mind if I gave you my email?" she asks. "In case some of them turn out, could you send them to me?"

"I'd be happy to," he says.

She finds a scrap of paper and a pen in her purse and writes down the address.

"Jenna?" he asks, looking at the paper.

"Yeah, that's my name," she replies.

A moan sounds from behind her. "Come on. I'm getting hungry," her friend whines.

"Well."

"Yeah." He watches the couple walk ahead of him for a few minutes before taking the path back to the parking lot. He wants to avoid any awkward moments that repeat their earlier parting. As a single traveler, he's been on the receiving end of those who overstay their welcome.

In the rental car, he accepts the mantle of loneliness that shrouds his heart on every expedition. These moments of levity, like the one with this couple, are wonderful while they're happening but are always a drain on his spirit afterward. These moments replay in his mind for days.

On the route back to Savannah, he spots a perfect picture. On the far side of the path, over the bridge, and beyond the Georgia brush stands the Savannah River. Green beacons of light provide a clear path for ships. Reeds and tall grass hold the muddy banks in place. The water pushes past him to the sea.

The sound of a door slamming behind him stops him from snapping the shutter. It's Jenna and the guy, using the rest stop.

"Hey, it's your photo buddy," the guy says, stepping from the turquoise public port-a-potty.

She says something inaudible from the small outhouse next to his. Much rattling takes place until she pops out and the door slams shut. "Oh, hey," she says.

"It looked like a nice place to take some shots," he says.

"She had to pee," the guy explains. "She always has to pee."

"Are you following us?" she asks with a coy and teasing tone.

"No, really, it just looked scenic," he replies. She's the last person he expected to see.

"Well, since we're all here, where would you like me to pose?" She smiles.

"Ah, let's try over here, and pretend you're thinking about a far and distant land." He points to a bench.

Her friend impatiently says deep and loud, "Hungry."

"You can wait in the car. It will only be a few more minutes," she scolds.

Her friend stomps off through the gravel lot, kicking little rocks to the grass like the eight-year-old he was twenty years ago.

He directs her to pose, to think, to dream, adjusting the camera's dials and buttons between shots for the perfect effect.

Finally, in the winter darkness, the camera goes silent, and the two giggle as they make their way to the parked cars.

"Thanks again for modeling. You're very good at this. Are you a professional?" he asks with a tenderness in his voice that is sincere.

"No, no don't be silly."

"Well, you could be, if you wanted, I bet," he says sheepishly.

"Enjoy your vacation." She gives him a quick hug and goes to her car. She turns to watch him dig in his pocket for keys.

"Thank you, you too. Enjoy your dinner," he says.

The two linger for a final moment, eyes locked across the distance of the two vehicles.

"Come on," her friend says from the muffled interior.

"He's hungry. He gets this way when he's hungry," she says before puckering her lips and blowing a kiss. "Email me those photos." Her head ducks into the car.

The friend backs out and then sprays gravel as the car pushes into the darkness of the two-lane road, headed west.

Alone once more, he can feel the sadness cover him like a heavy blanket, limiting his movements. There's no hurry to return to Savannah.

Finding a table for one at a restaurant is difficult enough, but during this time of evening, it's even harder. He finds a place at the bar of The Cotton Exchange on the riverfront and chats with the other tourists around him out for a fun night.

When he's done, he heads back to his hotel room to start work on his photos. He has big thoughts about what to do with the photos to impress Jenna. Setting up a private website for her, he decides, might be the best way to share files but is too big of a gesture. Maybe email is best. She might write him one day. Perhaps they will become online friends. The best he can hope for at this moment is "one day" and "perhaps."

Entering the hotel lobby, he's more than a little surprised to see Jenna standing next to her friend under the glow of a large chandelier.

"Oh my God!" Jenna says. "What are the chances?"

"You're staying here too?"

Her friend looks unhappy at his greeting.

"Did you find a good place for dinner?" he asks.

Jenna is nearly glowing with excitement. "Yes—it was the most wonderful little place, out of the way, only a few tables, hardly anyone there. A real find."

"Let's go to the room." Her friend tugs at her arm.

"Yeah, okay, it *is* getting a little late, and it's been a busy day," she says to the two of them.

The three walk to the elevator together.

"Which floor?" he asks politely.

"Three."

"Same as me." He presses the button.

The lift moves up, its hum the only sound.

When the doors open, he says, "Well, thanks again for all the modeling."

"It was fun," she says with some finality.

He follows the couple around the corner and down the hallway. He pulls the plastic keycard from his pocket, hopeful that the worst is not about to be discovered.

Leaning on the wall next to the door of the adjacent room, Jenna seems to be enjoying the lingering buzz from the cocktails after dinner.

He fumbles with the knob.

Her friend says smugly, "Pretty thin walls at this hotel. You get to hear everything."

✿ 13 ✿

THE DINNER PARTY

It wasn't like the Stockmans to be so late. Lauren and Scott had been such darling guests over the years. They were one of the original couples to attend the weekly dinner party. Lauren's grace and charm and Scott's bold stories of adventure had been cornerstones of the gathering.

"Where could they be?" Grace finally asked.

"It's certainly not like them to be a whole hour late," Dottie said. "Why, I don't recall anyone who's been a whole hour late to an invited event. Fifteen minutes may be fashionable. Thirty minutes and something unfortunate has occurred. Certainly, at forty-five, I would call my host and let them know I would not be able to join in due to an emergency. But sixty minutes without word. My lord, something terrible must have happened."

Mr. Shutters cleared his throat, took one more sip of his cocktail, and suggested, "Perhaps we should start without them."

Everyone looked at him as if he had stridently encouraged the evacuation of everyone's colons.

"Thank you for the suggestion," Grace said pertly. "But I do not think that would be very polite of us. Let's give them a few more minutes to provide word. Perhaps they will show."

"Of course," Mr. Shutter mumbled under the scrutiny of his peers.

A series of loud raps sounded at the door. The room jumped at the familiar pattern Scott regularly provided each week.

Grace scurried to the door, unlocking and opening it wide with a flutter of excitement. "Scott—Lauren," Grace greeted them and then stepped back in alarm at their discombobulated state. Lauren's hair was a mess, with a leaf-covered twig sticking out the back. Dark, dirty smudges were smeared across both their faces. Scott's jacket had a tear at the shoulder. Another rip at the trouser knee was soaked with fresh blood. Lauren, normally immaculate, wore dark stockings that were shredded and looked more like webbing, starting at the ankle and spreading up to the hem of her skirt and beyond.

A polite yet pained smile flashed across the couple's faces out of long practice and societal graciousness.

"Grace," Scott said, nearly out of breath. "So good to see you again. Sorry we're late. Can we use your phone?"

"So sorry. Need phone," Lauren said gnashing her teeth.

"You see, we had a little trouble in the park with the car and the like."

Grace, though concerned, was delighted to see them both, and she stepped out of the doorframe and swung her arm wide. "Please, come in. Let me get you a drink for your troubles."

Tenderfooted, the two entered.

Grace went to the liquor cabinet. "Sit," Grace insisted. "Irving," she called to her husband. "Help me with these. We need two potent cocktails."

He rose and quickly complied.

After drinks had been placed in the Stockmans' hands and they'd been comfortably assisted to their seats, the group waited eagerly for an explanation from the two.

"Well?" Dottie finally blurted out.

Scott looked at her and the group. The forced smile on his face started to melt away, replaced by a pained look. He took the paper cocktail napkin and pressed it to his knee.

"What happened? Was it something thrilling like your expedition to the rain forest?" Mr. Jones asked.

A quizzical expression flashed across Scott's face. "No, no that was just zip-lining during our trip to Disney World in Florida."

"Did you fall from a cliff like your base-jumping adventure in the Far East?" Mrs. Jenkins wanted to know.

Lauren looked at Scott and said, "You mean the parachute ride we went on in Atlantic City?"

Mrs. Jenkins nodded in agreement. "That's the one."

"Oh, oh, hunting and shooting a pack of rabid wolves like that journey to the new territories?" Mr. Taylors posed.

"That was a family trip to Mount Rushmore with our kids," Scott said with fading patience and politeness, "and I took a picture of a dog. That was, like, five summers ago."

"Don't any of you actually listen to Scott's stories? Our lives are not that interesting. Scott is not here to entertain you each week. We are not that exciting," Lauren said.

"Well," Scott interrupted in defense, "I did kill a guy."

The group gasped in disbelief.

Lauren nodded and said, "That's true. You did kill that man tonight."

"Dear God!" Grace exclaimed. "You killed a man?"

"Yeah, I did, in the park tonight," Scott explained.

"Why didn't you start with that? That's kind of big," Irving said.

"I don't know. It just happened. I'm not sure how to describe it," Scott said.

"That's okay. You're still in shock. You need time to think about how to tell the story." Irving patted him on the good leg.

"What? No. No, I need to call the police, or I just need a minute to think. We were on autopilot—it all happened so fast, and we just ended up here." Scott began to sound upset.

"So," Grace said. "There you were, driving over to our house, when . . ."

"What? No, this isn't some story to amuse you, some cocktail party story to tell. A man is dead, in a ditch, put there by me."

"Right, right," Irving said, steadying his wife. "Now, now. Let's give him a moment to breathe, to think through it, to form the story arc and exposition."

"What? We were involved in a death," Lauren said. "We should call the police. We should tell someone, tell the authorities. Where's your phone?"

The group looked at Lauren and Scott with growing anticipation. So Pavlovian was their desire for the weekly fix of another of Scott's stories that saliva began to build in their mouths as they waited with baited breath.

Finally, Mr. Taylor spoke up. "Well? What happened?"

"That's enough. I'm not telling this story to you. First, I'm telling it to the police," Scott said.

"Good idea," Grace said. "Let's call them. We can all listen in to the story while you tell it."

"No, no I don't think you're hearing me," Scott explained. "We need to—" He stopped mid-sentence and stood up. Hobbling from the twisted ankle and the loss of blood from the open wound at his knee, he made his way to the kitchen, where he guessed the phone was located.

His wife watched the bloody trail build across the long white rug Grace was so proud of finding at a textile outlet in Kentucky.

They all listened as Scott fumbled with the receiver and the rotary dial moved back and forth, clicking. "Hello, police?" he began. "I've been involved in an incident, and someone has died as a result of it. I need your help." There was a pause while the person on the other end spoke. "No, no. Please send an ambulance to this address. I'm injured and losing blood. I need . . ." He took a deep breath. "Is someone on the other line?"

Irving called out from the other room, "Sorry, sorry, just wanted to . . ."

"Please, Irving, I'm trying to tell the police about the incident. I'm feeling kind of dizzy." These were the last words anyone heard from Scott before the loud thump he made landing on the kitchen floor.

All eyes in the room turned to Lauren. Irving jogged into the room to be part of the conversation.

Lauren felt small on the large couch. The plush royal red was now marked with great Rorschach splotches of her husband's brown blood drying on it. "I should check on Scott," Lauren said, slowly getting up and wobbling to the kitchen. Her husband had landed on his side atop the dark Mexican tile that Grace and Irving had hand laid. The receiver of the yellow phone was still in his hand, with the coiled extra-long cord reaching back up to its wall unit. A voice burbled from the handset. She picked it up and explained to the officer the address of the house, who owned it, and repeated the request for an ambulance for her husband before hanging up. She took a deep breath and could smell the sandalwood incense that Grace had burning in the guest bathroom. In the avocado kitchen, Lauren spotted an open bottle of wine and helped herself to a large pour.

"Everything alright in there, Lauren?" Grace called from the other room. "Anything I can help with?"

"The police are on their way with an ambulance. You should be ready to greet them at the door." Lauren took another long drink.

Grace, who had been quiet in her approach, touched Lauren on the shoulder, giving her a start. "Honey, are you going to be alright?" she said sweetly, like a sister.

"Yes, yes I just . . . needed a moment to . . ." Lauren replied.

"Oh good. Now, it's just us girls. Tell me, how did the two of you get into this predicament?" Grace soothed her arm gently with a kind rub.

"Well, you see, we were driving here like we normally do. Instead of taking the main road, Scott said, 'Let's take the park.'" Lauren stopped, seeing the edge of an eye peering around the corner. She could hear heavy breathing from nearby. "Okay, guys."

The other guests, looking at their toes, ashamed, walked into the kitchen from the other room.

"We just wanted to hear what happened," said Mr. Taylors. "We just want to hear the story."

"I understand. Let's just wait, everyone. The police are sure to arrive any minute now. Why don't you all freshen up your drinks and sit in the living room?" Lauren held out her arms to encourage them as one would with a herd of cows.

"Yes, yes," Grace said. "Let Irving refresh your drinks."

"Grace, do you have something for my husband's leg? A towel, some bandages, a cloth?" Lauren asked politely.

"I do. Let me see." Grace opened the kitchen drawer. "You could try this."

Lauren looked up to see. "Oh, Grace, I couldn't. That's the cute flower print you purchased at Sears last month."

"That's true, Lauren. It is the one I had specially ordered. Still, your husband is bleeding. I would be remiss not to."

"I couldn't." Lauren hesitated. "It will break up the set."

"Well," Grace said, turning back to the drawer. "Let's try this one. It's a little older but clean."

"Perfect, thank you." Lauren took the yellow-and-white-striped Egyptian cotton hand towel and applied pressure to Scott's leg.

The doorbell rang. Grace left the kitchen to greet the men. Lauren could hear her offer each of the officers a drink to "quench your thirst." There was the rattle of a metal cart in the living room.

"Scott, they're almost here. Hold on, honey." Lauren kneeled at his side, pressing on the leg. Lauren became curious as to why the officers or paramedics hadn't joined her. She stood and peered into the other room where the guests, officers, and the medical team stood, full glasses in hand, smoking and talking. The cart she had heard was the serving cart rolling across the carpeted floor and the bloody trail of her husband's footprints. "Hey, over here! We have a man down," Lauren called out.

The officers and medical technicians looked up, as if suddenly remembering why they were there. As they set their drinks down before going to help, Grace called out, "Coasters, please. Coasters, please." It took another moment for each man to find a coaster and set his drink on it before moving to the kitchen.

The paramedics placed Scott on the backboard and strapped him on tightly. They injected him with something from a syringe and then cracked open a vial of smelling salts, waving it under his nose.

"Are they going to make him tell the story?" Irving asked the officer closest to him.

The bulky man in blue said, "What story?"

"Oh, officer, he's the best storyteller I know. We invite him and his wife here each week for our dinner party just to hear his tales of adventure," Irving explained.

Grace added, "They arrived all bloody tonight, said they had killed someone. Wanted to wait to tell the story until you arrived."

"Yes, do you think you could get him to tell us the story now that you're here? We'd love to hear what happened," Irving said.

The police officer gave the two a look of discontent. "Takes all kinds." He followed the paramedics who were carrying Scott, followed by Lauren, out the door and into the box cabin of the ambulance.

The doors slammed shut with Lauren and Scott inside. A double pat on the door from the officer gave them the all clear to proceed. The officer asked the group now on the lawn to stand back, give them room, and go back inside.

Lauren held Scott's hand and said, "I think we're clear."

Scott opened his eyes, and the technician began to detach him from the backboard. "Well," Scott said. "I think that went pretty well. We won't have to go to that dinner party again."

Lauren smiled, leaned in, and kissed her husband full on the lips. She drew back and gave a devilish grin. "Thank you for your help, boys," Lauren said to the driver and paramedic. "We couldn't have pulled this off without your help."

The man at Scott's side pulled the last restraint off and asked, "Were they really that bad? Couldn't you just decline the invitation?"

"It wouldn't be very polite to decline an invitation," Lauren said.

Scott added, "And in the morning we move to our new home, away from this crowd, never to be invited again."

The man asked, "Won't they just forward your mail to the new address?"

14

KILLING THE DEVIL

"There is a God to fear and a Devil to shun," he preached from the front of the congregation, his eyes squinted, brow covered in perspiration. "There is a heaven to gain and a hell avoid," he continued. He moved his hands up and down slowly to calm the energized crowd. "Now, close your eyes with me. If there is anyone joining us for the first time who doesn't have peace in their heart, if there is anyone here who has not accepted Jesus Christ as their Lord and Savior, I need you to raise your hands. Raise your hands high and acknowledge that you need Him, that you need the sweet Lord to enter your heart . . . or be cast out with Lucifer into a fiery lake, where your soul will burn for all eternity."

Tex Bryant stood at the back of the service. He had chosen this spot to best observe the Southern Appalachian congregation. The hundred tan folding chairs he had counted out of boredom during the sermon were not all filled, even though it was Sunday morning. Outside the double doors of the church, it was no more than ten degrees, but inside the brown-paneled walls, the room was sweltering from all the jumping, swaying bodies.

You have to respect a church this size with a full drum kit and a bass guitar, Tex thought.

Over the past three months of his crusade, he had seen his fair share of tambourines, folk guitars, ornate pipe organs, and even a few karaoke machines leading the worship. He loathed the incessant cabasa that seemed to be included in every church percussion starter pack. It seemed to scrape its rhythm across the crowd, chewing at Tex's every nerve.

"Anyone here," the pastor went on, "who has never accepted the word of God into his heart faces a choice today: everlasting joy at the right hand of our Lord and Savior or eternal damnation of fire licking at your heels."

Tex noticed the last comment was directed at him. The spiritual leader shot a tense stare through the crowd, toward Tex. Tex shook his head and waved off the pastor, who wore a well-tailored tan suit.

"Thanks, I'm good," Tex mouthed back at him.

The pastor tilted his head in return, demonstrating a lack of acceptance in the matter, then returned to his preaching. "Thank You, Lord Jesus. We thank You for the peace in our hearts today, the peace that transcends all understanding. We thank You for leading us down the path of light, of joy, of happiness. It is a path only You can provide."

As the pastor brought the three-hour service to a close, he walked down the center aisle toward the back of the church while the band played him out. He kept one eye on Tex the whole time. After he said a closing prayer, the congregation exited, each receiving a handshake, a pat on the back, or a hug of encouragement from the pastor.

Tex waited, just as he had done at every service since he made his decision.

WHEN HE'D TYPED "HOW TO KILL THE DEVIL" INTO THE INTERNET search engine, it had been on a lark. Online, he'd found the process described in four simple steps. First, find out who the devil is. Second, figure out the devil's weakness. Third, find the devil. Finally, kill the devil.

In retrospect, Tex thought that finding the information had been like taking the first hit of a joint: it had seemed simple and benign at first, but it wasn't until later that he'd realized it'd had an impact. Those few laughable words, such simple instructions, had planted a seed and taken root in his life. He'd found himself wondering what it would it take to kill the devil. Was there even a devil to kill?

That cold day in Abilene, Kansas, after typing those words into the search engine, letting the results stew in his mind while he showered, and eating dinner with his best girl, Tex had determined what he had to do.

He had to kill the devil.

⚜

WHEN THE DOOR CLOSED BEHIND THE FINAL PARISHIONER AND THE bitter cold stopped blasting into the church, the pastor's footsteps creaked over to Tex. He had such a tight, square squint that his eyes looked permanently closed. His salty hair, more white than dark, was about as square as it could get without being a military crew cut. He removed a toothpick from his pocket and let it rest on the right side of his lower lip, looking Tex up and down.

"They call me Pastor Bill," he finally said. "What do they call you?"

Sitting in the padded brown folding chair, Tex replied, "Tex Bryant."

The toothpick started to dance as Pastor Bill tickled it with his tongue from behind his pursed lips. "What can I do for you, Tex?"

"I'm looking for information," Tex said. "In certain circles, they say you're the one with answers."

"Certain circles, you say. What kind of circles are those?"

Tex wondered if this was just another dead end. There had been many along the way. Some found his quest amusing and would simply play along as if they had the answers. Some men who claimed to be holy seemed to think a profit could be made off a man seeking to kill the devil. More than once, Tex had found himself a pawn, being used as an excuse to pass the plate around one extra time at a service. He never saw a penny, of course.

"There is a brotherhood outside the village of Nendeln in Liechtenstein who have taken a vow of obedience to protect a wall in the cloister where a set of ancient weapons are kept," Tex began.

Two women full of smiles to demonstrate peace beyond all understanding entered the church hall and began straightening the rows of chairs in service to the Lord. A third entered with a vacuum.

Pastor Bill nodded toward the door. "Let's talk in my office."

Tex rose and followed him down into the basement, which was painted white and carpeted in a deep shade of brown. The church had been built on a foundation of ancient stone, now whitewashed. Chunks of painted mortar dangled loosely on the walls, ripe for picking. A Sheetrock wall with a doorframe separated the church supplies from the pastor's private sanctuary.

"C'mon in. Take a seat," Pastor Bill said, sitting down behind a hefty wooden desk.

"How in the world did you get that desk down those rickety steps and into this dungeon?" Tex asked.

Pastor Bill chuckled under his breath. "You don't mince words, do you?" He pulled the top desk drawer open, leaned back, and propped his legs up on it. "This was here when my daddy got the place. Don't know how they did it, but it got done. You can do anything you set your mind to. But you already knew that, didn't you?"

"Yep," Tex said, sitting in the chair facing the desk.

"I heard—from those certain circles you mentioned—that you might be on the way. What is it exactly you're looking for?"

"Pretty simple, really. I'm looking for the devil."

"Right. Well, you know that the devil is a spirit, an angel gone bad. Look around this world and all you see are the remains of his work. What you're looking for isn't easy to find."

Tex smiled. "Well, I've been on the trail, and it's brought me here to you. I understand you're a man who knows."

"Who told you that? The monks?"

"Yes," Tex said. "The details were limited. Only a few of them were allowed to speak, while the others were completely focused on the 'counsel of perfection,' on writing, and on prayer. During my three weeks there, the elders found me to be serious-minded. One night, a note was slipped under my door. It described a small church in the

Appalachian Mountains where a church leader watches over the lock of the devil's keep."

Pastor Bill dropped his feet down to the floor, reaching into the bottom drawer and pulling out an old bottle of whiskey and two small glass tumblers.

"None for me, thanks," Tex said.

With a huff implying weary patience, Pastor Bill filled both glasses, then reached behind the desk to a small refrigerator and took out a bottle of water. He handed Tex the bottle before quickly shooting down the first tumbler of alcohol, leaving the second for sipping. "There are a lot of churches fitting that bill."

"I know. I've been to nearly all of them. This is the last one on a long list."

Pastor Bill sipped again at his whiskey. He looked Tex up and down, seeing his lanky build before him, outfit shabby from miles, and breathing in the faint odor that had clung to him since his last shower. "What if I'm just a zookeeper, a jailer, a man with a key?" Pastor Bill took the drink in hand, leaned back in his chair, and propped his legs up again. He wore the expression of a man reminiscing. "I didn't know about him until I was older, a teenage," he said. "It was my father who caught him."

"So, it's a 'he,'" Tex said.

"Yes, I think so . . . when I see it . . ." Pastor Bill continued. "My father was getting older and weaker. His hair was always white, his skin ashy, and there seemed to be something eating away at him. When I turned sixteen, he brought me here, showed me the door, and explained what he had done."

"What exactly had he done?" Tex asked.

"Made the biggest mistake anyone could have: he'd let the devil loose on the world," Pastor Bill said, staring down at the glass in his hand. "Your monks? My father met them on a stormy night, lost in the mountains of Liechtenstein. He had been separated from his unit during a training exercise."

Tex listened as Pastor Bill explained his father's journey. As a young man stationed in Europe, stumbling upon the order of devout monks, Pastor Bill's father had entered an unknown world. Inside the monastery was a locked room where a normal man had begged to be let out, claiming that the monks were religious zealots who had imprisoned him unjustly. Pastor Bill's father had taken pity on the man and helped him escape. As the man had run away into the darkness, the pastor's father had realized the monks had, indeed, captured the devil. Each step running into the darkness had transformed foot to hoof, skin to scale, man to beast. He knew that it was now up to him to recapture and imprison him, so the world would not suffer his next reign.

Tex was beginning to doubt Pastor Bill's story. His leg had been pulled before, and he didn't want to be made a fool again. "You think this is funny? You think I'm a joke or a fool? You've just described an episode of the Twilight Zone. Thanks for wasting my time."

Tex stood up and turned toward the door.

"I guess you're right," Pastor Bill replied, cynicism in his voice. "There certainly couldn't be any truth in a tall tale like that one. No way that a young writer in the army could have heard this story from my father late one night in the barracks and written a screenplay about it. You're absolutely right. Run along, young man. Keep searching, wander the desert like the Israelites for forty years, that's what you do best."

Tex stopped at the doorknob. "A story based on truth, you say?"

Pastor Bill's faded blue eyes opened fully for the first time. He let his shoulders drop into a slouch, finally revealing himself. "You're the first one who didn't walk away," he said, wincing as he took another sip of liquor. "There is a devil," he went on, "and I can prove it."

THE HATCH IN THE FLOOR BORE A METAL CREST ON ITS THICK wooden planks. It was the same symbol Tex had seen emblazoned on the cloister wall where the ancient weapons were guarded. The hatch was heavy, and Pastor Bill used a rope and pulley to shift its massive weight. He unhooked several booby traps as he and Tex descended into the sub-basement.

Thick padding lined the walls and ceiling, dulling every sound.

Opening a door, Pastor Bill revealed a downward-sloping passage, leading even deeper into the earth. The two walked down the dark corridor, arriving at a heavy door with an eye-level metal slot .

Pastor Bill stopped in his tracks. "Tex," he said, "this is your last chance. If you have anything in your life worth living for, if there's something or someone you wanted to keep safe, if you have any doubt about going forward, this is your opportunity to turn back. Once you see this, it can't be unseen. There won't be a day that passes when you don't think of it, not a sleepless night without its image bubbling up again."

As the words of warning came from the Pastor's lips, memories flooded Tex's mind. He thought of the friends and family he'd lost and tried to forget. He thought of Jessica, his one true love, who was now little more than a painful sting of remorse in his gut. He saw their faces and knew that killing the devil was more important.

With that knowledge, the weight of his cares was lifted from his mind and he moved forward. "Open it," he said.

Pastor Bill shook his head. "No skin off my nose. I haven't had a good night's sleep in thirty years."

The man of God encouraged Tex to step closer. With a rusty drag, the heavy iron slot opened.

Tex expected something fantastic to happen. A beam of light. Fire and brimstone. He moved toward the slot and squinted, ready for anything. But all he saw was a sparse room, with a single light and a simple bed tucked in one corner. At a plain wooden desk sat a man, reading. He wore a short sleeve dress shirt with a pocket protector filled with pens and a small ruler. His belly, like his face, was round. His dishwater blond hair had a pronounced cowlick.

"Are you sure this is the right dungeon?" Tex asked, confused.

"What is it you see?" Pastor Bill replied. "The devil takes on many forms."

"Well, it's a guy who looks like he's from IT support, maybe an engineer."

A small voice, crisp and throaty, came from inside the room, "Oh, hello. Didn't expect company today."

Tex looked to Pastor Bill, "What is that accent?"

"My name is Louis," the voice from inside the dungeon came again. "Are you here to help me? Can you let me out, please?"

Tex and Pastor Bill exchanged a knowing look. The devil was a liar. Anything he said, any appearance he took on, was all a deception, no matter how convincing.

"It seems some crazy rednecks have kidnapped me," the man said. "Please, help me get out." With that, the man rose from the desk, dropping his book, and pressed himself up against the door, his face directly across from Tex's. "Oh, fresh air!" he said. "I can feel it, smell it. You brought some with you. I have been in here . . . well, I'm not sure how long I've been here. I can't keep track of time. What day is it?"

"Sunday," Tex replied.

"What month?"

"February." Tex watched as the trapped man dropped his head and leaned against the door.

"That makes five years. Five years in this hole. Help me," he pleaded, becoming agitated. "Help me get out. Help me get home. You have no idea what they do to me. They are mad. Mad, I tell you!"

"I'm told that you're the devil," Tex said.

"The devil?" the man asked, his mild manner returning. "Ha! That's a good one. I'm just a guy."

"What do you know about the devil?"

The IT man seemed to search his head for any answer that might help him escape. "I know a joke. Well, it's a story, actually. I am not very good at jokes."

"Go on," Tex urged.

"Let's see. It starts when the devil and Jesus are in heaven, standing in front of God, arguing about who's better at running a computer. Have you heard this one?"

"No, go on."

"The argument lasts for days about who is better, so God sets up this test. He's always testing the devil, you see. The test is three hours long and has a detailed list of tasks they need to complete. The test starts, and Jesus and the devil start running programs, typing command lines and the like. About ten minutes before the timer sounds, a bolt of lightning strikes, knocking out the power."

Tex watched the man through the slot in the door. His nervous little storytelling dance involved lots of hand motions and swaying from side to side.

"The devil," the IT man continued, "is outraged at this, knowing full well that God has added this as an extra test. He says it's a trick that God has played on him. Just then, the power returns, rebooting the computers, and Jesus starts printing out His final stats to complete the test. The devil is enraged. He's screaming and pounding the desk all mad, and then, the timer goes off. The devil starts yelling at God, saying that Jesus cheated, that there was no way He could have recovered all that work." The IT guy started to giggle to himself before the punch line. "And God says, 'Well, Jesus saves!'" The man looked to the eye slot, clearly anticipating a reaction. "You get it? Jesus saves! That's how he won!"

Tex and Pastor Bill remained silent.

Frustrated by the absence of laughter, the trapped man continued explaining. "It's a well-known tag line in the church. Jesus saves."

Tex, unfazed, said, "I guess it's just not that funny if you have to explain the punch line."

"Okay, fine, it's not that funny. But it's all I've got. You have to help me get out of here. I'm just a guy, not the devil. The devil would have a better sense of humor, right? He would have told a dirty joke. Do I look like the devil to you?" There was real fear in his voice.

The pity Tex felt came as a surprise. In his mind, he knew this was the devil, the dark lord of lies. But still, he felt doubtful. What if they were wrong? he thought. What if they were part of a crazy cult and just caught a man, a human?

"Be strong, brother," Pastor Bill said. "You know it's true. He is a liar, a deceiver, a serpent."

Tex looked back through the slot and said, "If you're a man, tell me about your life before they caught you."

The trapped man's face suddenly popped up in the slot, startling Tex. Now he could smell the body odor and bad breath.

"I am a computer programmer," the man said in a hushed tone. "I was sent here by my company to help a customer, you see. Just here to help. I got lost driving, and when I stopped to ask for directions, Pastor Bill and his family abducted me, brought me here. They have been keeping me trapped in this room ever since."

"What was the name of your company?" Tex asked.

"PaineWebber," the man replied.

Tex began a small chuckle.

"What? Why are you laughing?"

"They've been out of business since 2000, and they aren't a software company," Tex replied.

"No, I was in IT. I came over from Europe. They sent me to help a client."

"Okay, what was the name of your client?" Tex asked.

The man's face disappeared from view, and there was a long moment of silence. Tex thought the man might have stepped away from the door, into the recesses of his dimly lit dungeon. Tex balanced on the balls of his feet to get a better look inside the room, but suddenly, the man appeared in the iron window, sending Tex stumbling backward in shock. A loud howl of laughter filled the air.

"You got me, didn't you, Tex Bryant?"

More bellowing laughter erupted from behind the heavy door. Tex returned to the eye slot, his heart racing. Looking inside, he saw that the once mild-mannered man had now taken the shape of an old haggard beast-like person.

"You outsmarted me with just a few questions! Guess I'm out of practice with these little games. I should have said SAP." The kind, bespectacled eyes of the IT professional had now been replaced by a pair of seething, yellow eyes with black, horizontally slanted pupils, like those of a goat. The beastly man sat, staring at Tex, ass on the dirt floor.

"Be strong," Pastor Bill said. "Last year, he took the form of my wife and pretended to be trapped in there. He takes many forms, anything to gain an advantage." He extended his hand to help Tex to his feet.

"It is the devil," Tex said, standing up.

"No shit, Sherlock," the devil taunted from behind the door. "We have a real bright one here, don't we, William? Another one to test me! Someone to take your place, perhaps. You're old and feeble now. You can't even keep it up for your wife."

"Don't pay attention to his rants," Pastor Bill said. "He's not nearly as strong as he claims. If he were truly powerful, he would have gotten through that door by now."

"Oh, I can get out any time I want. I choose to stay in here," the devil said. "Plans are in play. Soon, your wife will be underneath me, screaming with pleasure. Your daughter's virginity will be next to go. You will watch as your precious women writhe in delight."

"I thought he would be more original," Tex said, looking at Pastor Bill. "After an eternity of torment and sorrow, I expected him to have thought of better ways to taunt us."

Pastor Bill, looking pale, grabbed Tex by the hand and dragged him a safe distance away near the passage entrance. "His words don't sting at first," he said. "He plants a seed in your mind. It's easy to brush them off . . . until you wake late one night and all you can think about is 'what if?' What if he gets out? What will he do? It haunts me. It's unshakeable."

"Yeah, but I see those types of things in movies, on television, in video games. It seems ridiculous."

"If he were to ever get out, these things would quickly become reality." There was a seriousness in the pastor's tone that moved Tex. "He must die," Pastor Bill continued. "I don't have enough energy left in me to do it. You have to end this."

"Can you get me in there? Without letting him out? Can you open the door for me to go in and kill him?"

"The fire hose next to the door. We have used it in the past to spray him and push him back into the corner. That's how my father and I used to keep him at bay. We pushed him away from the door with the hose."

"If you can get me in there, I can kill him," Tex said confidently. He unsnapped the pocket on the side of his cargo pants and removed a leather sheath. The knife's handle was of polished silver. Tex gripped the handle and unsheathed an ancient blade.

"Where did you get that?"

"The monks. It was one of the weapons they guarded. It is part of their purpose to keep safe the tools that would fight the devil. It's the only way."

"It's beautiful," Pastor Bill said, admiring the blade. "Will it work?"

"I have done nothing with my life until now. I am willing to risk everything to find out."

The two made their way back down the tunnel. Pastor Bill unraveled a circular fire hose. Next, he turned the wheel that regulated the water pressure, shifting it to full capacity. The pipes began to groan as the fabric hose filled up.

In the dungeon room, all was silent. Tex took his place beside the door, blade in hand. Pastor Bill readied himself, sticking his key in the enormous lock and picking up the pressurized hose. He leaned forward, looking through the eye slot to locate his target. Just as he pressed his face to the door, the devil appeared at the slot, shooting a mouthful of fiery spittle out at the pastor and hitting his target.

Pastor Bill dropped the hose, clutching his face. "It burns! It burns!" he cried.

Cackling laughter came from inside the dungeon.

"Are you okay?" Tex asked.

Pastor Bill raised his face, revealing the swollen slots of his eyes. Feeling for the hose, he picked it up and held it up to the slot. With one quick movement, the nozzle lever opened and a torrent of water burst out. Pastor Bill leaned into the pressure of the hose, holding it up and in place. As he moved the nozzle from left to right, the spray found its intended target.

The beast's laughter transformed into a gurgling howl of pain as he was pelted with the high-pressure stream of water.

Pastor Bill squinted through his swollen eyelids, staying focused on the writhing beast. "Now, now, now!" he shouted to Tex. "Go, go, go!"

Tex lunged forward, turned the key, and pulled the heavy door open, cracking through a rusted crust of seams. Then, he squeezed into the room before pulling the door closed behind him.

Leaning all his weight into the door, Pastor Bill helped to slam it shut and quickly turned the lock until it clicked. He continued spraying water through the slot, keeping the monster in place as Tex moved in on his prey.

The blade of Tex's holy relic glinted under the dull light of the single swaying light bulb. He struggled forward into the rising mud, moving closer to the blasting water and the weary beast.

A rumbling sound came from the water pipes. Pastor Bill turned his attention away from Tex just in time to see one of the pipes explode. Water poured from the earthen ceiling, and the hose went limp. Pastor Bill ran back to the main entrance, shutting off the main valve and locking the basement hatch, trapping Tex and the devil inside.

Tex looked at the beast lying on its back as the last trickle of water flowed from the hose and Pastor Bill slammed the sub-basement hatch. The devil displayed no apparent wounds, but stubbed horns protruded from his forehead and hooves had sprouted where his feet had once been.

"Just do it," the devil said, sounding exhausted. "End it. I am tired and old. Put an end to me." The devil rolled over onto his side, exposing the spot at the base of his neck that the monks had told Tex about. This spot, they'd said, was where the devil was weakest.

Tex took the opportunity and vaulted forward, blade in hand, aiming true. He felt the blade slide in and break off in place, with no chance for removal.

The devil flopped around and struggled to stand up. A mighty, razor-edged tail emerged from the base of his spine, swinging wildly. Leathery wings grew from his shoulder blades, and he attempted to take flight.

Tex fell backward, stunned by the transformation. The tail swung in his direction, and he felt it slice across his chest with great force. Tex fell forward, slamming his head against the bed frame and landing face-first in the ice-cold pool of muddy water. As the beast writhed above him, everything turned to black.

"YOU KILLED HIM."

The voice spoke directly to Tex. It had no corresponding body or shape but simply penetrated his mind.

Tex opened his eyes and found himself bathed in a beautiful light. He felt strongly and completely that there were no more worries. Fear was only a four-letter word. No emotion. No pain. All was golden, angelic, warm, and inviting. This, he knew, was the ethereal plane. "God?"

"It is I."

"I killed the devil!" Tex announced proudly.

"Yes. Why?"

Tex didn't understand the question and took what seemed an eternity to answer. Several things went through his mind. Firstly, he did not want to disappoint the Almighty, nor did he want to feel His wrath. Secondly, he didn't quite know how to answer the question.

"Well," Tex finally replied, "I entered into battle with him, and I won."

Silence in this holy place felt far more awkward than on a first date, much worse than a job interview. Instead, it felt like being on a large stage in front of a huge audience, naked and unable to remember your lines.

To find relief, Tex just began to speak, hoping that it might improve the situation. "There I was, in my mother's basement, with no real job, and this question popped into my head: why don't we just kill the devil? So, I looked it up on the Internet—" Tex paused. "You do know what the Internet is, don't You?"

There came no response, only the vast and great silence of the unknown.

"Of course You do, all-knowing, all-seeing God. So, this question sat with me all day. I took my best girl out for our anniversary dinner, and I explained to her this feeling I had, this need to do something more, do something bigger, and that it wasn't going to happen in Abilene, Kansas. She felt the same, that moving somewhere and doing something bigger was what we both needed to do."

As he recounted the story, Tex could remember the conversation clearly. That night still stung him deep in his chest. He realized that he should have handled the situation differently. How do I still know this pain and anguish in heaven? Tex thought. Where is the peace that surpasses all understanding?

"Why did you do it?" the voice came again, resonating deep in Tex's body.

"Finally, a full sentence," Tex mumbled. "All for You, my Lord. All for you." He let out an exasperated sigh. "I thought it was the right thing to do! I thought that killing the devil would remove evil, badness, and hurt from the planet."

"That's not how it works, Tex," the voice said.

"What's the deal here, Lord? I took down Your bad guy. Now, don't I get a reward? Aren't You happy? How does it work?"

"Thou shall not kill," came the reply.

Tex stepped back in shock at the simplicity of what he'd overlooked. "That applies to everyone? That covers the devil too? There is a lot of confusion about this subject on earth, You know. There are exceptions to that rule, like in war, abortion, euthanasia, or, say, the devil where killing is all right."

"Thou shall not kill."

"So, that is an absolute rule. Got it. There are people, like Pastor Bill, representing You on earth and encouraging the opposite of Your absolute rule, and You saw how that played out."

"Pastor Bill is not My best representative."

"No? If he was not Your best representative, then how did he and his father capture the devil?"

"If you kill the devil," the voice explained, "you take his place. The beast you killed was Pastor Bill's father."

"Wait, go back," Tex interrupted. "If you kill the devil, you take his place? I've never heard that before. It seems like it should be covered in the top ten rules."

"Thou shall not kill."

"That is clear to me now."

"It is time," God replied. "You will now take the place of Lucifer, the original adversary. Go, spread his lies. Encourage pride, envy, wrath, gluttony, lust, sloth, and greed."

"Why would You have me do that? What kind of fucked up system did You create?"

"Tex, I love all of My own creation. The devil is part of that balance. Kill him and you upset the balance. Without choice, humanity would be nothing more than a group of robots who do nothing but worship Me. I give you choice, free will. You need the devil. You need to have choice."

"Oh," Tex replied. "I didn't think of it that way."

"I know," God replied. "I was watching you."

"When will it happen?" Tex asked. "When do I become the devil?"

"It has already begun."

"Do You have any advice? Words of wisdom?"

"Read My commandments, and do the opposite."

Tex started to feel a tingling inside his body that quickly progressed into a burning sensation. He became annoyed by God's answer. "Fuck that!" he spat in return. "I thought I was doing the right thing before, and now, here I am, the devil himself."

"See? You're already doing a great job."

"No further advice, I suppose," Tex said angrily. "You're just going to drop me back down there and tell me to do the opposite of what You would."

"The power you have is the power given to you by the sinful and by the doubtful. If you seek, you shall find."

"Screw You. Get me out of here."

"You're going to be great at this."

TEX SAT UPRIGHT IN THE ICY WATERS OF THE MUD BASEMENT. "UGH, this shithole."

The smell of something like burnt skunk hung in the air as the leathery remains of the former devil began to bubble and melt away into a fog.

Tex tried the door. It was locked. He pushed harder. He could feel that the earth holding it in place was loose. After a few more minutes of pushing, the whole doorframe fell over. Tex walked back up the earthen corridor to the hatch. He knocked on it in hopes that someone might answer. He called out to Pastor Bill. When no answer came, Tex tried to visualize the hatch in his mind. He thought of the way the counterbalance was arranged, the metal locking mechanism, and he imagined it all melting away. The harder he thought about the silly door and the metal symbol on it, and the more he visualized that rope burning, the more real it all seemed. He could almost smell the smoke.

Opening his eyes, he realized that there was actual smoke. The rope was on fire. Then came a thud that sounded like the counterweight falling to the floor. Molten silver began to drip through the wood's imperfections. Tex tested the hatch again, and it opened with ease.

Stepping up into Pastor Bill's office, Tex could see that the fire was spreading. The heavy desk was now timber, fueling his burning anger. Looking around the office, Tex saw the collection plates, the envelopes filled with tithes, and shoved them into his pockets.

With a turn of the knob, he was in the supply room. He climbed up the steps, along the whitewashed walls, out the large double doors, and into the icy wind. He walked a quarter mile up the road to the first house and knocked on the door.

From behind the glass panes came the voice of Pastor Bill. "You stay away from here, devil. You are not welcome in this home. In the name of Lord Jesus, you stay away."

Tex touched the knob and watched it melt away beneath his grip. He pushed the door open, and the sound of both hammers striking the shells of the double barrel clicked. There was a thunderous noise and a spray of gunpowder struck Tex's body, but it had no impact.

Devil Tex tried to walk into the home, but he couldn't make it over the threshold. It was just a matter of stepping forward, yet there was something preventing this simple action. He remembered what God had told him, that he only had the power others gave to him. Admission into his home was not something Pastor Bill was going to give.

"How long can you stay in there, Bill?" Tex asked.

"Long enough."

"Seems like you weren't being entirely honest on this whole project, were you?"

"I had a promise to keep. He couldn't be the devil any longer. He couldn't take it."

"A hell to fear, a devil to shun? You've been a bad boy, Bill. You made a made a deal with the devil, or should I say 'daddy'? Let the next fool take his place," Tex said.

There was another click, followed by the sound of opening the barrels to remove the empty shells. One more click and both barrels were full with fresh shells.

"You know that won't stop me," Tex said, pointing at the weapon.

"Might slow you down some," the pastor replied.

"Spoke with God about you. He doesn't seem to like you much. Said you were not a good representative of His Word." Tex felt pleasure as his words stung Pastor Bill, whose pain discharged onto Tex like the warmth of a radiator on a cold day. It was a new kind of nourishment for him. "How long can you wait in there, William? A few days? Maybe months? One day, someday soon, you are going to put your big toe on this porch and I will be here. I have all of eternity to wait."

"We will see," Bill said. "We will see."

"Your daughter and wife are in there. I can smell their fear," Tex said, his nostrils flaring. "Might be a nice spring day when your daughter finds a new prize on the porch and can't resist the temptation of bringing it inside. Then, I'll be in, Bill. Inside your home. Wasn't that your fear in the pit? It's what the last devil warned you about— your precious wife and daughter."

A click sounded, followed by the thunder of both barrels ripping pellets through the air. Tex stood unchanged, reveling in his invincibility. It was clear to Tex that this was a mental game. The fear, hate, and negative emotions of these earth-bound mortals would feed him. He only needed to make the suggestions.

SNOW CRUNCHED UNDER HIS FEET, EACH STEP PLUNGING KNEE-DEEP into the fresh powder. He had to raise his legs high as he moved forward. Making the turn through the pines, Tex saw a small cottage bathed in the glow of hearth and light. He trudged forward, eventually reaching the porch that wrapped around the front of the home. He wasn't cold. He wasn't hungry. There was no sense of thirst. There was only the sense of being there, in the moment.

He sat in the rocking chair that had stayed out for the season. Closing his eyes, Tex could sense that there were two people inside. He knew that it was a man and a woman. He could feel that they were good people and that their kindness was a weakness. He could use it to take advantage of them.

Tex stood and pushed the rocker over, making a loud thud, then got down on his knees, pretending to be desperate, feigning confusion.

The front door opened a sliver, and warmth and light poured out onto Tex's snow-covered body. A woman's head poked out, and the door opened wide when she saw Tex.

"What is it, honey?" came a male voice from inside. "Another deer?"

"It's a man," the woman said, stepping out quickly to help Tex. "Get some blankets! Put the kettle on! And add more wood to the fire!"

The woman bent over Tex and tried to help him to his feet. Tex feigned slow progress, starting by balancing on the flipped chair, then putting his weight on her shoulder, and finally sliding each foot under him to move forward. Near the door, the man appeared and helped to bring Tex inside, seating him by the fire in a very comfortable chair.

The woman helped Tex remove his jacket and shirt before placing a warm blanket around his shoulders. Tex watched the flames for a long time, listening to the two talk about him as if he weren't even there.

The storm had come on strong. They would be there for days, maybe even a week, before the roads would be clear enough to get help. They decided they would just have to do their best with the stranger. After all, they agreed, it was the Christian thing to do.

Tex took delight in hearing these words. These would be the perfect conditions for him to find out just how much power he had.

The man stooped at Tex's side and said, "Mister, what's your name? I'm Glenn, and this is my wife, Mary. And you?"

Keeping up appearances, Tex was slow to respond. "Tex," he said eventually.

"Tex," Glenn repeated. "That's a great name. How did you get here, Tex?"

"There was so much snow," Tex replied, telling the couple precisely what they wanted to hear. "I got lost on the roads. Then, the car just wouldn't move. So, I started walking."

"Kind of what I figured, Tex," Glenn said.

"Thank you for letting me inside," Tex said. "Mary, thank you for letting me in."

"Of course, Tex. I heard that loud noise and had to see what it was. Can't leave you out in this kind of weather."

Mary was attractive. She had long brown hair that went past her shoulders and lightened at the tips. Glenn looked like a capable man, wiry and strong, with a thick, untrimmed beard. Both looked to be somewhere in their late twenties or early thirties.

"I really appreciate it," Tex said, looking back to the fire. He could feel the worry Mary had in bringing him inside. He sensed her uncertainty. Glenn, on the other hand, was more like the static and white noise of a television set on the wrong channel. Tex was not sure if this was a result of the three empty beer cans on the kitchen counter or just a lack of any meaningful thought from him.

"We don't have much, but you are welcome to it," Glenn said.

"Are you hungry, Tex? We have some meatloaf from dinner. I can cook you a potato. Do you like salad?" Mary asked.

"That would be great," Tex said, focusing on the fire. "You sure are nice to offer. I would be grateful."

Tex could feel his senses heightening in a way he had never experienced before his transformation. He listened to the two in the kitchen area. There was the scrape of Glenn dragging out a large plate from the cupboard, the sound of the refrigerator seal breaking when it was opened, and the tinkle of cheap utensils being removed from the drawer. There was a shift in the air of the small cabin as the two moved around. He could smell the ash and soot from the long-burning fire.

When the meal was ready, Mary and Glenn helped Tex to the table and watched him eat. He wasn't sure if this attention was from having someone new in the cabin or if he himself was particularly interesting.

"This is very tasty, thank you," he said to Mary.

"It's my mother's recipe. She's a good cook," Mary replied.

"Don't get to see her much, do you?" Tex asked.

"Not as much as I would like, but we talk on the phone."

"Lives pretty far away, does she?"

"No, not really, just an hour from here. We just don't drive over that often in winter."

Tex sensed that the blame for this lay on Glenn. Mary wanted to see her mother, but she blamed Glenn for preventing her. "Glenn, when this all melts away, you should drive your beautiful wife over to her mother's. There may be more recipes as good as this one that Mary will bring back."

Glenn chuckled. "Yeah, we should do that."

For the first time, Tex got a flicker from Glenn. It felt like spite, almost hate, for the word "mother" and all it signified. It wasn't necessarily Mary's mother; it could have been his mother or all mothers.

"Very good," Tex said lightly. "Is it just the two of you here?" he asked, trying to make innocent conversation.

Although Mary and Glenn were nothing but smiles, Tex sensed that this question too ignited all types of harsh feelings. Their silent suffering was feeding him even more than the meatloaf.

"Just the two of us," Mary said, placing her hand on Glenn's and looking him lovingly in the eyes.

"Built this place myself," Glenn bragged. "Took me a year, and I still keep adding to it."

Tex felt the nourishment again. Inside these two seemingly kind and charitable people were dark feelings that had been building over the course of their relationship. Tex felt stronger. He felt smarter. Something inside of him began to grow the more turmoil he observed.

"Kids?" Tex asked innocently. With that word, a full blossom of emotional energy radiated from the couple, and Tex started to feel full and satisfied.

"One day," Mary said.

"Maybe, when the time is right," Glenn added.

Then came the dessert. Glenn's "maybe" opened a tap of frustrations that had been festering in both. For Tex, this was like eating a full Thanksgiving meal, consuming more than one normally might, going back for more, unbuttoning one's pants, and adding on the toppings. He was feeding on the dark feelings they'd held for each other over the years.

Mary offered Tex the couch, and he lay under a blanket, listening to the two bickering in the kitchen while they cleaned up.

"Look, even a starving man couldn't eat your mother's meatloaf. See how much he left on his plate?" Glenn whispered.

"He said he loved it," Mary replied.

"He was being nice."

"What was your 'maybe, when the time is right' answer? You know full well I want children. You can't keep coming up with excuses."

"Excuses? Do you want to raise a child in this tiny cabin? It's already crowded with just one more person here. Let me finish the place first, that's all I am asking."

"Glenn, you are slower than molasses when it comes to building. Two years? They built Prudential Tower in four, and this is just one cabin."

With each harsh whisper, Tex felt stronger. The energy continued to build for some time, even after the two had gone to bed. As the two lay awake, refusing to speak to one another, Tex was fueled even more.

HE WOKE TO SOUNDS FROM THE KITCHEN IN THE MORNING. MARY had gotten up and was making breakfast.

"Did you sleep well?" she asked when she saw him stirring.

"Yes, thank you, Mary. You have a most comfortable couch," Tex said as he got up, stretched, and looked around. "Where's Glenn?"

"He was up before light. Wanted to do some hunting. Said it would be easier to track deer in the snow."

Tex, naturally aroused in the morning, was not ashamed or modest about these things anymore. He watched Mary move. Her top was loose, and when she leaned, Tex could see that she wasn't wearing a bra. She wore what looked like yoga pants, tight, reminding Tex about all the things he liked in a woman.

He was slow to approach her. He enjoyed watching. "I am sorry to put you out like this," he said.

"It's no trouble. You're not putting us out," Mary replied.

"Well, I don't mean to pry, but I could sense that my being here may have caused some trouble between you love birds here in your nest."

"Oh, that? That was nothing, really. When you've been married for twelve years, that's normal. You are no burden."

Tex stood behind Mary, who was facing the sink. He leaned in close and started to whisper in her ear so she would feel his hot breath. "Normal? Normal to dedicate yourself to one man for so long? To spend this much time and energy on him, to think of all the little things he likes, and he won't even let you visit with your mother?"

Almost in a daze, Mary asked, "How did you know?"

His words began to dazzle. "All you want is to be a mother yourself. He doesn't understand you. He is tough, mean, and insensitive to your desires. All the boys in school chased you, and now, you're stuck in the woods, alone with this brute, who won't give you a child, who can't even make you feel."

Mary's body pressed back against his. She started to push her butt into his groin. He could hear her breath changing, becoming deeper. He moved his hand under her top and began to massage her breast while his other hand started to explore the band of her yoga pants. Slowly, he peeled them down. She did not resist or complain but willingly complied with his directions and suggestions.

"You want a baby?" he asked.

"Yes."

"I can give you one. You want to have my baby?"

"Yes," she replied feverishly. "Yes, I want you."

Like a bending reed, he pushed her in half over the sink and began to thrust his pleasure into hers. Her moans of delight filled the little cabin like they never had before.

When it was over, Tex went to the bathroom and helped himself to the shower. He dried himself with the first towel he found. Seeing the two toothbrushes in the cup on the counter, he felt the need to put both in the toilet for a good lap in the bowl and return them, as if untouched, to their holder.

Tex got dressed, taking Glenn's jacket, socks, and boots as easily as he had taken Glenn's wife. There was no second thought about whether it was right or wrong. It was just what he wanted.

He sat at the table, and Mary served him breakfast. She watched Tex eat and drink coffee, smiling as if nothing out of the ordinary had happened.

"You are going to be a good mother," Tex said. "I just know it. You're going to raise my boy right and never tell Glenn it isn't his."

Mary smiled and nodded in agreement.

"Or you might even think about going to live with your mother. When the roads clear, you should pack up and do that," Tex said, dragging the toast across his plate to sop up the last of the yellow from the egg.

Once he was finished, Tex got up from the table, grabbed the scarf and hat hanging on the back of the door, and said, "Mary, it was my pleasure."

She turned with a smile and waved, watching him close the door behind him.

Tex began to make his way down the drive through the deep snow. It was taking longer than he had hoped, and he heard Glenn call out from the woods. Tex stopped and waited for him to catch up. "Good hunting?" Tex asked.

"No, didn't see a thing," Glenn said, trying to catch his breath. "Where are you going?"

"I don't know. Next town. Whatever I find," Tex said almost gleefully. "This is all one big, new adventure for me."

"Is that my jacket?" Glenn asked.

"Why, yes, it is. How generous it was of you to give it to me."

"I didn't give it to you."

"Sure you did, Glenn. Last night, you said I was welcome to whatever you had. So, I took what I wanted."

"Oh." Glenn looked both disappointed and confused that someone would take advantage of his kindness in such a way.

"Mary was delightful this morning," Tex added. "We had breakfast. I'm off now."

"I understand," Glenn lied.

"You know, Glenn," Tex said, turning back, "in a place like this, so isolated from the rest of the world, if you didn't have Mary, well, it might drive a man to drink. That sure would be a dark place to find yourself. Drunk, depressed, alone."

Glenn looked at him strangely, almost shaken.

"Yes, sir. I would worry about Mary leaving if it were me. I'd hate to be alone out here, to wake up one day with a bottle in my hand and a rifle in my mouth, all by myself in an empty cabin of lost hopes and dreams." Tex shot Glen a wicked grin and a wink. "But you have a great day, Glenn. Thank you for your hospitality."

Glenn smiled and nodded silently, watching Tex make his way through the snow in the direction of the main road.

15

LIVING THE DEVIL

(The Devil is a friend of mine)

The golden laurel of the 1984 Cadillac Coupe hood ornament pointed north, and Tex's hand rested on the wheel. Six weeks had passed since his transformation. Each day had brought new insights into his practical powers and abilities. Walking back roads, he'd gained a new appreciation for what he was up against. Everyone had a secret—not all could be exploited.

Two weeks earlier, Tex had found the Cadillac on a lot. Its owner had offered it to Tex, free and clear, after just a few whispers in his ear. The outside of the car was a brassy brown color, and it had a faded vinyl roof. The interior would have been the original golden tan installed by the manufacturer had every square inch not been covered with nude cutouts, laminated in transparent plastic and adhered to every surface. This led to severely distracted driving. If Tex didn't keep himself focused on the road, he was faced with hundreds of images of boobs and bush. A special surprise waited in the rearview mirror as the driver needed to look between the legs of Dorothy Stratten for any view out the back.

The previous owner had had a great deal to make up for in his life of misdeeds. Covering the interior of a beautiful Cadillac like this was an obvious sin, but darker, more unmentionable sins had radiated off the man. Tex could see them, even from a distance. Tex had honed in on him like a heat-seeking missile. He had whispered things that only he, the devil, would know. And within moments, the car had been his.

It was late in the evening when Tex came across a scruffy hitch-hiker on the side of a lonely road. He stopped and picked him up in an instant, just for the company.

"Thanks, mister," the hitchhiker said, plopping into the passenger seat.

"My pleasure. Tex Bryant."

"Arlo Marley," the hitchhiker said, shaking Tex's hand. Then, he turned and saw the decorations. "Jesus Christ!"

"Wrong one." Tex chuckled.

"So many pictures. You sure do like the ladies," Arlo said.

"Oh yes, the finest collection of women from the end of the last century," Tex boasted. "I hope they don't offend."

"No, no. I am down with that. Just, well, never got to see something like this. How are they fixed?"

"Superglue."

"Not coming off any time soon." Arlo laughed.

"No, they are not. Trapped in here with me, the happy driver. Where are you headed?"

"Well, I'm headed to New York City. Gonna try my hand at theater. But it would be cool if you could take me as far as you're going."

"New York City, you say? Let's go there," Tex replied.

"Really?"

"Absolutely."

"Is that where you were going?" asked Arlo.

"I had no plans. I was just in Georgia, looking for a man named Johnny who had my fiddle. Couldn't find him. So, now I'm ready for anything. And you? Where are you coming from, Arlo?"

Arlo laughed. "Was it made of gold?"

"What's that?"

"The fiddle? Isn't that a song? You were funning me, right?"

"Yes, it was made of gold. No Johnny, no fiddle."

Arlo laughed again, thinking his host was a very quirky man. One had to be of a certain mind to pick up hitchhikers so late in the evening.

"Do you know anyone in New York?" Tex asked.

"I have a cousin in school there," Arlo explained. "He said I can crash with him for a while until I figure things out." Arlo watched as the road passed and the rain started to fall. In a few minutes' time, the rain exploded onto the windshield in sheets that sounded like thousands of tiny ball bearings pouring onto a tin roof. "Sure am glad you picked me up, Tex. I would hate to be out in this weather."

"My pleasure. I could use the company."

"Tell me, Tex, with pictures like this all over your car, are you cool?"

"Am I cool?"

"Yeah, do you partake?"

"Partake?"

"Are you opposed to smoking a little of the devil's lettuce?"

Tex grinned. "Are you asking if you can smoke weed in my car?"

Arlo had a big smile on his face and nodded slowly.

"Sure, go ahead. Hotbox the thing," Tex said.

Arlo took out a thick blunt, and his thumb made a pushing motion, scratching the little wheel of his weak lighter.

"Here," Tex said, pushing the lighter fob in the dashboard. It popped out a red glow that he held up.

Arlo leaned in and took a big drag. "Woah, that's cool. Is that special?"

"No, that came standard with cars for decades." As the smoke slowly filled the compartment, Tex opened the window a slit so that he could see out the windshield. "The devil's lettuce." Tex laughed. "Where did you get that name?"

"You've never heard that before?"

"That's a new one for me."

As Arlo continued to hit at the blunt, his movements slowed. His stare became distant, reaching out the window into the miles unseen. "Have you ever wondered what hell is really like?" Arlo asked.

"Often."

"I mean, you always think of this place where bad things happen, right? Like, if your sin was to eat too much, you'd be forced to eat more than you ever wanted for eternity."

"Ironic punishment. Like Homer Simpson being strapped to a chair and forced to eat donuts."

Arlo had a stoner's laugh that was filled with a series of smaller, tight laughs, conditioned from years of holding cannabis smoke in his lungs. "Yeah," he laughed, "but Homer Simpson wants more donuts. There aren't enough in hell, so the devil gives up."

"You know," Tex started, "that idea of hell is not from the Bible."

"It's not?"

"Nope. It's from a painting. A type of painting called a triptych, which shows three wooden panels. The first panel is supposed to be the bliss of the Garden of Eden. On the center panel are all these people partaking in earthly delights."

"Earthly delights!" Arlo cheered.

"Finally, the third panel shows the worst parts of earthly delights. So if you liked to have dirty sex on Earth, you were forced into nonstop bestiality."

Arlo cringed and wiggled at the thought. "You're harshing my high, dude. Don't bring me down."

"A Dutch painter named Bosch painted it."

"Why do you know that?"

"I saw it in Madrid when I was searching for something in my last life."

Arlo didn't know what to make of the driver, so he just took another hit.

"If you go to hell, Arlo, what do you think you will be doing for the rest of eternity?"

Arlo thought hard, then burst into chirpy laughter again. "Smoke down."

Tex grinned. In an even, almost hypnotic voice, he said, "You will be forced to smoke down for the rest of your life, smoke more than you will ever enjoy, become so addicted to it, you will do anything for one more puff. But that won't be enough, will it, Arlo? You are going to want to taste Mephistopheles's Molasses, black tar, heroin. And it won't stop. The high will never be enough. You will always want more."

Arlo's distant look turned to fear as reality found its way through the fog of marijuana and into his mind. He took another hit. He couldn't really stop himself, even if he didn't need or want it. He looked to Tex. "You. You're—"

"The devil? Yes. Pleased to meet you."

Arlo looked worried, as if Tex's voice was all he could hear, urging him to take another toke. A single tear rolled down the side of Arlo's face, and he knew that he'd made a huge mistake.

"New York. The Big Apple. Think you're ready for it? I could use a sidekick, a minion, someone I can trust to do my bidding. The position is open if you want it. Or do you want to get out here? From the look on your face, maybe New York is not for you anymore. What do you say?" Tex asked.

Arlo, joint still stuck to his lip, muttered, "Here."

"Here it is," Tex said.

The car rolled to a stop. Arlo, discombobulated and stoned, opened the door and stepped out. Tex said goodbye, and when the door closed, he started to slowly roll down the road in his pornographic Cadillac.

Through the spread legs of Dorothy Stratten, he could see Arlo realize where he had been dropped off: at the front door of a small-town police station. Two blue uniforms, outside on a cigarette break, looked to Arlo stepping from the car and right to their feet. Evidence of an illegal substance was stuck to his lip, and a baggie just over the federal limit was sticking out of Arlo's pocket where Tex had stuffed it.

EVERYTHING IN NEW YORK SEEMED BIGGER. THE TELEVISION screen covered most of the wall in Tex's luxury apartment. Changing channels, he landed on a station where a well-respected retired judge was being interviewed. The screen was high definition, revealing more than the human eye could see and making every pockmark on the old man's face larger than life.

"Why do we sign treaties that ban torture?" the judge argued. "Why do we enact articles? There are four of them that prohibit the use of torture. Why enact statutes that prohibit torture? Why do we expose those who order it and perpetrate it as war criminals? Why do we prosecute those who use it abroad, where the president's commutation and pardoning power is useless? Why do we undermine the very values of the Declaration of Independence and the Constitution? To demean our morals and superiority, both of which uphold our inalienable rights as persons?"

"Because war is hell?" the interviewer interrupted.

Judge Richter agreed, "War is hell, but war is fought by rules."

"So, there are rules in hell?"

"There are," Judge Richter said definitively.

Tex heard a clank from the kitchen and muted the television. "Everything all right?" he asked.

"Good," she replied, just loud enough.

Tex liked the apartment. Getting past Manny, the doorman, was nothing but a whisper. His host had looked surprised opening the door when he'd knocked, but she had quickly let him in when asked to do so.

Tex got up from his lazy, Bacchus-like position on the couch, then stretched and made his way to the balcony door. As he opened the sliding doors, a strong wind entered, setting the drapes and sheers dancing. Above the city, overlooking the park, he could still hear the faint noise of the cars below. He wondered if from this height, he could die from falling or if only the arsenal that the monks guarded could do the deed.

All of a sudden, Tex remembered the children's Bible he had grown up with. He thought of the hard-worn cover of brown parchment, with images of headscarved disciples walking across the front. Inside, there had been a picture of Satan tempting Jesus. In the image, Satan, winged with stubby horns, stood atop a mountain ridge next to Jesus, Lord and Savior, who was wrapped in white and blue, resisting the food and words offered Him. It disgusted Tex to think of the smug expression on Jesus's face, but his curiosity was piqued by the thought of the wings. Could he fly? When would he take that leap to test it?

So far, he had stayed with the one thing he knew he could do well: swaying the will of the weak. He felt a burning desire to break laws, especially those of physics. But now, on his perch above Manhattan, he still only felt confident enough to break moral codes. One day, though, he would work his way up to breaking laws.

"Would you like your sandwich out here or at the table?" Ms. Hudson asked.

"Thank you, Janet," Tex replied with a wicked grin. "I'll take it at the table inside. He followed the beloved personality to the table, where he sat watched her serve him. It was a very good sandwich, and she had made her own sweet potato chips to go along with it, as well as a delicious salad and freshly squeezed juice.

Janet Hudson had been a professional homemaker on television for decades. She was billed as the ultimate hostess. Each week, her viewers could watch the amazing things she did, and each month, they would receive a delivery of her instructional magazine or shop for her brand-certified items at the big box stores. She was the epicenter of entertainment. Movie stars, politicians, athletes, musicians, and all types of celebrities wanted her advice. Many hired her team to help with their extravagant parties.

"I hope you enjoy it," she said. "It's the least I could do after you looked out for me at Alderson prison."

Tex continued to eat, barely acknowledging Janet beyond allowing her to tend to his needs. She eventually just sat at the other end of the table and watched him.

"Janet," Tex said, finally breaking the silence, "you're on television. Do you know this Judge Richter?"

She thought for a moment and said, "We've met on occasion, but I don't know him."

"No phone number? No 'I can have my agent contact his agent'?"

"I don't think so. There are so many people. But I know he lives three blocks from here."

"Well, that's a good girl, Janet."

She provided Tex with the building name and wrote down what she thought were the cross streets. He determined that the interview he'd just watched was live and that it might be some time before the judge went home.

"Janet?"

"Yes?"

"Why don't you wait in that closet? Having you watch me is a bore."

Janet hesitated. "You know I don't like—well, I'm just not a fan of the dark, and that's why we made that agreement about Alderson. The tight spaces, the darkness. You know I don't like that."

He could hear the tremble in her voice, feel the nourishment of his spirit feeding on her fears. "Now, Janet, I know pretty girls are used to getting their way—"

"But, could I leave the light—"

"Now, Janet!" Tex shouted, slamming his hand down on the rich wooden table.

Janet followed her orders grudgingly. Her sadness and fear filled Tex up as she approached the closet.

"All the way," he commanded.

There was a click of the spring-loaded latch snapping the door shut.

Tex took her cell phone from the counter charger. Scrolling through the list of contacts, he saw familiar names from entertainment, politics, and news. She was at the center of a Venn diagram of major modern influencers. They all wanted that better life, a taste of her food, that little touch of elegance that only Janet could bring.

"That lying minx," Tex said. Whether it had been a lie or a misremembered piece of information Tex didn't know, but Janet did have Judge Richter's phone number.

Tex went into the bedroom and lay on the luxurious fitted comforter. It smelled of lavender lotions and flowery fragrances. Slowly, his weight carried him deeper into the mattress as he texted, Judge, would love to catch up. Coffee? and pressed send.

Tex took a good hour-long nap, followed by a long shower, before he was ready to leave. Entering the main room, he noticed a pool of yellow liquid on the tile floor near the edge of the closet door. He could hear a whimper and faint crying from inside. It had been such a wonderful sleep, he'd forgotten all about her. "Janet?"

"Yes," she whimpered.

He could feel that old familiar sense of fear and anguish fill him once again from the other side of the door. "Why don't you count five hundred Mississippi and then come out of there?"

"Five hundred?"

"No, better do a thousand."

"A thousand?"

"Want to go for a million?"

"One Mississippi, two Mississippi . . ."

With that, Tex headed for the door. Within minutes, Tex was looking into the little coffee shop, where the judge was waiting at a table for two. "Judge Richter?" Tex asked, approaching.

"Yes," the judge replied, looking up from his coffee and tablet.

"Tex Bryant. Big fan of your work. Love what you said in the interview this afternoon." Before the judge could say a word, Tex sat down across from him. "You are one of the greatest legal minds of our time not sitting on the Supreme Court," he continued. It was a small but painful slight.

"Thank you," the judge said, shifting his weight uncomfortably.

Tex could feel a swell of vanity fill him. "And you mentioned something in the interview today that, well, caught my attention. You said that there are rules in hell."

"I did?"

"You most certainly did. Emphatically, in fact."

"You see, that was a response to the interviewer. We were talking about the president's executive order. I think the interviewer was getting a little funny. It was more of a quip."

"A quip. I see. Well, not to beat a dead horse, but are there?"

"Are there what?"

"Rules in hell?"

"Look, I'm a retired judge—"

"You are the perfect person to provide this insight."

"Really?"

"Absolutely. You see, I've talked to many people about the topic of heaven and hell, good and evil. Most quote Scripture, but the problem is that you must believe the author was right—or a witness—in order to believe what it says. It just goes in circles. If there are rules for a game, wouldn't you consult an expert or a referee when play was on the field?"

"A referee . . . like a judge. Okay, you make a decent point."

"I do. When you talked of war criminals, torture, undermining the value of inalienable rights, well, I just knew we had to talk."

The judge tilted his head in consideration. He looked carefully at Tex before speaking. "What did you do with Janet?" he asked.

Tex dismissed this question, saying, "Let's leave her out of it."

"It's clear you have questions, but you've brought me here under the guise of a dear woman who is an acquaintance of mine, and I do not believe you are an ordinary man."

Tex stopped feeling the sense of nourishment. "I am not an ordinary man," he said flatly.

"What are you then?"

For the first time since his transformation, Tex felt nearly human again. His mind moved from hatred to focusing on the moment. He had finally met someone who could see what he had truly become. "I am the devil."

Judge Richter nodded and raised his hand for the waitress. "I'll have another coffee, please," he said, before turning to Tex. "Anything for you?"

"Coffee, black."

The waitress went back toward the bar, and the judge turned back to Tex.

"I believe you, if you can believe that. Tell me your story."

With a clear mind, Tex explained his long hunt for the devil, speaking of his foolish obsession and his journey through a world of ancient sects and religious orders in Europe and Asia. He told of how he had stolen a blade from the monks, even after they'd told him of its purpose and why it was never to leave the grounds. He spoke of his arrival in America and how he'd found the devil in a basement and killed him. Finally, he described the unexpected conditions that had followed and how he'd been forced to take the devil's place. He only left out the details of his despicable and evil actions over the months following his transformation.

"That is an amazing story," Judge Richter exclaimed, his second cup of coffee now nearly empty. "What is it you're looking for that you think I can help with?"

"The only guidance I have ever gotten, the one useful thing that was told to me, was that the only power I have is what people are willing to give me freely."

"That sounds like a great deal of power."

"Does it?" Tex asked.

"Certainly," the judge replied. "Look who we give power to: totalitarians, tyrants, those who kill and destroy. Think of the literary choice explained by John Steinbeck in East of Eden. Consider his focus on the difference between the King James, American Standard, and the initial Hebrew Bibles: thou shalt, do thou, and thou mayest. 'Thou shalt' gives hope that men will surely defeat evil as a matter of providence, 'do thou' orders men to fight and win over evil, but 'thou mayest' gives men control, free will, because thou may or may not. The first two provide humanity cover, while the third forces a decision."

"Is 'mayest' a real word?" Tex asked.

"Consider the power of words in creation itself. Anyone who went to Catholic school, like I did, will remember what the nuns had us diligently study. It took God six days to create the world and the devil two sentences to undo it." The judge then quoted Genesis, saying, "'Has God indeed said, you shall not eat of every tree of the garden?' Eve then replied, 'We may eat the fruit of the trees of the garden; but of the fruit of the tree which is in the midst of the garden, God has said, 'You shall not eat it, nor shall you touch it, lest you die.'"

"Not eat or touch?" Tex said.

"'You will not surely die,'" Judge Richter replied. "'For God knows that on the day you eat of it, your eyes will be opened, and you will be like Him, knowing good and evil.'" He paused. "Creation is long and complex; the critic is short and destructive."

Tex professed, "I never considered that."

"As a judge, I hear all types of stories and study all aspects of life." He leaned back in his wooden chair. "When I was a little boy, I loved the circus. My parents took me to see the elephants. Here is this giant pachyderm, skin thick, powerful, capable. Yet it lets these little men push it around, order it to lift tent poles, to drag carts. You would think that if it didn't want to do those tasks, it would just walk away. Nothing could stop it."

"That's right—it's a powerful beast," said Tex.

"My father explained that when the elephant is little, it is chained to a stake. Sometimes it's beaten with a stick. The little pachyderm can't resist the men. It doesn't understand how to escape or what's happening to it. Over the years, it grows, tugging on that immovable stake, unable to break free, beaten down. Then, by the time it's mature, powerful, and fully able to break free, the elephant won't even try. It has been conditioned to a world where it's chained to a stake. It can't break free, doesn't even know the power it has. If you truly are the devil, and I don't have reason to doubt you, the power you have is considerable."

Tex considered the parable in silence for a moment. "People have a choice," he finally said. "But as they get older, they struggle less, resist less, forget the choice that's in front of them because of the choices they made in the past."

"Thou shalt, do thou, thou mayest," the judge repeated. "Providence, command, or choice?"

"Choice," Tex replied.

"I am an active decision maker. I have eaten of the tree of knowledge. I know good and evil. I recognize evil. I've met it in countless forms inside my court. I choose not to side with evil."

"Thank you, Judge Richter."

"You are welcome." He paused. "I should warn you that I am not on your side. However, every person has the right to representation, and if you need a lawyer or a representative, I am bound by law to uphold your interests and not to disclose what you say to me."

"Attorney-client privilege?"

"I am not your attorney, but pay for my coffee and consider us locked in agreement."

✾ 16 ✾

KEEPING THE DEVIL

Somewhere 35,000 feet over Iowa, en route to Los Angeles, Tex finally perfected his ability to deceive. In the small airplane mirror, after nearly eighteen months of repeated attempts, he found that he could hold the appearance of the well-known celebrity Malik Goodwin for as long as needed. This infuriated the real actor, of course.

Goodwin had been photographed stealing apples, getting into bar fights, jogging in Times Square dressed as the Naked Cowboy, and, the final straw in yet another marriage, having nasty public sex with underage women beside the stage at a Simon and Garfunkel reunion show.

Tex could hold this appearance, voice included, while denigrating an airline attendant from behind the locked bathroom door for a good ten minutes. He had been able to keep it up for the last two and a half hours of the flight.

Satisfied and unembarrassed, Tex opened the door, pulled up his pants, slapped the man on the ass one last time, and returned to his seat. It was another spectacle Malik Goodwin would have to contend with. In front of passengers and flight attendants with cell phones, the moment was well captured. As he snuggled back into his first-class seat, Tex wondered how Malik might try to get out of this one. Would he be able to work again? Time after time, he kept getting caught up in outrageous acts, badmouthing of presidents, and drunken evils, yet the community kept welcoming him back with open arms. Would this finally pop the throbbing vein in his forehead?

The news being broadcast on the headrest monitor in front of Tex's first-class seat was all about the raging fire in Washington, D.C. Cries for another Dolly Madison came across the airwaves, with pleas to save the important historical documents now at risk. No one knew where or how the fire had started, only that it was building in strength and couldn't be stopped after the funding cuts to the local fire brigade and police force had taken hold.

Most of the world had followed suit. There was a burning uneasiness in people that the future would not be good. Regional wars continued to grow over ancient disputes and boundaries. Poverty and sickness seemed rampant on every screen. Famine, drought, and death were highly reported. Was it true? It didn't matter. It was repeated on every broadcast and website. It was the perception of the truth Tex intended.

Walking up the jet bridge to the terminal gate, Tex dropped the Goodwin façade, slipping back into his normal lanky body as he passed by a crowd of soon-to-be-disappointed photographers and journalists who had jammed into the gate for a first interview on landing. Toying with them, Tex announced, "He ran down the jet bridge, across the tarmac."

This sent the mad gang scurrying in all directions to find the escaped star. In the scramble, at least three were trampled, once again fulfilling Tex's seemingly insatiable appetite for pain. But this was a new high. Greed wrapped up with an unadulterated lust for power and a thick coating of pride was sweet euphoria.

Tex's year in Washington had gotten him hooked, but he needed to find a new fix. Tex needed someone he couldn't break as easily as a politician. He wanted a group he could feed off of without sending them home to their constituents, without them literally dying of embarrassment.

Stepping out the doors of LAX, Tex could feel the loneliness enveloping the city, from oceanside to mountaintop. All these millions were trapped together, yet all were isolated. What had brought him to Los Angeles was the same thing that had kept him away from small towns in the Midwest. Though there were few people in these lands and great distances between them, they still felt like part of a community, all standing together. It was the great American irony.

Tex saw a 1960 silver Porsche convertible pull up to the red zone marked for loading and unloading only. The driver popped out of his seat and jaunted through the electric doors to the baggage carousel. Tex took advantage of the opportunity and helped himself to the classic car, driving off to find a place for dinner.

As the sun began to fade in the distance, Tex drove up to what seemed like a nice restaurant, Patina, near the concert hall, and entered. After a quick whisper in his ear, the maître d' sat Tex at the best table in the restaurant. The Patina wait staff and sommelier treated him with the highest regard.

Two couples arrived at the door. Tex recognized one of the men as Ephraim Wiese, whom he had seen in his in-flight magazine. Ephraim, who was president of the largest studio in North America, could greenlight any project for cinema, television, cable, or the generalized bucket of new media that supported the other three.

The maître d' turned and looked at Tex, as he had done with the previous three guests, but this time, Tex nodded his approval. With this, the maître d' ushered the two couples over to Tex's table and introduced them to their host for the evening. The couples were a bit surprised by this and looked as though they were about to protest when Tex addressed them.

"Welcome. Please, sit down," he said, and they obeyed. "I am your host tonight, Tex Bryant, and boy oh boy have I got an evening planned for you."

Ephraim, in turn, introduced his wife, Nora, as well as his VP of planning, Gary Lark, and Gary's wife, Ann.

"Well, now that we're all cozy, let's get started," Tex said.

Tex ordered some nice wines recommended by the somm to start. When Ephraim explained that he had been sober for six years, Tex insisted that he have not just the glass of wine, but that they all start the night with shots of tequila as well.

This was all good fun for Tex. Between the appetizers and main course, he started to explain his plans. "I think there is a real opportunity for more revenue with violence. Nothing sells like fear, you see, and I want to see more violence in video games, in movies, and on television."

"But there are rules," Ephraim said. "There are ratings."

"Pish-posh and gobbledygook," Tex replied. "Thirty years ago, all that PG-13 movie crap came out. Today, those same films would easily be rated PG or G. We must push the boundaries of what is acceptable to stay ahead of the market." Tex watched Ephraim study the glass in his hand and grinned. "Need another one, Ephraim?"

"I . . . I could use another," Ephraim said uneasily.

Tex raised his finger and asked for the bottle to be brought to the table. "I've just spent that last year in D.C., and I left the place on fire —literally." Tex chuckled. "I think they would be willing to bend and shape some new rules in that city if we ask real nice. They will do what I say." Tex spread that devilish grin of his wide and changed the subject to keep everyone at the table engaged. "Nora! Ann! I know all about the work of your husbands, but tell me more about you. Are you part of the yoga and spa group? Maybe you love to shop. Tell me, do you take the kiddos to church? Synagogue? Temple?"

Nora smiled. "It's what's held us together these past few years. Between all the hours at work and the meetings, our family time is wrapped up in going weekly."

"Well, I don't know whether that's such a good idea. I hear, on good authority, that God is a dick. In fact, I wonder if He is even real sometimes." He waited for her reaction. "Don't you?"

"I do," Ann chimed in. "I wonder that all the time."

"I do wonder, from time to time," Nora said tentatively. "When bad things happen. Still, there has to be something."

Tex took her hand. He looked into her eyes with a sense of empathy and feigned concern. "I know, I know, dear Nora. There are so many bad things in life, I wonder about them all the time. It must be tough to even leave the house scared; there are bad people all around us, waiting in bushes, ready to carjack us. They all have guns. They all have knives. Poor, dear Nora, it must keep you up nights with worry."

Nora's face changed. She was no longer that sweet kind woman listening to Tex's words. Now, a streak of real fear gripped her. She began to appear uncomfortable, even itchy, and looked to the exit on more than one glance.

"Tex, you can stop there," Ephraim said in a calm and steady voice. "There's no need to say more to Nora or to Ann. Lark and I agree that violence in movies, in gaming, and on television has always worked for us. Play up the fear. I hear you."

A shark-like toothy grin spread across Tex's face. Not only was he getting the agreement to move forward with his demand, but he also now knew this man's weakness: his wife. This was how Tex would destroy him. After dinner, Ephraim may be able to quit drinking again, the two might be able to go on as they did in the past, but he couldn't do anything without Nora. Tex nearly salivated at the destruction he could bring to the world through this man once he sunk his teeth in deep. "Of course, of course," Tex said softly. "But there is more to consider."

"More?" Gary interrupted.

"Well, have we considered just how important smoking is?" Tex asked.

"Marijuana or cigarettes?" Gary asked.

"Both, of course," Tex replied. "There should be a show about God too, I think. It's a documentary, and every week, we focus on a different god. Jainism, Buddhism, Islam, Judaism, Sikhism—if it has an 'ism' attached to it, let's investigate. Let's compare. Saturate and dilute religion into a thin syrup of the past that only old fools could believe in —the more comparison, the better. Show that religion is a way to control the masses and turn key organizations into power structures that only seek control."

"Morgan Freeman could narrate," Gary said.

"I like your thinking," Tex replied.

"What about Christianity?" Ephraim asked. "You didn't mention that in the group, and there is no 'ism' there."

"Everyone knows Christianity is fake. Don't they, Ann?" Tex asked.

Eventually, Ann nodded in agreement.

The main course arrived. Tex had ordered off-menu. Each of his guests received a bloody, rare steak sitting in a pool of red juice. The four began to feast, blood dripping down their faces. Each felt compelled to chew every morsel of grit and fat.

Tex enjoyed his spinach salad. He insisted that they all get dessert, but only once their plates had been licked clean. The literal interpretation of the comment let him know he had captured their full attention that evening. Dabbing the edges of his mouth with a white linen napkin, Tex said, "I find this whole traditional marriage thing rather limiting, don't you?"

"Absolutely," Ann and Gary agreed in unison.

Looking to the Wiese couple, Tex saw that they were reluctant to even look up. Something deep between the two was keeping them connected. "Well, maybe not for all of us, but for kids these days. I say, who needs the license? Who needs the ring? Just, you know, be young. Go with what you feel. What could go wrong?"

Tex watched as Nora and Ephraim slowly began to cave in under pressure. Their heads, ever so slightly, nodded in agreement.

"We can work on that one," Tex said, letting them off the hook. He dabbed one last time at the sides of his face and stood up, making certain his appearance was acceptable.

The waiter brought the check, handing it to Tex.

Instinctively, Tex opened and looked to the sum, which was close to $6,000. "You will take care of this one, won't you, Ephraim? Loved that wine selection." Tex tapped Ephraim on the back, dropped the leather-bound bill holder on Ephraim's plate, and walked out the door.

THE LITTLE PORSCHE ROLLED UP TO THE GATE OF THE STUDIO LOT. A few subtle words and the security agent pointed him toward the prime parking spot outside the offices of Ephraim's media empire.

The main building was like any corporate office. Around the reception desk, the bland walls were covered in art and product offerings.

Beyond that, there was a series of passageways with doors, meeting rooms, and people desperately attempting to stay employed, hoping they made a difference. Soon they would all align to his thinking, Tex thought. They would all be talking about his priorities, following the goals he put forward. Ephraim would certainly help.

President Wiese had a very nice office. Soft, deep seating for marathon meetings faced the desk he sat behind.

Tex walked right in. "Ephraim, good to see you again. Hope you're feeling well because we have a lot of work to do."

Ephraim looked to Tex, uncertain what to make of him. "Let me call you back. Something's just come up," Ephraim said, hanging up the phone. "I thought you might have been last night's bad dream."

"Nope. Here I am, in the flesh, ready to help guide you to a bright future," Tex said, taking an obvious glace toward the liquor cabinet.

Ephraim was overcome by a craving and looked helplessly at Tex.

"Oh, don't mind me. Go ahead. It's only nine in the morning, but I won't stop you."

"Can I offer you something?" Ephraim asked.

"Bottle of water, ice cold."

Ephraim leaned over and tapped the intercom button. "Jessica, could you please bring our guest an ice-cold bottle of water?"

"You have a guest, Mr. Wiese?" the voice asked.

Tex smiled and said, "I just let myself in."

There was something about that voice on the intercom. It was so warm. It was inviting, welcoming, soothing. It sounded like home. The feelings the voice brought on nearly dropped Tex to the floor. And when the owner of the voice entered the room, he fell back, landing on the armrest of the leather chair.

"Mr. Wiese, I'm sorry. I didn't see anyone come in." Jessica walked toward the desk with a bottle of water that made her delicate hands look almost blueish.

"Jessica?" Tex stood up, mouth agape. It was as if a hard blow had struck him in the chest and all at once he couldn't breathe.

"Tex?" Jessica asked. "Is that you? I haven't seen you in, well, I don't know. How long has it been?"

"Too long," Tex whispered.

She looked to Ephraim, then back to Tex, remembering her place. "I'm sorry, Mr. Wiese, you have business. I don't mean to interrupt."

Tex looked to Ephraim and back to Jessica. There was something so human about his feelings. The hatred, the burning desire, and the drive to destroy were all extinguished in her presence. "Ephraim, you got the CliffsNotes last night. You don't need me to carry on, do you?"

"I have already started the changes you suggested," he replied.

"Jessica and I are going to step out. You don't need us."

"I don't. I'm fine here," Ephraim said in a trance-like state.

"Jessica, you drink coffee. Would you let me buy you a cup?"

She blanched. "Sure, yeah, if Mr. Wiese won't need me."

"He's fine, just said so himself."

The studio cafeteria looked like one of the most magical places on earth. Zombies from the television lot were sitting next to nuns, while cowboys were grouped at another table. There were recognizable faces mixed in with the corporate staff, all looking for an inexpensive place to grab something within walking distance of the office.

Tex looked at Jessica across the table through the steaming vapors of a hot coffee and thought to himself that she had not changed one bit.

"There's something different about you, Tex. I can't put my finger on it, but you're different."

"Different good or different bad?" he asked.

"Not sure. Just different," Jessica said, squinting one eye. "It's not your hair, and you aren't wearing glasses, but there's something . . . I'll figure it out."

He wanted to scoop her up and carry her away to some distant place. He wanted to forget what had happened since he had decided to leave and pursue the devil, transformed into that thing he hated, and roamed the world, acting on his pleasures and desires. Her lips were so kissable, and he would be so happy to press his against hers one more time. He wanted to bury his nose in her hair and breathe her in. He wanted to feel her legs wrap around him and hear her call out his name.

She interrupted his vivid daydream with a simple question. "So, what have you been up to?"

The truth was not something he could deal in easily—not then and not now. "Travel, making things happen, you know, keeping busy."

Jessica's smile was polite, as if she knew it wasn't the full truth. "Now you have business with Mr. Wiese?"

"Yes."

"You must be doing well. I haven't left L.A. since I got here." An uneasy silence hung over the hot steaming beverages. Jessica blew on her coffee to help it to cool down.

"I found what I was after," Tex said simply.

She was excited for him. "That's great news."

"Mixed results."

"Oh," she said with a sad and empathetic tone.

"I mean, I got it. Getting what you want isn't always what you think it will be."

She sighed with a deeper understanding of that truth in adulthood. "Yeah. I understand that."

"How about you? What are you doing? What have you been up to?"

Another awkward moment hung over the table. Jessica seemed to have things to say but couldn't really articulate them.

"Hey, it's me," Tex said. "You can tell me anything."

"Can I?"

"Sure you can. You always can." He instantly regretted his offer once Jessica started talking.

She explained that after Tex had left town, she'd felt lonely and afraid that she might end up like her mother and sister, hooked on home shopping and living from paycheck to paycheck. So, she'd saved what she could and moved out to Los Angeles. Most of her time had been spent building a reputation as a trusted assistant, until she'd been recommended to Mr. Wiese by his wife, who knew her distantly through a friend.

Still, Jessica had felt just as alone in L.A. as she had back home, as the men here tended to be cruel or want just one thing. She'd found a man named Steve who didn't hit her, wasn't bad looking, and could keep a job. Nothing exciting—accounting and finance—but he was always employed. He had made for a good investment.

It was then that Tex noticed the ring on her hand, modest but true.

In an instant, Tex realized that that was what Jessica had always needed, not someone to slay monsters, grab the devil by the tail, be rich, or command the souls of another realm. Not that he was any of those things, but he was certainly not modest and true.

Seeing that his chance for a pure reunion with Jessica had faded, Tex felt a familiar tingle inside. It would not be dormant any longer. He started to take delight in his work again. He despised truth and true love and hated modesty. He did his best to resist the physical cringe it brought to his body as Jessica talked about her husband.

As she spoke, Tex started to plot and plan. He decided to set aside the work he'd started in New York and continued in Washington. His new plan would be to split Jessica up from her husband. Instinctively, he knew no one could be good enough for Jessica. This new man in her life would need to perish by Tex's hand or live in torment without her.

"He sounds like such a great guy." Tex smiled. "I would love to meet him sometime."

"Really?" Jessica said, tilting her head inquisitively. "Are you sure?"

"Of course. I would love to meet the man who made my Jessica happy."

Jessica saw past this sinister grin and saw him for the man she knew he was: the man from Abilene, Kansas, the man she used to love. "Great! Why don't you join us for dinner tonight?" Jessica wrote her address on a napkin and handed to him. "Six?"

"Six, six, six! I can't wait for six."

Tex joined them later that night for dinner at their house in Pasadena. It was what he thought the perfect suburban life might be like.

With one handshake, Tex sized Steve up. He watched him move. He listened to his words. Even took his hand and held it over grace at the table for dinner. After the small talk and getting to know one another better, Tex said to Steve, "You say too many prayers to be an innocent man. What is your real story?"

"Tex!" Jessica scolded. "Steve is a saint."

"I have learned to recognize my own kind over time," Tex explained.

Steve seemed somewhat shaken by Tex's astuteness. As the kind of man Jessica thought he would be, Steve confessed, "Tex is right. I am not the saint you think I am. Before we met, Jessica, I was a troubled man. I would regularly cheat and steal. There was a time when I didn't have a penny to my name, skipped payments on bills, and could barely keep from swiping my meals from busy grocery stores. A few days at a time, I learned how to turn that around, apply myself, get a job, and do right. When I met you, I just knew I could keep it up longer. I could be the man you needed me to be."

Tex sensed there was more to this story than Steve was letting on. His imagination raced to Hollywood pedophile rings, drug dens, street workers being assaulted with razors and chains. Then, Tex remembered hearing Jessica's voice that morning. He remembered how it had knocked him off his feet. Suddenly, he had the sense of falling back into himself on their comfortable couch. He saw her face, and for a few short minutes, Tex was himself again. He could remember his old life and the time he was in love with Jessica.

"Tex, are you all right?" Jessica asked.

"Tex, buddy," Steve said, "what's going on?"

Tex sat at the dinner table. The smell of Jessica's lasagna filled the air. Tex looked across the table to see her smile, those lips he had kissed and taken for granted. There was a sadness in seeing her, knowing how much evil he had done since they'd last met. "Steve," Tex finally said. "I take you for a good man, someone who has found redemption. What was the trick? How did you do it?"

Steve looked at Jessica, then back to Tex and replied, "There is no trick, no easy answer. Each day, you must decide if you are going to be a better man. Every day, Jessica is a reminder to me that I want to be a better man."

"Jessica," Tex said, "I want to be a better man, but I just can't."

"You can't?"

"I'm sorry I left you in Abilene—"

"You don't need to apologize," Jessica interrupted. "There is no need to be sorry."

"I came here tonight with such bad intentions, Jessica. I came here to break you and Steve up."

"Don't be silly. You couldn't have. There is good in you."

"There isn't. I'm a bad, bad person, Jessica. I am evil."

Both Steve and Jessica laughed.

"You're being a little dramatic, Tex," Jessica said.

Tex stood up from the table, clinging to the humanity that still lived in him. "I know what I have to do," he announced. "You may hear things about me, awful things, but know that"—Tex began to choke up as he spoke—"I want to be a better man for you."

He thanked the two for dinner, for welcoming him into their home, then proceeded to the front door. Jessica followed Tex to let him out. He turned to her and gave the most warm and tender embrace he could possibly muster. Her arms held him. He could smell her sweet scent, forgotten and buried in his past. His heart must have taken a single beat in that moment, for he felt human and whole with her.

With a quick peck on the cheek, Tex said, "I wish you nothing but the best."

⚜

JUDGE RICHTER EXPLAINED THAT IT WAS INTELLECTUALLY DISHONEST for the government to have the devil in its borders and do nothing about him. He, after all, was the most severe threat to national security that might ever have existed.

Witnesses were plentiful, starting with Pastor Bill, moving on to Mary, and then to all the lives he had destroyed in a systematic matter. Even Malik Goodwin was finally able to clear his name. Judge Richter could confirm that the devil was trying to control the media and spread wickedness and corruption across the globe by any means possible. The trial had been one for the history books, and Tex had watched it all play out in his front row seat.

When he'd had the chance, Tex had whispered into the sitting judge's ear, "Put me in supermax and throw away the key."

Within a matter of hours, Tex was counting the twelve gun towers along the lonely Colorado road. He allowed himself a crooked smirk at the number of guns surrounding him, none of which could do a thing to stop him.

Camera after camera lined the corridors of locked gates until he was introduced to the 8x4-foot room where he'd been sentenced to spend the rest of his days, no matter how many there might be. He had been promised to never see the sun again. There would be no warm ocean breeze. His plans to bring down the world, collect souls, and cast doubt in God had been extinguished.

Tex knew one thing: he'd had a chance to love and to be loved by Jessica, but he'd thrown it away for a crazy and foolish desire to kill the devil. He could now only remember that last embrace, the smell of her hair, the last moment he'd felt human in her arms. Every day, he fought to remember one thing: he could choose to be a better man.

Each night, his mind would take him through the catalogue of evil deeds he had done. Every tortured face wretched in pain pleading for mercy and craving another chance at life would torment him. Each night, he chose not to do evil. He decided not to turn into a mist, seep under his prison door, and visit the butchers, mad hatters, and black-guards that kept shop in this block of the neighborhood. He chose not to rally forces, break free, and work in concert to chew through the landside in cannibalistic acts of mayhem the world had not witnessed since dark ages. He focused on Jessica to be a better man.

Pastor Bill had been right that day so long ago. There was a hell to avoid and a heaven to gain. Tex's personal hell was living with his choice. And like the old man of Crete in Dante's Inferno, he was a man, frozen in tears, begging to see his love one last time.

Tex imagined that Jessica had passed peacefully after a long and full life with Steve before his first life sentence was even served. Tex knew that he could have grown wings and a spiny tail and broken free from the supermax prison. He could easily have hunted down Steve, forced Jessica to fall under his spell, and done whatever he wished with her. Still, she would never have truly love him in return or fully forgiven him for leaving in the first place.

Screams from the supermax kept him awake nights. Death walked the corridors, keeping watch on all. There was no escape, and Tex kept to himself for centuries. While the prison walls wore down and were eventually rebuilt, while inmates came and went, Tex stayed in his cell and tried keep evil thoughts away, killing the devil inside and choosing to be that better man.

It was some 500 years later when his gate was finally unlocked and Tex was rolled out of that cell to see daylight. Old and frail, he still wouldn't die. The world had gotten better while he'd been locked away. Cures had been discovered, wars had been few, and people had lived longer and in happiness.

"I forgot how big you are," Tex said when he saw the brilliant sun. He then requested to be returned to his cell, which was in everyone's best interest.

As the guard turned to lead Tex back inside, a young man moved in front of them, blocking their path. Slowly, he removed an ancient and broken blade with a short shard of a point just long enough to do the job.

"Tex Byrant," the young man started, "I am here for you."

Tex recognized the blade. He knew it could release him from his burden or might even be a chance for redemption. "I never thought I would see that blade again," he said.

"It took me two years, but I found it and am here for you."

Tex took a final breath. "A word of warning, boy: you can't kill the devil without facing your own hell."

17

A WING AND A PRAYER

Father Juan Francisco, the chaplain for Detroit Metro Airport, stood on the far side of the scanning maze, waiting to meet the new member of what he called the "Mobile God Squad." One of the blessings he found in this specialized line of service was the opportunity to learn about the similarities between Catholicism and other religions, between his and others' ways of worshipping. It had been some time since a new member had been added to the team. He was hoping to learn more about the Muslim faith.

He held a hand-lettered sign, similar to the ones limousine drivers hold, on which he had printed the name "Aazad Khamenei." It had seemed like a good idea that morning.

Before he could try his cell phone, he saw a man wave to him from the top of the escalator. The imam's bright white teeth shone through his bushy beard as he smiled widely. Aazad seemed younger than Father Francisco had imagined he would. Father Francisco extended his hand to greet his new team member, saying, "I'm Father Francisco. It's a pleasure to meet you."

Khamenei took the father's hand and shook it. "Imam Aazad Khamenei," he said. "It is indeed a pleasure. I look forward to working with you." Aazad kept a firm grip on Francisco's hand until Juan pulled away.

"How was the security line today?" Francisco asked.

Aazad's undeterred smile beamed. "It was long."

"Once the TSA team gets to know you, things will go more smoothly. It took a few months of them seeing me every day before they began to know me. A staff badge will help too. Let's go get you started."

Before the two began the tour of the mile-long terminal, they filled out some paperwork, and Khamenei had his photo taken for a security badge. They took the series of moving walkways from one end to the other, Francisco pointing out places he thought would be important in the imam's first week. At each gate, he took time to introduce the new member of the "Mobile God Squad" to the airline agents. "Just call us if you need help with anyone or if a situation arises," he said.

Beyond the numerous thirty-minute services or prayer sessions the "God Squad" held, the biggest job his team had at the airport was to comfort unruly passengers or people who were flustered, confused, lost, or troubled. Francisco knew the manager of every hotel in a half-hour radius, and he kept a pocketful of vouchers for all the restaurants on the mile.

At the center of the terminal was a small corridor with four rooms. One was for Protestants, one for Catholics, one for Jews, and one for Muslims. Francisco introduced Aazad to Rabbi Silverman, who had just finished consoling a traveler. The imam greeted the rabbi with the same warmth and enthusiasm with which he had two hours earlier greeted Juan.

The three joked and laughed for a good hour, sharing with one another. It was one of those moments one later remembers in which everything clicks into place.

Finally, Rabbi Silverman looked at Father Francisco with a bit of trepidation. "I don't want to spoil things—this fellowship has been so wonderful—but have you told him about *Los Tres Demonios?*"

The imam was puzzled. "The three devils?"

Father Francisco reached out and touched the imam's arm. "I

wanted to wait until the two of you had met so the rabbi could corroborate that I wasn't playing a practical joke on your first day, Aazad."

"Please, tell me about *Los Tres Demonios*," Aazad said with a slightly smaller smile. "It can't be that bad."

They all took a seat before Father Francisco began.

"Everything was new and pristine at the airport when it first opened, so much better than the older, confusing terminal. I was the only person here at the time, and I was asked to serve all the faiths when the program started. I was very busy. When flights were delayed, I would get a call to stand at the gate or talk with travelers. Just showing up in my formal collar would often cool tempers.

"So, near the end of that first week, I got a call from Gate 1. One of the throwers—"

Aazad interrupted. "Throwers?"

"Baggage handlers. I know they're supposed to handle your luggage with care, but they call each other 'throwers.' So, I get a call that one of the throwers has mishandled an animal container. Usually, when I get this call, it means that someone has lost a pet and is grieving, but it was different this time. Some birds had escaped from a container and had gotten into the aircraft. From the aircraft, they flew into the jetway and into the terminal."

"Let's take a walk," Rabbi Silverman suggested.

The three went to the nearest loading area for the tram that ran between gates. There was a large sign that read "Bird Recordings" in big bold words. Under it, the text read, "You may periodically hear what sounds to be birds in distress. These are recorded devices that help us reduce the actual bird population in the terminal without harming the birds. We appreciate everyone's understanding in this matter."

"The three birds that escaped that day," Juan explained, "were African grey parrots on their way to the Detroit Zoo."

"Oh, parrots! They are so cute. People keep them as pets," Aazad said.

"They might look cute, but these are not your average, everyday parrots," Rabbi Silverman said.

"Zou-Zou is the leader, Mr. Pink is the muscle, and Yo-Yo is the beauty," Juan said.

"You describe them as if they are a gang. They're just birds, aren't they?" Aazad asked.

"At first, they were just escaped birds who would occasionally poop on things. The cleaning crew would spot them from time to time in the trees or ceiling. Mr. Pink is easy to see with his bright red color in the spring. Then, I started to get more calls about arguments on the mile." Francisco explained that many of these disputes were a matter of harsh words between strangers, but both parties claimed the other had started it. There were also problems with inventories at the food court. Fruits and vegetables went missing, and staff members were getting into trouble.

"I became a witness," Francisco said. "I watched Zou-Zou fly down from a rafter into the fake plastic tree at the sitting area by a gate and say, 'Get out of my chair, asshole.' Pardon my language, but that's what Zou-Zou said. The two passengers seated back-to-back turned and started to argue. At the same time, Mr. Pink and Yo-Yo waited above the food court. When the two yelling men began to draw everyone's attention, the two birds swooped in and grabbed large stashes of food. You wouldn't think a bird that size could carry items bigger than itself."

"Hold on, Father Francisco," Aazad stopped him. "You're telling me that these birds can talk like humans and are stealing food from vendors?"

Rabbi Silverman, with a somber look, said, "Every word of it is true, my friend. I have witnessed it as well."

"You see," Francisco explained, "African Greys are very smart. They are known for having large vocabularies and being highly adaptive to their environment."

"But you are talking about real intelligence," Aazad said, "not some mimicry or clever animal behavior."

Rabbi Silverman said, "Let me put it this way: God's creatures are very good at certain tasks. Getting food is one of those tasks. Zou-Zou can mimic sounds, all kinds of sounds. We've listened to him repeat announcements from the loudspeaker in several languages or sound exactly like the coffee grinder by the snack shop—even a popular cell phone ring. He also can mimic words that instigate fights."

Father Francisco went on to tell how the birds were able to avoid being captured. He told how thirty men, animal wranglers, had been hired to catch all the birds in the airport. They used sounds to confuse them, nets to catch them, and tranquilizer darts to put them to sleep. All these efforts caught the dozens of smaller average birds but never Zou-Zou, Mr. Pink, and Yo-Yo.

ASH WEDNESDAY WAS ONE OF THE BUSIEST DAYS OF THE YEAR FOR Father Francisco. Rabbi Silverman was assisting him with a series of thirty-minute services throughout the day.

Imam Aazad Khamenei was walking the mile with his phone on, ready to be at any gate in five minutes. He enjoyed the walking this role provided. He enjoyed that so many friendly people worked at the airport. He had made good friends over the past month with gate agents, security, shopkeepers, and the airport authority. It was a real community that merely happened to have thousands of travelers passing through it each day.

After many trips back and forth over two hours, Aazad decided to sit for a few minutes in one of the comfortable black leather chairs by the food court. The patter of footsteps had become a comforting background noise. That's when he first heard "Get out of my chair, asshole" from behind him. Aazad turned to see a large muscular man with a brush cut dressed in a camouflage uniform and looking at him in similar confusion.

As the two were twisted halfway in their chairs, they heard the voice again say, "I said, 'Get out of my chair, asshole.'"

Aazad looked up into the plastic tree near them, and the man in uniform followed his gaze. There, in the center of the perfectly placed green foliage, was an orange beak on the front of the fully gray face of a bird. It began to sway back and forth on the branch. Its tail was a shock of two red feathers sticking out from an ashen-gray body.

"Zou-Zou?" Aazad said.

Zou-Zou turned his head at the sound of his name. His beady bird eyes looked especially menacing with the short feathers along his lore.

Aazad turned to look at the food court. A bright red bird the size of a football was perched at the top of the coffee house logo, watching. In the distance, to the right of the sandwich shop sign, Aazad could make out a gray ball of fluff cooing and watching him as well.

"Hey, what's going on?" the man in camouflage asked.

"I think that parrot knows some wicked phrases," said Aazad.

"Yeah, I think you're right. That's pretty cool. Come here, birdy," the large man said, slowly approaching Zou-Zou.

Zou-Zou turned his head as only a bird can. He watched the man approach with his finger extended. When the man came close enough, Zou-Zou's bright beak struck, drawing blood. In a flutter of feathers and profane language, Zou-Zou was gone and the man left bleeding.

Aazad took the man to the nearest first aid kit, cleaned the wound, and dressed it. It was much deeper than he'd first imagined. The cut was also not clean. It was misshapen and jagged, with a good deal of skin torn away. He recommended that when the man got to his destination a doctor look at it again to see if stitches were needed. The man said, "It's just a scratch. I'll be fine."

Later, after sharing the events of that day with the father and the rabbi, Aazad said, "I must confess, you were right about those birds. They are devils."

It had been a very long day for the father and rabbi. They looked equally tired from having served so many souls, a never-ending stream of foreheads with ashen crosses on them.

"Oh ye of little faith," Juan said with a smile.

"What can we do about this?" Aazad asked.

Francisco shook his head. "What is there to do? The airport authority knows about it. They've installed the random birdcall recording."

Aazad was unsatisfied with the predicament. "I don't think it is working. These birds are big and fat from all the food they steal. They can live as long as a man. Do we have decades ahead of us in which to face"—he searched for the right word and was happy to have found it —"these bullies?"

The rabbi, who had patiently listened to the two, shared his insight. "If we are talking about intelligent creatures . . ." He paused, knowing the path it could take the conversation down. "*If.* We should consider a test to see if they are intelligent and not just very good mimics and hunters."

"What did you have in mind?" Aazad asked.

"There are different ways scientists measure intelligence." The rabbi slowly eased into the conversation. "For example, squid have been tested by being put through mazes to get to food. Scientists found that they have a very sophisticated way to solve these problems." He gauged the faces of his friends to see if there were any concerns with this argument so far. "One of the best ways to test for this higher level of problem solving—what I'll call 'intelligence' for now—is to put the subject in front of a mirror."

"Fascinating," said Aazad. "What does this show the scientists?"

"Well, the example that seemed most interesting was with dolphins. They put a mirror in the water tank with the dolphin, and they observed the animal looking at itself, trying to see around the mirror, until it seemed to recognize itself." Still looking into his colleague's eyes, waiting for a rebuttal on evolution or soulless creatures, he continued cautiously. "Finally, the dolphin starts to observe itself, look at parts of its body it has never seen before—what the dorsal fin looks like, what its tail looks like."

"How can they tell what the dolphin is thinking?" Aazad asked.

"Well, they observe the reactions of the dolphin. It is normally a very chatty creature, making noise, but during the mirror experiment, it's silent. Normally, the dolphin is a very playful creature, but with the mirror, it is very intent, focused on the mirror."

"Interesting, very interesting." Aazad looked to his right. "Don't you think so, Father?"

"Yes," Juan said. "Very interesting. But birds usually have mirrors in their cages to keep them company, don't they?"

Rabbi Silverman nodded. "Which makes it an ideal test if we are ever able to conduct it."

"You're right. If we were able to put the parrots in front of a mirror, I agree," Father Francisco said.

As the three men left the room to the corridor, they looked up to notice that Mr. Pink, Zou-Zou, and Yo-Yo were perched that late night on a vendor sign on the mile, looking down at them.

"You don't think they know we were talking about them, do you?" Aazad pondered.

"I don't know," replied Father Francisco.

The three birds cooed and turned their heads like normal, healthy birds, watching the "Mobile God Squad" walk past them to the main corridor.

"They really are getting big," Rabbi Silverman added.

THE NEXT WEEK, FATHER FRANCISCO ASKED IMAM KHAMENEI TO join him at the weekly airport authority meeting. It was another business meeting. Usually, the group ticked through annual goals, metrics that had been achieved or missed, upcoming news, and changes in policy or programs. Howard Brown was a bookish administrator who ran the airport and these meetings very efficiently.

Howard announced at the start of the meeting that they were going to focus on one topic exclusively—birds—and return to the regular schedule the following week. "We all know about the bird problem here on the mile," he continued, "so I've spent a good amount of time researching how we can resolve this issue. I've hired one of the best animal wranglers in the world, and I'd like to introduce him to you. Nero Blackstone." Howard Brown gestured toward the new face at the table.

Nero Blackstone rose from his chair, dwarfing Howard Brown, and looked over the group of transportation professionals. He was a man of colossal stature, his hair was jet black and slicked back, and he had thick sideburns. Three old scars, about the right size and distance from one another to be from talons, marred his right cheek.

"You may see Mr. Blackstone on the mile over the next three days while he observes our problem," Howard added. "If you have any questions for him, now would be a good time."

"Mr. Blackstone," one of the lead gate agents started, "how will you be solving this problem?"

"I'll be using two trained falcons to hunt and kill the three birds you call Zou-Zou, Mr. Pink, and Yo-Yo," Nero said.

"Don't you think there's a more humane way of addressing this issue?" another person asked.

"No," he said plainly. "From what I can gather, your situation has gotten out of control. The birds are too wily to be trapped, and you've tried all the other options."

"What kind of support will you need from us?" a maintenance person asked.

"The center fountain. You'll need to turn that off and emptied as soon as you can."

Another person spoke up in protest. "But the dancing fountain is the centerpiece of the design. It's a symbol of the airport—we can't just turn that off."

"You can," Nero said, staring the man directly in the eyes, "and you will."

Howard Brown spoke in the eerie silence of the room. "Well, maybe we're going to have a short meeting this week."

Aazad, unmoved by Nero Blackstone's attempts at intimidation, decided that they would be trading one bully for another if they allowed him to act. "Mr. Howard, why such drastic measures? Are the birds that large of a problem? Is business down? Are complaints up? Are fewer people coming to Detroit because of our 'bird issue'?"

"I know you are relatively new here, Imam Khamenei," Howard Brown started. "Our concern is not only that these three continue to be a problem, but that they will also—let me say—propagate it. Yo-Yo is a female. We believe she is at the age to begin nesting. Our problem could multiply each spring."

"Your solution is to kill them," Aazad said, "not to transplant them, not deliver them to the Detroit Zoological Society as originally planned."

"That's correct," Howard Brown said.

Aazad looked at Juan. "Tell them about the dolphins," he said. "Explain that the birds might be intelligent."

Father Francisco looked to his new friend with understanding and then to Howard Brown, softly asking, "Mr. Brown, do you hate these birds?"

"No, Father, this is just a matter of business. We've tried other methods. You've been a part of those efforts. I don't see another practical way."

"Do you feel vengeance in your heart toward these animals?" Francisco asked.

"No," Howard Brown replied.

Father Francisco turned to Aazad. "I am sorry, my friend. I do not see another way at the moment."

The imam sighed and said, "If anyone kills a person—unless it be a punishment for murder or for spreading mischief in the land—it is as if he has killed all people. And if anyone saves a life, it is as if he has saved the lives of all people."

"I understand," Father Francisco said to Aazad. "But these are birds. Mischievous birds."

Aazad nodded and turned back to Howard Brown.

"Okay then," Howard Brown said. "Maintenance will shut off and drain the dancing fountain. Nero Blackstone will be granted access to the mile to hunt and kill Zou-Zou, Mr. Pink, and Yo-Yo."

On the first day, Nero Blackstone walked the mile with his notebook and camera. He was easy to spot. At times, he looked as if he were wading through the masses of people, like a swimmer coming up a beach. Occasionally, he'd stop, click off dozens of photos with his high-powered zoom, and then take a few notes.

He spent a good amount of time at the food court in the afternoon, sitting near the fake trees, hoping to catch one of the birds with his bare hands, his banana-sized fingers wrapping around the winged creature and squeezing.

There were several concerned travelers that day who reported a suspicious-looking character scoping out the airport to security. After the eighth such report, the security captain assigned two of his uniformed staff to patrol with Blackstone, ending further reports.

Aazad arrived early the morning of Blackstone's second day. He felt compelled to help the three birds escape or be captured rather than executed. He took every opportunity to walk the mile and try to find the birds before Nero.

By evening, it was clear that Nero Blackstone was not going to kill the birds that day. He had not even brought in the falcons he'd mentioned in the meeting to hunt them. Aazad took comfort in this as he sat in the deep leather chairs near the executive lounge, exhausted from running back and forth on the mile that day. As he sat in the chair, air hissed, escaping from the cushion. Once settled, he glanced up, surprised to see that the three birds were only a few feet from him, perched on the solid branch of a large potted plant.

"Nero Blackstone is here to kill you," Aazad spoke softly to them. "I don't know if you can understand me, but you need to leave the building before he finds you."

The three birds acted just like birds, sitting and cooing, pecking at one another from time to time, turning their heads in impossible directions. Aazad hoped he would be able to communicate the situation, no matter how foolish it seemed. He reached into his robe pocket and pulled out a small shaving mirror. Slowly, he rose from the chair and approached the three birds. Remembering the gash Zou-Zou had made in the soldier's hand during their first encounter, he continued with caution.

Arm extended, he held the mirror like a small shield. Once close enough to the birds, it caught their attention. They could see one another, and they could see themselves next to each other. It stopped their movement and ticks.

"Zou-Zou." The bird said its own name. "Zou-Zou," he repeated.

"Yo-Yo, Yo-Yo, Yo-Yo," the female said, repeating her name rapidly.

"Zou-Zou," the lead parrot replied.

"You *are* intelligent," Aazad said with surprise.

A loud single clap came from behind. Aazad turned to see that Nero Blackstone had discovered them and dropped his notebook while scrambling to get his camera. The loud noise drove the birds to flight.

Aazad held up the mirror to Nero. "They are intelligent. You can't kill them—they are intelligent."

Nero did not know what to make of the moment. He looked into the mirror and was puzzled by the reflection of a beast looking back at him, his head tilted, trying to comprehend. Giving up and returning to instinct, Blackstone looked at the little man in a funny robe holding out the mirror and wrinkled the scars on his cheek with a grin. "That doesn't matter. They are going to die tonight."

৺৵৺

AAZAD, NEARLY OUT OF BREATH, CAUGHT HIS TWO FRIENDS AS THEY were packing things up for the night and explained what had happened —how he had found the birds, how he had used the mirror test successfully, and how they had known their own names. He told them about Nero Blackstone finding them and that he must have gone to his truck for the falcons to kill the three birds that night.

Francisco had already started to dial Howard Brown before Aazad had finished the story. Rabbi Silverman started to open doors, looking for something. Aazad was not sure what or if anything could be done, but he was excited at the activity and enthusiasm of his friends.

Rabbi Silverman returned from another room with a large plastic pet carrier that had been left by one of the throwers "just in case."

When the three began to walk the mile, it was late, and the airport was desolate. The pet carrier was bulky and took both Rabbi Silverman and Father Francisco, one on each end, to keep pace with Imam Khamenei.

By the time they reached Gate A65, they could see that the hunt had already started. Nero Blackstone stood at Gate A70, looking up, his extended arm covered in a brown leather glove. Yo-Yo's body wiggled in the cloth bindings on the cold white stone floor with a hood over her head.

One of Blackstone's falcons dipped and turned in the air, chasing the football-sized Mr. Pink in aerial combat, the parrot using skills a WWI ace would have envied. Just when it seemed the falcon had caught his prey, Mr. Pink stopped in midair, letting the faster bird pass him and smash into the large screen monitor showing news. But from a ledge only five feet away, the second falcon, which had been waiting motionless, took flight and surprised the tired Mr. Pink with a calculated strike. In an instant, everyone knew that this had been the plan: lure the tough Mr. Pink into a trap by getting Yo-Yo first.

Deflated, the three men of faith watched as one falcon returned to Nero Blackstone's glove-enshrouded arm on command. The second falcon circled and returned to his perch, ready for the next ambush.

Blackstone smiled his menacing grin and said, "I guess we're not worried about babies anymore. One more to go."

It had been in vain, these efforts, these hopes the three men had shared at saving these souls. They returned to their rooms of worship, dragging the crate with them. Not a word was spoken. What could be said?

"Well," Rabbi Silverman said with sadness, "maybe this was part of—"

Before he could finish his attempt to comfort the other two, a flutter of activity sounded at the open door. "Sanctuary!" cawed Zou-Zou. "Sanctuary!" he screeched once more, landing on top of the pet cage.

Father Francisco quickly got to the door and slammed it shut. He could hear a loud thud on the other side followed by scratching on the floor.

"Open the cage," Francisco said. "Get him in the cage."

Aazad complied. He opened the metal wire door and stepped back, and Zou-Zou peered in. "You have to get in there, Zou-Zou. It's the only way we can protect you."

Zou-Zou looked up at Aazad and over to Rabbi Silverman, and then he stepped into the cage as if it were the most natural thing to do.

A loud knock came from the door. Rabbi Silverman latched the lock on the cage and gave the father a nod.

"Mr. Blackstone, how are you this fine evening?" Francisco said, opening the door and putting himself in the entrance. He could see a dazed-looking falcon finding his footing on the slick stone floor. "Must have hit his head, poor little guy."

"I want Zou-Zou," Nero Blackstone seethed.

Howard Brown turned the corner of the corridor just in time to hear this.

"Ah, Mr. Brown. Good to see you this evening," Francisco said, still blocking the doorway to the airport chapel.

"I got your message, Father, and came right over." Howard Brown looked at Nero. "Mr. Blackstone, when I called your emergency line, you did not answer the phone as you said you would."

"I was in the middle of something," he muttered.

"Yes, yes you were. You were able to take care of Mr. Pink and Yo-Yo?" Howard Brown asked.

"He was. I am able to confirm that," Father Francisco said.

"Well, I guess we're done here," Brown said.

"There is still Zou-Zou," said Nero. "My job is not complete until I have Zou-Zou."

Father Juan Francisco puffed out his chest a little and looked Nero Blackstone directly in the eye. "You are not going to get him."

Rabbi Silverman and Imam Khamenei smiled at the fortitude of their friend.

"Zou-Zou has requested sanctuary in my chapel and my associates and I will be providing it," Juan said.

"I guess you are done, Mr. Blackstone. Be sure to send me an invoice for your services." Howard Brown turned to walk away. "Oh, and please clean up your mess before you leave. We have a midnight flight landing in a few minutes."

IT WAS ONE OF THOSE UNEXPECTEDLY BEAUTIFUL SPRING DAYS IN Detroit. Green buds were starting to blossom, the warmth of the sun was refreshing, and the air was filled with the laughter of children.

Aazad thought it was a bit unusual to see his two friends out of their traditional work attire when he spotted them waiting by the hippo statue outside the front gate. Before leaving work the previous night, the three had agreed to meet and visit with their old friends who had been living at the zoo for many years.

They enjoyed each other's fellowship just as much as that day when they had first met. They walked the asphalt path past the butterfly pavilion, beyond the bear fountain and reptile house, to the new home of exotic birds.

Zou-Zou looked as if he were plotting a prison break with the others when they first arrived. The men noticed he was not as bright in color or as well-fed from stolen fruit. But he was clean, well kept, and as happy as a bird in captivity could be. His glass partition kept children from hearing the profane phrases he knew and teenagers from teaching him new ones. The three men smiled when Zou-Zou recognized them and landed on the branch nearest the window.

Mr. Pink and Yo-Yo cooed and cuddled away from the plots and planning Zou-Zou was preaching to the others. The two still bore the scars from the hunt that day in the airport. Mr. Pink could not fully extend his wing, and Yo-Yo had a bare patch at the back of her neck where the talon scar remained from the knockout blow.

Father Francisco's smile was a bit crooked at the edges, almost weepy with joy, when he said, "We saved them. We saved them!"

18

THE ILLUSIONIST'S DAUGHTER

"*There are beautiful lies all around us.*" Trinity sat in the auction hall, remembering her father's last words to her. They had seemed overly dramatic at the time, so very much like him, full of flair and showmanship. That had been his life. She only wanted hers to be normal.

It had been an unusual day. This was an extraordinary auction. It had been billed both as the greatest assemblage of magic tricks and illusions to come before the public since the death of Houdini and as the largest of its type to ever have been held in North America.

Trinity was now forced into the position to preserve her father's legacy by buying all of his work at auction as her mother, Jasmine, was only interested money and not art. Members of this tight community knew the story. For the last thirty-three minutes, Trinity had been the only bidder. The hall, filled with hobbyists, amateurs, professionals, and aficionados of the world of illusion, had all gathered out of respect for her father. Absent a funeral, this was the best way they could pay homage to the man known as "The Great Makuakane, Father of the Spirit World." When his properties hit the block, no one else bid, allowing Trinity to buy back her birthright.

Trinity and her mother had never been close. She suspected it might have been jealousy because her father had spent his time and devotion on her. It could have been that her mother was ashamed to be seen with her in public. Jasmine certainly blamed Trinity for the changes that had happened to her body during pregnancy, transforming her from a highly desired contortionist to a mother with roomy hips. It was when Trinity discovered her mother with one of the stagehands in the dressing room just two years earlier that their relationship had ended. She couldn't believe that after decades of marriage, Jasmine would cheat on her father; later, she discovered this had happened frequently.

"And now we come to item 437," the auctioneer announced to the room. "The first of the 'Air Trilogy' illusions from The Great Makuakane."

These were her father's signature works, "The Firetrap" and "The Diver's Dilemma." The third was the illusion that had killed him. Even Trinity did not know exactly what it was he'd built while she was away at school. She only knew it involved a giant fan used to train skydivers, capable of creating a wind of such velocity it could hold a human body aloft. Word about her father's death had spread quickly throughout the community, as had the high drama of her mother's infidelity.

When the auctioneer first entertained bids for "The Firetrap," the crowd was silent as before out of respect for the dead illusionist. Trinity raised her paddle, assuming that she would now gain one more piece of her inheritance. But as she lowered it, the auctioneer found another bidder across the room.

Her head shot up to see who it was. Jasmine's latest lover representing her out of spite? Someone else? Did she know him?

Trinity quickly bid again, raising her paddle high so everyone, including the new bidder, could see it. He quickly countered. Her hand shot up again, accompanied by an ardent little grunt. The auctioneer recognized her and then recognized yet another counter bid.

Her budget had been clearly calculated. There was little room for anything exceeding the minimum set by the house. Rather than give Jasmine more money, Trinity stopped bidding.

"'The Firetrap' goes to number 248," the auctioneer said, closing the sale with a rap of his hammer.

Trinity closed her eyes and cleared her mind. This was not supposed to be emotional. This was supposed to be about economics. She still had enough for the last two illusions.

But she lost her father's "Diver's Dilemma" just as quickly to the man with paddle 248.

The last illusion, the one that had killed him, would be hers. She now had the money she had budgeted for three illusions to spend on this final one. Nevertheless, the man with paddle 248 was relentless and seemingly deep-pocketed, and the bidding quickly escalated to a price beyond any Trinity could afford.

By the time the auction had resumed, offering up for purchase the next group of items, she had lost all interest. Some of her father's friends sitting near her gave her words of encouragement, while others cursed the man who had outbid her. But none of it mattered. Jasmine would make as little profit as possible, and Trinity now had nearly all of her father's work.

At the conclusion of the bidding, Trinity met with the auction house personnel to give instructions on the wire transfer of necessary funds and the delivery of her purchases. She picked up the itemized bill of lading for each property.

"Trinity?" a voice said behind her.

"Yes?" She turned and found herself face-to-face with the man who was number 248.

"I wanted to introduce myself. My name is Alan Forsyth. I was a huge fan of your father's."

"Really?" Trinity said. "Most of the people in the hall were his fans as well, but you didn't see them bid against me."

"I was stunned by that at first," Forsyth said. "Why would such a thing happen?"

"They refused to bid out of respect for him so that I might own his work. You must be new to the community."

Alan shook his head. "But the illusions were up for auction. I was allowed to bid on them."

"You were, you did, and now you own them. Good luck."

"Why are you so angry? You've got everything else."

"You're right, Mr. Forsyth. I don't know why you didn't deprive me of them." Her voice was cold. "But you got the masterpieces. Enjoy them."

"Wait. I'd like to make you an offer."

"I'm not selling what I have," Trinity said. "They're all that's left of my father. But I certainly would be happy to take the ones you bought at a much lower price than the one you paid for them."

Alan laughed quietly at the suggestion. "I was thinking of something else. After all, you and your mother, of course . . ."

"Jasmine," she interrupted.

"As you say, you and Jasmine are the only people in the world who know how these tricks work. I'd like to hire you as an instructor to teach me the illusions."

"Owning the physical equipment is one thing," Trinity said. "But the illusion itself is intangible. How it works is the artist's most prized secret, worth far more than the device. It's what sets each artist apart from his competitors." Trinity thought out loud for a moment. "Jasmine only knows one of the three."

"Even more reason I should hire you rather than Jasmine," Forsyth said.

"Give me your card. I'll think about it."

He reached into his jacket pocket and handed her his card. "Don't think too long," he said, "or I'll contact your mother."

She turned on her heel and stalked out of the auction house and out to her car. Sitting behind the wheel, she could feel the weight of the business card in her hand. The tip of her finger stroked the engraving. It was the sort of card designed to convey the impression that the owner was someone with money and power, simple and straightforward.

"Who does this Alan Forsyth think he is?" she said and hit the horn hard. Trinity had met many men like him over the years, each of them projecting an aura of prowess and importance, only to discover their impotence in the end. These were the men who thought nothing of leaving a room key backstage for a fifteen-year-old.

She had decided, as she drove away, that he had to be either very naive or very ignorant for buying her father's equipment. Perhaps, she thought, he believed that money would gain him access to the secret world of illusions. Either that or he knew nothing of them and thought they were merely something to collect—like antique cars or paintings. Surely he understood nothing of the world of the artists. He was a simple fanboy. Worse, he was a fanboy with money, enough to gobble up whatever interested him at the moment.

Trinity thought about Forsyth for another three days. His arrogance astounded her. She couldn't get him out of her mind. Finally, she called him. She learned quickly that her speculations had been correct as far as they went, but that they hadn't gone far enough. Alan Forsyth was a businessman with an obsession with "magic." She was quick to correct him on his terminology. Magic had gone out with hocus pocus and top hats and rabbits; what the artists did now—what he had purchased—were called illusions, not "tricks."

Forsyth's plan was to start a dinner theater in an area of Los Angeles on the economic rebound, one that would be ideal for tourists visiting Anaheim but close enough so that families in Orange County could come up. He was already "networking," a word that made her cringe, with the illusionists at work in the area in order to build a schedule of performers.

When she arrived at Forsyth's theater, Trinity was struck by how familiar the building looked to her. But she only had to step into the lobby to see that Alan Forsyth had visited her father's theater in Honolulu—this was as close to a replica as one could be. Hanging on the wall were framed posters of her father's act from his youth, the rare and highly sought after 1893 photo of "The Brothers Houdini"—Harry and his brother Dash—in Coney Island before they were famous, and the haunting stained-glass cross of St. Anatolia her father had saved from a small church in Italy. All of them were items Jasmine had likely sold to him.

"Thank you for coming," Forsyth said. "I appreciate it."

"It's your dime," Trinity said.

"Let's go look at the stage."

"I think I've seen it before."

"Really?"

"As you are all too aware, this is my father's theater."

"I told you before, I'm a huge fan of your dad's work. You know, not many performers have a mind for business as well as the artistry necessary to be a great illusionist. Sure, they have the ingenuity to dream up tricks—pardon me, illusions. They have a flair for showmanship, a flip of the cape, a puff of smoke. But your dad had a real mind for the business part of show business."

Trinity's father had spent a lifetime on his craft. As a wily child under the big top, he'd been rewarded for ingenuity and excelled at being a tinkerer. He had surpassed all others in the design and construction of highly complex devices of illusion. He had been smart and meticulous in the rehearsal of movement.

The illusionist had built a reputation for being generous to new talent. Each year, a select few performers just starting out would work at the theater. Their main responsibility was to warm up the audience and keep them engaged between acts. Successful starters bonded with the illusionist, creating relationships that had lasted a lifetime. The illusionist had kept a collection of all the letters and postcards he'd received from the people he'd mentored pinned to a wall backstage; they told of travels and bookings and thanked him again for the opportunity he'd given them.

"It's the responsibility of each good performer to keep his art alive for future generations," her father had told Trinity frequently. Inside the community, they'd called him the "Father of the Spirit World," but the world had known him by the Hawaiian translation: "The Great Makuakane."

Trinity and Alan walked to the stage, and she could see that the illusions Forsyth had purchased were partially assembled in the wings.

"Where should we start?"

"Well, Mr. Forsyth." Really, the man was impossible. All she'd done was agree to meet him.

"Please. Call me Alan."

"Alan, if I must. You told me you were lining up a slate of performers. There's no reason I should tell or show you anything. I'll wait until the performers are here—and that's only if I finally agree to help you."

"Who did you expect would be performing these illusions?" Forsyth asked. "I didn't buy them for someone else's glory."

"You?" Trinity asked, incredulous. "You yourself?"

"Why, yes," Forsyth told her. "I'd like to be able to perform these three."

Trinity was dumbfounded. Didn't this man understand it took a lifetime of experience? You didn't learn to read with Nabokov's *Pale Fire*.

"Alan," she asked him, "what's your passion?"

"Pardon?"

"What are you passionate about? Your car? Your business? Your wife?"

"I'm not married."

"Oh." She quickly tried to recover. "I assumed you were."

"I enjoy taking an idea and making a profit from it. I've done this on several ventures."

"You," she told him, her voice rising on a wave of derision and contempt, "are not the man for this. My father spent hours every day of his life practicing the smallest hand movements, the rhythms of his patter, the way he would breathe. You have no idea how many years it took him to reach the level of these illusions. And you certainly don't seem like the type of person with that sort of attention to detail."

"I understand," Forsyth said. "Perhaps you're right. But I've also learned that one never gets anywhere without trying. I'd like to perform at least one as part of my business."

"Okay, fine," she said. "We'll go with the least arduous one. I'll show you how 'The Fire Trap' works. We'll take it very slowly and see how it goes."

Under Forsyth's direction, two stagehands brought the elements of "The Fire Trap" into place on the stage. Trinity was curt and efficient as she gave the men instructions as to how to lock things down. She double-checked the mechanisms as she had done six times a week for years.

"The Fire Trap" looked like a giant glass candle. The cylinder was transparent so the audience could see the artist, who was bound by several locks and ropes before being placed inside. A high-velocity gas burner that sent up a sensational flame sat on top of the cylinder. Before entering the chamber, the artist would explain to the audience that fire needed oxygen to stay alive as did the artist himself. The two would share a single source of oxygen—the air in the transparent cylinder. It would be a race to see which of them would expire first.

"So how does it work?"

"I tie you up, put you inside, and see what you can do," she said with a straight face.

"No. Really. How does this trick—" He caught himself. "How does this illusion work?"

She smiled. "Good effort. There are actually two cylinders, one inside the other, but it's impossible to see that. The inner chamber—the one the artist is in—draws its air through little holes in the floor of the platform. The air is pumped up past the performer and keeps you very cool. The outer cylinder is made of a high-quality acrylic–silica blend that was developed for NASA and supplies the flame's air. There's one tiny hole in the bottom of this outside ring, allowing the flame a limited amount of air, enough for the dramatic flicker. But as the air is sucked out of the outside cylinder, it gets very hot and contracts; the acrylic–silica is what's responsible for that scary compression sound."

She instructed the stagehands to ignite the burner. The flame shot into the air with a whoosh like a jet engine, dramatic and loud. At forty-five seconds, as the flame sucked the air out of the outer cylinder, the acrylic walls began to bow inward as the vacuum inside succumbed to the pressure. At sixty seconds, the eerie sounds of plastic stretching and torqueing started to overtake the rush of fire. By ninety seconds, the flame was flickering down to nothing. Just as the large red digital clock at the side of the equipment reached 120, Trinity yelled, "Cut!" The flame went out, and the cylinder slowly started to return to its normal shape.

"Even without an artist inside, that's an impressive-looking illusion," Alan said.

"It's the 'show' in show business, Alan. Theatrics."

"So I have a hundred and twenty seconds?"

"Yes, you would have to escape from your bindings in two minutes. What can you get out of now? A straitjacket? Handcuffs? Knots?"

"Well, none of those. I'd have to learn that part too."

"That's a lot to learn, Alan."

"Start with the easy part. Do the setup for the audience."

When she turned to the empty seats of the theater and began that perfect pattern of banter her father had recited each night, she was unexpectedly overcome by a rush of emotion. The numbness she had felt since her father's death vanished, and a chill, like a blast of cold air from a walk-in freezer, rushed over her. Her eyes welled and then over-flowed with tears. "I need a moment," she said as she left the stage.

After thirty minutes alone in the backstage bathroom, she had managed to get herself under control. The fierce grief she'd been holding at bay had overwhelmed her, and now she splashed cold water on her face, dried it, and tried to repair her makeup. She heard a gentle knock on the door and then Alan's voice softly convincing her to go to lunch.

They didn't speak during the drive to the restaurant and were seated, napkins on their laps before Alan spoke again. "This is one of the best kitchens," he said. "I know it's only a small place, but the food here is great."

The lunch did not start well when a passing family's child knocked Trinity's coffee into her lap. She remained cool and controlled under the circumstances.

"Are you okay, sweetie?" the waitress asked. "That was fresh coffee."

With lots of blotting from the napkins and towel the waitress brought her, she removed the hot liquid from her upper legs.

"I'm fine. I'm fine, really," she assured everyone. "Just some bubble people living in their own world."

When things had quieted down again, Alan resumed their conversation. "What was it like working with The Great Makuakane?" Alan asked her.

"I don't know." She felt a glow of affection thinking of her father's theater. "For me, it wasn't so glamorous, really. There were lots of rabbits biting me while I tried to feed them and bird poop to clean. I've made so many balloon animals for the kids in the audience, watched them smile on stage with my father. It's hard to say."

"Have you ever thought of having kids?"

"No. I think my father was into having kids, but once Jasmine had me, things changed."

"It must have been fun to grow up in the theater, to know all these cool tricks."

"Illusions," Trinity reminded him. She sipped her new coffee. "I'll tell you when knowing those tricks came in handy—in college. For some of the brightest minds in America, my peers were soft. I went through high school in three years and college in another three."

"How old are you?" he said bluntly.

"Twenty-two."

"Really? You're as callous as an old sailor." He laughed. "Jasmine is your biological mother, right?"

"I've never had a DNA test done, but I'm told she is," she said wryly.

"That's kind of a cold thing to say about your mother."

"How old are you?" she shot back.

"Thirty-one."

"How did you make all your money?"

"Hard work?"

"Not buying it."

"I built up many restaurants over the years and invested well," he said with more conviction than the first time.

"Now you want to dabble in the dark arts of illusion."

"I like dinner theater. I saw your dad's show a year ago and offered to buy the rights to make a chain."

"I didn't know that," she said.

"He talked very highly of you. He was very proud of you from what I could tell."

"I hope so. I wanted him to be."

"Did you ever want to be a magician's assistant?"

"Illusionist. I didn't have much choice in the matter, did I? I was my father's daughter. But I was good at it, even though it was exhausting. After all, assistants do more of the work," she explained.

"They do?"

"Certainly. The illusionist talks a good game, but the assistant is the one who has to curl up in the device. She has to have great timing. She has to run all over the stage and duck into secret spaces."

"Well, that makes sense," he said.

She realized that Alan had jumped into this new project of his without the slightest knowledge of theater. "Jasmine was a contortionist and acrobat before she met Dad. That's part of why he was so good. She could squeeze into anything."

"Really?" He was amazed. "Is that the hardest part?"

"I'm really good at getting into really small spaces no one else will fit into, but I'm not as fast as others at getting across the stage."

"What are you best at?" He kept the conversation focused on her.

"I'm good at sleight of hand."

"Why don't I see more female magicians?"

"Illusionists," she corrected.

"Why don't I see more female illusionists?"

"Witchcraft."

"Pardon me?" he asked.

"Witchcraft, wicked witchcraft. People were quick to assume that any women involved with magic were witches and would chase them out of town, or worse. You might find this interesting. One of the first times The Disappearing Woman was performed—you know this trick, right?" She felt the need to double-check. "A woman goes into a box, the illusionist says the magic words, opens the box, and she's gone."

"Yeah, I know that one," he said.

"In the 1860s, the English were running India as their colony, and they first saw the illusion being practiced by Indian fakirs who made the woman disappear, but she was never seen again. Who knew what had happened to her? To the English, this was savage and unacceptable. They decided to add a twist—they brought the woman back and, in doing this, set themselves apart from the savages."

"Illusions come from India?"

"Most of the traditional ones," she said.

"Who do you think invented them?"

"I don't know. Yogis, I suppose," she replied. "Anyway, being on stage, you need to be in command. You need to display power and dominance over the audience. Lead them to that place where what you are showing them is real—it's all about perceptual constancy."

"What's that?" he asked.

"You're not going to do well in this business unless you do your homework, Alan."

"We just started. What is perceptual . . ." He tried like a poor student.

"It's a beautiful lie, Alan. Every day, I see things. I understand that they should have a certain weight, a certain heft, a certain length. I know what a table should look like because I have seen so many of them. I know what a hollow box should look like. I expect that, when I see one of those on stage, it will look like what I'm accustomed to seeing. But on stage, we make things look like they do in real life when they're actually not."

"Sounds easy enough." He laughed.

"It isn't," she said seriously.

By the end of lunch, they had agreed on a basic working construct and price. She would teach him; he would listen and learn. She would also help him find a permanent assistant that was not Jasmine.

There was a certain Peter Pan quality about Alan she could see. He jumped into situations that looked fun, refused to grow up, and the things he liked were more like play than work. The art of illusion was not for this type of person. It took time and practice and study. Still, there was something about Alan's Pan quality that brought out the Wendy Darling in her. Trinity felt rather normal when she was around him, and she liked that.

BY WEEK'S END, THINGS HAD BECOME MUCH MORE COMFORTABLE between the two. Trinity had lowered her guard now that she was working with the illusions again. Forsyth was still working hard at becoming a bad illusionist. She had tied him into the straitjacket time and again, hoping he would eventually escape, taking small pleasure in tightening the straps, which was followed by disappointment on loosening them again. Forget making it look good; just getting out would be a valiant first step.

She had contacted a few local agents, looking for an assistant for Alan. None were good enough for him. They were too tall, too decorative, uninteresting, unable to perform; he listed dozens of defects after meeting them.

During an evening cocktail and dinner, they planned for the next day's work. To avoid the conversation she was trying to have with him, he implemented a social cheat. "You may be the most interesting woman I've ever met."

Trinity, who was not new to speaking to men, found herself blush. This was unexpected. They had been spending a good deal of time together over the last weeks. The thought of the two of them together was something she had tried to keep at bay.

"Your life is fascinating to me," Alan said.

She looked down at her drink, wondering if it was going to be as strong as Alan had said his was. With a small sip she could tell immediately that it was. Her tolerance for alcohol, she had discovered in college, was very low.

"I told you they made them strong here," he said in a hushed tone.

Halfway through the meal, she could feel the effects of the drink. She felt warm and unrestrained, as if she could tell Alan anything. "I've thought about you that way."

"Really? I've thought about you too."

"I've thought about us," she slurred, "together."

"I've thought about us together too."

Alan gestured for the check while she finished her cocktail.

They left the restaurant, got into his car, and drove to her hotel. She fumbled with the key card. To her, it was all a fast blur.

He continually found himself catching her. At points, he may well have been carrying her. She seemed light and fragile in his arms. Once the two were through the door, he began to kiss her. His hands worked their way to her neck and helped her remove her jacket.

She leaned forward, kissing, and they tumbled toward the bed. His shirt and pants came off with a speed she hadn't expected.

Having been down this path time and again over the years, he let his experience kick in and slow the moment down. He took time and care to help her remove her blouse with small kisses in certain and unexpected areas around her neck. His hands, large and gentle, moved slowly along the skin of her arms. He turned her around so her back pressed up against his chest. He started to discover her waist and work up to her breasts. With little effort, they were bare, and her bra landed on the floor. Her small moans of pleasure encouraged him to move lower, where he began to blindly seek the button of her pants.

"Alan," Trinity whispered. She had to say it again louder. "Alan."

"Yes?"

"Alan, we should . . ." She tried desperately to be sober.

He had found the button, followed by the zipper. He began to peel her pants down in the dark room.

"Alan," she said, getting his full attention.

He stopped.

This was the first time she had found herself in this situation. "Would you turn the light on, please?"

"Oh, sure." He went to the lamp.

"Before you do," she said and took a deep breath, "close your eyes and sit down."

Alan smiled at her shyness. It was so out of character for her to seem embarrassed about her great body. Perhaps, he thought, she was inexperienced. He followed her instructions, touching the lamp, closing his eyes, and sitting on the edge of the bed.

"You should know something before we go any further," she said.

"Hey, we can go at your speed. There's no rush here." Alan had used this line on other women throughout his life. "This is not a race, it's a marathon we can both win."

"Oh, no, it's not that. I've been . . . well, you should know that my legs . . ."

Alan opened his eyes before she finished.

"Of all the things you've seen, all my father's great accomplishments, there are a set of devices I am more proud of than anything else. My father made my legs."

Trinity stood before Alan wearing only her underwear. A few inches below the line of her pink form-fitting panties, halfway above the knee, were two prosthetic legs. The difference between the color of her skin and the synthetic appendages was hardly noticeable in the dim light. In disbelief, he lifted the lampshade for a better view.

"Oh my God, Trinity! That's"—Alan could not find another word

—"amazing. I said to myself that you had great legs and a perfect ass, but you have perfect legs. That's—amazing."

She looked down at her legs as she had every day of her life. She had forgotten just how spectacular they were.

"Your father made those legs?"

"Yes. This pair and others." The romantic moment had passed, but the alcohol's potency still had an effect. "My father made my legs." She sat down on the edge of the bed. She pressed a button on the appendage, which caused the sound of air rushing into a vacuum. With a turn at the top, she removed the right device, revealing a sock-covered stump.

He took the leg she handed him and began to inspect it. It was light in weight, it felt like skin, not rubber, and a wealth of small veins, razor nicks, and imperfections speckled its landscape. "It's amazing."

"So you said." She detached the other leg and set it against the bed. Alan did not notice the oddness of Trinity moving across to the pillows using only her hands. "I have to warn housekeeping and security when I travel so they don't think I'm an ax murderer."

"Amazing."

"Father made a pair of legs for performances as well. They have hidden compartments where I can hide doves or keys to handcuffs. They even have a quick release so when he would cut me in half . . ." She paused, thinking about her father. "He made the most beautiful legs, a few each year. Well, you can imagine the rest." She took one of the legs and held it in her hands. "This, Alan, this is my beautiful lie. Others see what they want, but they don't know the truth."

Alan finally stopped looking at the leg and turned his attention to Trinity's eyes. He could sense that the memory of her father had spoiled any romantic moment they had been building. The big reveal of her legs had also helped in that.

"Hotel rooms have the ability to allow people to open up in ways they normally wouldn't," he said, lifting the covers.

As the two crawled into bed, Trinity could feel the weight of the blanket, the smoothness of the sheets, and the touch of Alan's skin. They began to kiss some more. Then, for a while, she would talk, and he would listen. By the time they fell asleep, they had made love several times. This was the most normal she had ever felt with another human. No childhood taunts, no odd stares in her direction, and no mother embarrassed to be with her in public. They were just a man and a woman together. No secrets, no tricks, no illusions between them.

"'There are beautiful lies all around us,'" she told him. "Those were my father's last words to me before I left for school."

"Trinity," Alan said, "*you* are your father's greatest illusion."

ABOUT THE AUTHOR

Top-selling author Paul Michael Peters is an American writer best known for his take on the quirky tangents and morals of contemporary life and his recent novel, Insensible Loss.

His upcoming novel, Combustible Punch, is a thriller scheduled for release in 2019 that explores the psychological dance between that most unlikely of odd couples: a serial killer and a high school shooting survivor.

Stay up to date with Peters' latest book releases and author news by visiting his website, where you can sign up for the newsletter as well as find more short stories and other online content. https://paulmichaelpeters.com/

THE SYMMETRY OF SNOWFLAKES

Hank Hanson's family is not only blended; it's pulverized by the weight of its own perfect symmetry

To the casual outsider, Hank Hanson's life might seem idyllic. As a successful businessman on the verge of a major business deal and an all-around good guy, few get close enough to see the troubled soul underneath his open face.

The product of a family fractured many times over by his parents' multiple remarriages, Hank spends his Thanksgivings running a miserable, thankless gauntlet of visiting multiple family members.

One Thanksgiving, he takes an unscheduled detour and meets Erin Contee, a woman who might just be too good for him – but at the same time, perfect. As the two grow closer together, Hank believes he has finally found the missing piece in his fragmented life.

He has a beautiful girl, great friends, a business, and a family – so why does he feel so bad?

Just as Hank starts to believe that he has finally found everything,

Erin reveals a dark secret own past, shattering Hank's romantic vision with the blunt force trauma of reality.

As Hank struggles to come to terms with Erin's past and their future together, he must also deal with his family's drama creeping into his home and business. Will Hank be able to do the right thing – or will he succumb under the weight of his own mistakes?

The Symmetry of Snowflakes is not just another contemporary love story. Peters has created an intricate, yet symmetrical world for readers to explore and ponder on the endless complexity and fragility of human relationships – and the unyielding drama that inevitably accompanies emotional realities outside of the romantic ideal of true love.

INSENSIBLE LOSS

If you had the chance to live forever, would you take it?

2053: An old man, Viktor Erikson, lies on his deathbed. Alone and with no known relatives, he is tended to by Olivia, a nurse. He has only one request: that she reads to him.

The request is not unusual, but the battered, leather-bound tome she must read is no ordinary book. Written in 1839, it chronicles the discovery of the fountain of youth by Morgana de la Motte – and Viktor Erikson.

What starts off as a swashbuckling adventure on the high seas in search of riches and eternal life soon transforms into something quite different: a clash between two personalities bound by love and deceit, locked together by a terrible burden of necessity.

What lengths would you go to – and what price would you pay?

As Oliva reads through the ancient book, she discovers a quest for truth and meaning as Viktor and Morgana relive the greatest sufferings and sorrows of humanity, over and over again.

In such a timeless loop, can Viktor or Morgan save their own true selves? Or will their unstable alliance, forged on the fine line between love and hate, turn into a tangled web of deception?

Insensible Loss is a dark historical thriller, breathlessly following Viktor and Morgana through a centuries-long adventure. Switching between the present and the past, Peters' masterful storytelling make this fast-paced, imaginative epic a bold exploration of a past spiraling out of control – and a future that has never been more uncertain.

CPSIA information can be obtained
at www.ICGtesting.com
Printed in the USA
LVHW092201210920
666678LV00001BA/288

9 781793 259707